PRAISE FOR MARIE FORCE

"I will never be the same after reading this book."

—5-star review for *Five Years Gone* from *As You Wish Reviews*

"There is not a doubt in my mind that this book will be one of the top books of 2018 for me."

—5-star review for *Five Years Gone* by Julie from Hey Girl HEA

"Simply put: *One Year Home* made my heart happy. Through all of the ups and downs, angst and darkness, unexpected love and insurmountable odds, this powerful novel pulled at my heartstrings and left me breathless."

—Top pick from Sara at *Harlequin Junkie* for *One Year Home*

"*Treading Water* isn't your typical romance where you're positive you're going to get the happy ending you were hoping for at the beginning. It will rip your heart out at times and have you weeping for joy at others. A stunning story about learning to love again and learning when to let go of those you love."

—Night Owl Reviews, reviewer top pick

"I love, love, love anything to do with the Gansett Island residents! They are real! They love, suffer, and succeed just as any human being would. Following this group of characters through all their ups and downs is addicting."

—*As You Wish Reviews*

How Much I Feel

OTHER TITLES BY MARIE FORCE

The Gansett Island Series

Book 1: Maid for Love (Mac & Maddie)
Book 2: Fool for Love (Joe & Janey)
Book 3: Ready for Love (Luke & Sydney)
Book 4: Falling for Love (Grant & Stephanie)
Book 5: Hoping for Love (Evan & Grace)
Book 6: Season for Love (Owen & Laura)
Book 7: Longing for Love (Blaine & Tiffany)
Book 8: Waiting for Love (Adam & Abby)
Book 9: Time for Love (Daisy & David)
Book 10: Meant for Love (Jenny & Alex)
Book 10.5: Chance for Love (Jared & Lizzie)
Book 11: Gansett After Dark (Owen & Laura)
Book 12: Kisses After Dark (Shane & Katie)
Book 13: Love After Dark (Paul & Hope)
Book 14: Celebration After Dark (Big Mac & Linda)
Book 15: Desire After Dark (Slim & Erin)
Book 16: Light After Dark (Mallory & Quinn)
Book 17: Victoria & Shannon (Episode 1)
Book 18: Kevin & Chelsea (Episode 2)
Novella: A Gansett Island Christmas
Book 19: Mine After Dark (Riley & Nikki)
Book 20: Yours After Dark (Finn & Chloe)
Book 21: Trouble After Dark (Deacon & Julia)
Book 22: Rescue After Dark (Mason & Jordan)

The Quantum Series

Book 1: Virtuous (Flynn & Natalie)
Book 2: Valorous (Flynn & Natalie)
Book 3: Victorious (Flynn & Natalie)
Book 4: Rapturous (Hayden & Addie)
Book 5: Ravenous (Jasper & Ellie)
Book 6: Delirious (Kristian & Aileen)
Book 7: Outrageous (Emmett & Leah)
Book 8: Famous (Marlowe & Sebastian)

The Treading Water Series

Book 1: Treading Water (Jack & Andi)
Book 2: Marking Time (Clare & Aidan)
Book 3: Starting Over (Brandon & Daphne)
Book 4: Coming Home (Reid & Kate)
Book 5: Finding Forever (Maggie & Brayden)

The Green Mountain Series

Book 1: All You Need Is Love (Will & Cameron)
Book 2: I Want to Hold Your Hand (Nolan & Hannah)
Book 3: I Saw Her Standing There (Colton & Lucy)
Book 4: And I Love Her (Hunter & Megan)
Novella: You'll Be Mine (Will & Cameron)
Book 5: It's Only Love (Gavin & Ella)
Book 6: Ain't She Sweet (Tyler & Charlotte)

The Butler, Vermont Series

(Continuation of the Green Mountain Series)

Book 1: Every Little Thing (Grayson & Emma)
Book 2: Can't Buy Me Love (Patrick & Mary)

Book 3: Here Comes the Sun (Wade & Mia)
Book 4: Till There Was You (Lucas & Dani)
Book 5: All My Loving (Landon & Amanda)

Single Titles

Five Years Gone
One Year Home
Sex Machine
Sex God
The Wreck
Georgia on My Mind
True North
The Fall
Everyone Loves a Hero
Love at First Flight
Line of Scrimmage

Historical Romance

The Gilded Series

Book 1: Duchess by Deception
Book 2: Deceived by Desire

Romantic Suspense

The Fatal Series

One Night With You (A Fatal Series Prequel Novella)
Book 1: Fatal Affair
Book 2: Fatal Justice
Book 3: Fatal Consequences
Book 3.5: Fatal Destiny (The Wedding Novella)

Book 4: Fatal Flaw
Book 5: Fatal Deception
Book 6: Fatal Mistake
Book 7: Fatal Jeopardy
Book 8: Fatal Scandal
Book 9: Fatal Frenzy
Book 10: Fatal Identity
Book 11: Fatal Threat
Book 12: Fatal Chaos
Book 13: Fatal Invasion
Book 14: Fatal Reckoning
Book 15: Fatal Accusation
Book 16: Fatal Fraud

How Much I Feel

MARIE FORCE

This is a work of fiction. Names, characters, organizations, places, events, and incidents are either products of the author's imagination or are used fictitiously.

Published by Montlake, Seattle

www.apub.com

ISBN-13: 9781542021319
ISBN-10: 1542021316

Cover design by Hang Le

Printed in the United States of America

How Much I Feel

CHAPTER 1

Carmen

It took only one day for my dream job to turn into a nightmare. Actually, that's being generous. In reality, it took one fifteen-minute meeting with the hospital president to throw years of studying, planning and dreaming straight out the window into the blistering South Florida sunshine.

Nowhere in the elaborate job description I was given at my interview to be Miami-Dade General Hospital's assistant director of public relations did the word *babysitter* appear. Let's face it, if I'd known what they really wanted me to do, I wouldn't be wilting in the scorching early-morning heat waiting for Dr. Jason Northrup to arrive for his first day.

"Anything he wants or needs, get it for him," Mr. Augustino instructed. "Just keep him away from the executive offices."

"But today's my first day, too. Wouldn't it be better to have someone who knows the facility meet and escort him?"

"I want you to do it," he said, leaving no room for further argument.

"Should I bring him up here to speak with you?"

"I'm with the board of directors all day. Don't bring him anywhere near the conference room."

Something stinks to high heaven about this whole thing. Why isn't the hospital rolling out the red carpet to welcome Dr. Northrup? Mr. Augustino referred to Northrup as a world-class, board-certified pediatric neurosurgeon. If he doesn't warrant the red carpet, who does? Most puzzling of all is why Mr. Augustino would let the newest person on his staff handle such an important task and not want to be there himself.

My boss's late directive gave me no time to research my first "assignment," which has me unprepared and out of sorts as I wait for him. Mr. Augustino gave me a photo of a sinfully handsome man with dirty-blond hair, golden-brown eyes and the perfect amount of scruff on his chiseled jaw. I can only imagine Northrup's type: privileged, pampered and pardoned for his sins. Now it's my job to kiss up to him and make him feel "welcome."

After years of waitressing and taking care of actual children to put myself through college and graduate school, being told to babysit him infuriates me. All the carefully cultivated marketing and publicity plans I put together in anticipation of wowing the bosses on my first day are still stashed inside the leather-bound portfolio I clutch to my chest, useless in light of the task I've been given for the day as I roast in dense late-June humidity.

One thing I'll say for Miami-Dade General Hospital is the grounds are gorgeous, with lush landscaping, colorful flower beds and grass kept green in the summer heat thanks to artfully hidden sprinklers.

Naturally, the good doctor is late, which gives me far too much time to consider my limited options as I try not to completely wilt in heat that makes my armpits feel swampy and has my ruthlessly straightened hair starting to curl. I could go to HR and tell them the position isn't a good fit after all. With less than a day on the job, it won't show up on my permanent record, especially since I only just completed the paperwork needed to enroll in the hospital's payroll system and health insurance program. I could still put a stop to it.

But then I recall how proud my parents and grandmothers were when I landed my first big job following years of school. After moving back home when Tony died, I'm finally on my own again in a new apartment I recently rented near the hospital in Kendall. And there's the wardrobe of power suits I purchased on credit so I could present a professional appearance at work. Paying for all of that is dependent upon my new cushy salary, which will be lost if I quit.

Quitting isn't an option.

Not when I haven't even given the job a chance. Besides, I'm not a quitter. My beloved Abuela would be so disappointed. She and my equally beloved Nona were happier about me landing this job than I was. Not to mention my top goal has always been to make Tony proud of me. I'm convinced he's close to me, and I want him to see me surviving and thriving, not walking away from a challenge the first time it gets tough. I can't disappoint everyone in my life by walking away from this opportunity. I've restored a bit of steel to my spine by the time the roar of a sports car draws my attention to the hospital's long driveway.

I watch in disbelief as a sleek black convertible Porsche growls its way up the half-circle drive with Northrup at the wheel and a bottle blonde in a sexy red dress riding shotgun.

"What a cliché," I mutter as he brings the low-slung black car to a halt two feet from where I stand ready to "welcome" him.

He alights from the car with catlike grace, tall, muscular and even handsomer than his photo—of course. As he comes toward me, he flashes a cocky smile, and damn if every cell in my body doesn't stand up and sing "Hallelujah" in a loud chorus of tightening nipples and dampening panties, which infuriates me.

I don't want any part of me reacting to any part of him, but I'd have to be dead not to notice this man. And while I might've been mostly numb for the last five years, Dr. Northrup is living proof that I'm still very much a living, breathing woman who recognizes a hot man when she sees one.

He props Wayfarer sunglasses on hair that's messy from the convertible. On him, messy is sexy. His golden eyes sparkle, his smile is straight out of a toothpaste commercial and his body . . . *Wow.* He must've spent as many hours in the gym as he logged in medical school.

I realize I'm staring but can't seem to bring myself to blink. Have I ever seen a more perfectly beautiful man in my entire life? The thought makes me feel disrespectful to the memory of the only man I've ever loved and snaps me out of the stupor I slipped into at the sight of Northrup.

I clear my throat and clutch the portfolio more tightly to my chest, desperate to hide any evidence of my ridiculous reaction to him. "Dr. Northrup?"

"That'd be me. And you are?"

"Carmen." I extend a hand that I pray isn't sweaty. "Carmen Giordino, assistant director of public relations. Welcome to Miami-Dade General Hospital."

"Pleased to meet you, Ms. Giordino." Somehow he makes the act of taking my hand, squeezing it lightly and releasing it into an erotic sex act that once again steals the breath from my lungs and the starch from my spine.

I hate him for making me react to him the way every other woman with a pulse has probably responded to him since puberty. I hate him even more when I discover he's pressed a fifty-dollar bill into my hand. I'm about to ask him what it's for when he fills in the blanks for me.

"Do me a favor, and please take Betty to the cafeteria, buy her some breakfast and send her off in a cab," he says in a low tone that only I can hear.

"But—"

"Did someone ask you to meet me and see to my *needs*?"

The way he says the word *needs* has me imagining him sweaty, naked and at my disposal, which infuriates me. I'm not sure who I'm more pissed with—him or myself. I feel my face go hot, and when I open my mouth to respond to his outrageous request, nothing comes out.

"What I *need* is for you to take care of her." He gives me an imploring look, and it's all I can do not to swoon. "Okay?"

It's insulting enough to be asked to babysit a neurosurgeon, but being asked to babysit his bimbo one-night stand is another story altogether. "I'm sorry, but I'm not willing—"

Ignoring me, he turns and gestures for "Betty" to join us on the curb. "Come on over and meet Carmen Giordino. She'll help you find the cafeteria and a ride to the airport." He kisses the blonde's cheek. "It was good to meet you, but I've got to get to work now."

"Thank you so much for *everything*, Jason," Betty says with her worshipful gaze fixed on his perfect face.

Northrup flashes his version of a sincere smile. "My pleasure."

I roll my eyes, imagining what "everything" included in this case. The pang of jealousy that nips at me only serves to further annoy me. What do I care if she got to take a spin with him?

He tosses his car keys to me, and I have the immediate choice of either catching them or letting them hit me in the head. I grab them a second before they would've hit me. "Can you find the staff lot and get Priscilla settled for me?" Winking, he adds, "Thanks. I owe you one." Glancing at Betty, he flashes that brilliant grin. "Or maybe two."

"But where're you going?"

"To check out my new digs. I'll catch up to you after a while."

"I'm supposed to—" I stop myself when I realize I'm talking to his back. So now I'm babysitting a bottle blonde *and* a Porsche 911? This day just gets better and better. I've never been prouder of the years I spent sweating my way through college and graduate school than I am in this moment.

My low growl has Betty stepping back from me, tottering on sky-high heels. "I'm not really all that hungry." Her nervous titter bugs the crap out of me.

I release my tight grip on the leather portfolio and let my arms drop to my sides, feeling utterly defeated an hour into my new "dream job."

Betty's eyes go wide, her red lips forming an O.

"What?" I look down to see what Betty is so focused on and notice that the veneer on my "leather" portfolio has baked onto the front of my very expensive and still-not-paid-for navy power suit. I let out a shriek of frustration.

"I'm sure it'll come off at the dry cleaner." Betty's kind smile makes me feel bad about the nasty thoughts I've had toward an innocent bystander to my career implosion.

Deciding I have nothing to lose by making Betty my ally, I glance at the other woman, who towers over me thanks to those four-inch heels. "Could I ask you how you came to meet . . . *him*?"

"It was the oddest coincidence."

Aren't they all?

"I was at the luggage thingy in the airport waiting for my bags that never came and my now ex-boyfriend who never showed up to get me." Betty swipes at a tear. "Then the airline couldn't book me on a flight home until this morning. I used all my money and maxed out my credit card flying here to see the *jerk* who stood me up. No luggage, no money, no jerk. Jason saw me crying and asked if he could help. Thank God for him, or I would've had to sleep in the airport. He even took me out for a nice dinner and bought me a bottle of my favorite wine."

"And what did he get in return for all this hospitality?" The question is out of my mouth before I can stop it. Horrified, I'm about to apologize for my rudeness when she continues.

"Nothing." Betty doesn't seem insulted by my question, which she absolutely should be. "He did me a favor and asked for nothing in return. He even slept on the sofa so I could have the bed. Then the alarm on his phone didn't go off. He was running late for his first day and was all stressed out. Do you know what time it is? My flight to Philly is at ten thirty. I'd like to see if they found my bag before then."

I check my phone, see that it's almost nine and eye the Porsche. "Get in." I wonder if it's possible to be fired on my first day. I'm about to find out as I slide into the scorching leather driver's seat and kick off my heels so I can drive this thing. The car starts with a growl that vibrates through my body, reminding me of the tingling reaction I had to its owner. His car smells the way I imagine he does—citrus and spice and hot man.

I'm thankful to Tony for teaching me to drive a stick in high school. That skill is about to come in handy.

If my palms were sweaty before, they're downright wet now as I navigate onto the busy interstate in a car that costs more than I'll make in ten years. Dr. Northrup told me to park it, not drive it nine miles each way to the airport. What if I crash it or hit something? The thought makes me sick to my stomach, as does pondering what the humid breeze is doing to hair I spent an hour straightening earlier.

It occurs to me in a sickening moment of dread that I never got the chance to tell his royal highness to steer clear of the executive suite. He won't go there, will he? Oh God, please let him be more interested in operating rooms and laboratories than conference rooms.

Mr. Augustino instructed me to babysit Jason Northrup. In turn, he asked me to babysit Betty. So in reality, I'm just following orders by driving Betty to the airport, right? This has to fall somewhere under "other duties as assigned," doesn't it?

In the highly unlikely event that Betty ever returns to South Florida and encounters a medical crisis, she'll remember the fine treatment provided by the staff of Miami-Dade General. There. I've done my part for public relations today.

"This is really nice of you," Betty says as we take the airport exit.

"No problem at all." I pull up to the curb at the departures level a few minutes later and release a sigh of relief that I didn't hit anything on the way.

Oh my God!

My purse, wallet, driver's license and cell phone are stashed in the top drawer of my desk back at the office. So on the return trip, I can also worry about being arrested for driving a "borrowed" car without a license. Fabulous!

The cop directing traffic at the drop-off area picks that moment to blow his whistle, which startles me and causes my foot to slip off the clutch. The car lurches forward and stalls. I miss hitting the car in front of me by less than an inch. It's official—before this day is out, I'm going to suffer a nervous breakdown. Hopefully I'll be back at the hospital when that happens.

Betty leans forward, stretching her neck to view the distance between the two cars. "That was a close one."

"No kidding."

"I'll get out of your hair so you can get along back to work."

"It was nice to meet you. I'm sorry you had such a lousy trip."

"It wasn't all bad," Betty says with a shrug. "I found out there're still nice people in the world willing to help a stranger in need."

First impressions, I'm finding, are often misleading. "Take this." I hand the fifty from Northrup to Betty. "He gave me this for your breakfast and cab fare."

Betty eyes the money with uncertainty. "I wouldn't feel right taking his money after all he did to help me."

"Look at his car. I bet you need it more than he does. Take it. Get yourself home, and then you can write to him at the hospital and pay him back."

Betty brightens at that idea. "I'll do that. Thanks again, Carmen."

"My pleasure." I watch Betty scurry into the terminal, as well as anyone can "scurry" on four-inch heels. Her jerk of a boyfriend missed out on a gem, that's for sure.

I return my focus to the task at hand, which is getting Dr. Jason Northrup's Porsche back to the hospital without a scratch or dent and without getting myself arrested.

CHAPTER 2

Carmen

The metal door slides shut with a loud clank that makes me jump out of my skin. Looking through the bars, I begin to laugh hysterically. This was *not* how I pictured the first day of my professional life unfolding. It wasn't even my fault. The car in front of me swerved, startling me into swerving, too. Of course, the cop behind us only saw *me* swerve and pulled me over.

When I couldn't produce my driver's license or proof that I had permission to drive the car, the officer said he didn't have any choice but to take me in and impound the Porsche until I can produce my license and prove I didn't steal it.

At the thought of my parents finding out I'm in jail, I choke on my laughter while my hands tremble uncontrollably. I've never even been to detention, let alone *jail*. How can this be happening?

They let me call my office at the hospital—you know, where I started my dream job *today*—to leave a message for Dr. Northrup. I asked him to call the station to confirm I didn't steal his Porsche. That was a tricky proposition—having the admin in the executive offices track down the new neurosurgeon, whom I'm supposed to be babysitting, because I need him to confirm I didn't steal his car.

I'm wondering how that sentence will look on my first performance appraisal.

If or when he makes that call and gets me out of lockup, then I'll retrieve the car he calls Priscilla from wherever they towed it. God, what if they damaged it? Will he expect me to pay for the repairs? How much will it cost to get the car back?

And what if he says I *did* steal his car, since he didn't exactly give me permission to drive it off the hospital campus? When it settles in that I'm probably going to be here awhile, I turn away from the bars to examine the tiny cell. At least it seems somewhat clean. The second I notice the toilet sitting against the back wall, I feel the urgent need to use it. But the thought of going where anyone can see me is unimaginable, so I'm determined to hold it until I have some privacy.

I lower myself gingerly to the narrow bunk. What if no one comes for me? What if Northrup reports the car stolen? What if I have no choice but to call my parents to bail me out? The thought of them coming to get me *here* has my stomach surging with nausea.

I have no idea how long I'm there. Judging by the discomfort coming from my overtaxed bladder, it has to be more than an hour.

The tingling sensation that dances over my skin is the first indication that Jason Northrup has materialized outside my cell. I have my own cell. Awesome.

"Fancy meeting you here." He flashes the sexy grin that made my heart race and my panties go damp earlier.

I'm in the biggest fight with my heart *and* my panties.

I jump to my feet, which I immediately regret thanks to the aforementioned bladder situation. "I didn't steal your car."

"Then how'd it end up getting impounded on I-95?"

"I gave Betty a ride to the airport. You told me to take care of her. She said her flight was at ten thirty. If I'd called a cab or Uber, she would've missed the flight."

His eyes drop to my chest, and just like that my nipples react.

Now I'm in a fight with them, too.

He returns his golden-eyed gaze to my face. "What happened to your jacket?"

Okay, so he was looking at the stain the portfolio left and not at my breasts. Try telling my breasts that. "Industrial accident."

His eyebrows come together in a stern expression that's just as sexy as all his other expressions. "And why are you dancing around like you've got ants in your pants?"

"Because." I can't believe I'm going to have to say these words to him, of all people. "I have to pee, if you must know."

He glances at the toilet in the cell and then at me.

"Not happening. Tell me you brought my purse so I can get out of here."

He points to the purse tucked under his arm, which I hadn't noticed.

A guard materializes and unlocks the cell door.

I'm so anxious to get out of there that I bolt forward and tilt awkwardly on my heel.

Northrup reaches out to stop me from falling, and for a brief, terrifying moment, I nearly lose control of my bladder.

"Please find me a bathroom with a door."

He takes me by the elbow and steers me through the corridors to a restroom in the lobby.

I have to go so badly I don't take the time to contemplate the wisdom of allowing him to touch me, but my body has plenty to say about it. Tingling, goose bumps, pebbling, moistening. And all he did was place his hand on my elbow. This is *not* good—and it's so, so *bizarre.* I've never in my life reacted to *anyone* the way I do to him, and that makes me doubly mad. My late, beloved husband deserves far more respect than what he's been getting from me since Jason Northrup showed up.

In the restroom, I manage to tear my hose in the urgent quest for relief. Afterward, at the sink, I catch only a brief glance of myself in the mirror, but it's enough to see wild, frizzy dark hair thanks to a convertible and the South Florida humidity.

Resting my hands on the sink, I take a moment to gather myself, to summon the fortitude to resist the ridiculous attraction to Dr. Jason Northrup, who is so not my type it's not even funny, and prepare to face my new coworkers after a brief stint in jail. Hell of a way to start a new job.

My reaction to him has me rattled. It's been years since I've experienced anything resembling desire. I've almost forgotten what it feels like.

Tony has been gone so long sometimes it feels like we happened in a dream. The memories of him and the time we had together are fading with the passage of time, as much as I wish that wasn't the case. I'm terrified of forgetting him, and my reaction to Dr. Northrup makes me feel disloyal to the man who loved me with his whole heart.

I can't be attracted to Jason Northrup. Not like that. He's a professional colleague, and thus off-limits.

Besides, any guy who looks like him, drives a car like his and carries the title of "brain surgeon" has to be the romance equivalent of poison ivy. It would serve me well to remember that and keep my focus on repairing the damage I've done to my fledgling career in one calamitous morning.

I do what I can with my hair, which is basically nothing, and leave the room with a brisk, determined stride—barreling straight into the unyielding chest of Dr. Jason Northrup. Damn, of course he smells as good as his car. Better, if I'm being honest. Releasing a choppy sigh, I take comfort in the knowledge that this day has to end at some point.

"Feel better?" That teasing grin sends shivers down my spine—and probably the spine of every red-blooded woman in the universe.

I step back from him, forcing him to drop the hold he has on my arms. "Much better. Am I allowed to leave?"

"You have to pay the ticket and sign some stuff."

"I'm getting a *ticket*?" My driving record is impeccable—or it was until now.

"'Fraid so. Driving without a license."

"But I *have* a license. I just didn't have it *with* me."

"And therein lies the problem." Nodding to the window where a stone-faced cop waits for me, Northrup withdraws my purse from under his arm and hands it to me.

"How did you, um, get here?"

"Took an Uber."

"And your car?"

"Impound lot. We'll go there next."

I do some fast mental math and figure that after the recent apartment deposit and wardrobe spending spree, I have about four hundred dollars available on my credit card. Beyond that, I'm in deep trouble. "How much will it cost to get it out?"

"No idea. I guess we'll find out."

Swallowing hard, I step up to the window, hoping Northrup isn't zeroing in on the tear in my hose. Almost as if I gave him the idea, I can *feel* the heat of his gaze on me and wonder if he is having the same puzzling reaction to me. Then I decide I do *not* want to know the answer to that question.

"Sign here," the cop says gruffly.

My signature is as wobbly as the rest of me after my hour in jail.

"That's three hundred twenty dollars."

I gasp. "For driving without a license?"

"And swerving out of your lane."

"But I swerved to avoid hitting another car that swerved into *my* lane!"

The cop looks up at me, his mouth falling open. "Carmen?"

My eyes dart to his name badge. PAULSON. Oh dear God. He was Tony's sergeant during his first year on the job.

"What the heck are you doing here? Hey, you guys, it's D'Alessandro's wife, Carmen."

A couple of other officers I don't recognize come over to the window to say hello, each of them asking me how I am and what I'm doing here.

Before I can respond to the barrage of questions, Paulson rips up the paperwork. "You should've said something. You're free to go, sweetheart."

"Oh, um, thank you." The gesture and the reason for it bring tears to my eyes that I can't deal with right now. I force myself to hold it together, to not let the grief overtake me. Not when I have too many other things to contend with, such as the doctor standing behind me who turns me on just by breathing.

"Your friend, Dr. Northrup, assured us it was all a big misunderstanding."

"Did he, now?"

"I did," Jason says from behind me. "She had permission to use my car."

"I can't do anything for you at the impound lot, though," the sergeant says. "That's out of my hands."

"Not to worry," Jason tells the kind sergeant. "We'll take care of it. Come on, Carmen. Let's get going."

"It's real good to see you, Carmen. I think about you and . . . Well, I think of you often. I hope you're doing all right."

"Thank you. I'm doing okay. Today being a notable exception."

"Glad to hear it." The sergeant gives me a sympathetic smile. "Don't be a stranger, you hear?"

"Well, I hope I don't see you again in this capacity."

Paulson laughs. "If you ever get arrested again, tell us who you are. We take care of our own."

"Good to know." I was so freaked out by being arrested, it never occurred to me to tell them who I am. Tony and I weren't married long enough for me to get around to changing my name, which was why the intake officers didn't recognize me. That and the fact they were probably in high school when Tony died. "Thanks again."

"No problem. Impound lot is two blocks that way." He points to the left.

"We'll find it."

Once again, Jason takes hold of my elbow to guide me out of the police station.

I tell myself to shake him off, to *tell* him off, to let him know I'm perfectly capable of walking without his assistance. But the minute I step out of the frigidly air-conditioned station into the warm sunshine, I begin to tremble again as the reality of my time in *jail* sinks in.

"You're fine."

I latch on to his soothing tone despite my resolve to keep my distance from the temptation he represents. As he runs a comforting hand over my back, I tell myself it's of no consequence to me that he immediately tuned in to my distress and said just what I needed to hear.

"It's over. No big deal."

"Sure. No big deal. And when my mother calls tonight to see how my first day went, should I mention my stint in jail?"

"You might want to leave that part out. You could tell her you went joyriding in a Porsche on company time. That's exciting."

I scowl up at him and find him looking down at me with a warm, friendly expression and the potent grin that makes me want to climb all over him. Our eyes meet and hold as a zing of awareness passes between us like an electrical current, confirming he feels it, too. Doubly fabulous and all the more reason to keep my distance.

Over my body's strenuous objections, I move away from him. "I can walk on my own."

"Suit yourself."

"Thank you, I will."

"Someday you'll laugh about all this, you know."

"I highly doubt it. Giordinos don't get arrested. They don't get handcuffed and fingerprinted and photographed. They don't get searched and tossed in a cell."

"They *searched* you?"

I can't bear to relive the humiliation of it. "Yes."

"*Strip*-searched?"

"Just about. They made me remove my outer garments to ensure I wasn't concealing any weapons." Single most humiliating moment of my life.

"Huh."

"What does that mean? *Huh?*"

"I'm getting a visual of you in sensible white cotton underwear, and it's rather . . . appealing."

I whirl on him, prepared to punch him or at least smack the smug grin off his face, but his grin isn't smug. It's not smug at all. It's rather tortured, and when I venture a glance below the belt of his black dress pants, *smug* isn't at all the word that comes to mind. *Impressive* is more like it. Very, *very* impressive and very, *very* aroused. Over the thought of me in my underwear. Oh God.

"I do *not* wear sensible white cotton underwear," I spit at him, furious at myself for letting my eyes venture down *there*. For reasons I'll ponder later when I'm far, far away from him, it's important he know that my underwear is neither white *nor* cotton.

"All the more interesting." He runs a finger over my cheek, the caress sending a torrent of heat and light and energy to every corner of my body.

Stunned and totally unnerved by my reaction to him, I take a step back. "I don't know what kind of game you think you're playing—"

He drops his hand. "No game. The last thing I need right now is any kind of romantic entanglements."

"Good. We have that in common. So don't touch me again."

"I apologize."

We walk the two blocks in uneasy silence that he breaks right before we reach the gates to the impound lot. "What was that about back there? Why did he tear up your ticket?"

"I . . . um . . . I used to know someone with the department." The most important someone in my life, someone I loved and lost in the worst way imaginable. A shudder of agony goes through me, transporting me right back to the darkest days of my life. Grief is funny that way. It can come at you out of nowhere, smacking you in the face with memories so painful they can still take your breath away five years later.

"Are you all right?"

I nod, because that's all I can do.

Inside, we learn they want six hundred bucks for the car. Before I can process that number, Jason hands over a black American Express card.

"I'll pay you back."

Somehow.

I should've called an Uber for Betty. My carefully calculated budget has no room for even incremental payments on a six-hundred-dollar debt. I'll have to pick up some extra shifts at the restaurant to settle my debt with him as soon as possible. So much for thinking my waitressing career was over now that I have a big new job.

"Don't worry about it. I need to get back to the hospital, so can we please expedite this transaction?"

"Fine," I say through gritted teeth as he reminds me that my disaster is affecting his first day of work, too. I step back to give him room to sign the credit card slip. Sneaking a glance, I find his signature remarkably legible for a doctor and then berate myself for caring.

After one of the workers delivers the Porsche to the parking lot outside the office, Jason takes a long measuring walk around it, checking every inch for damage.

I twist my hands together and say two Hail Marys while I await the verdict. "Is it . . . Did they . . ."

"She seems fine."

They probably hear my sigh of relief all the way up in Broward County.

Jason opens the passenger door and gestures for me to get in.

I let out a yelp when my ass connects with sizzling leather seats.

"Watch out, the seat might be hot."

"Gee, thanks for the warning."

Needing to do something with my restless hands, I reach for the seat belt and have it secured by the time he slides into the driver's seat. Here I am sitting in the world's sexiest car next to what could very well be the world's sexiest man with a rat's nest on my head, a seat burn on my bum, holes in my hose and a vinyl smear on the front of my pricey suit. This could happen only to me.

"I really will pay you back as soon as possible." If I have to waitress every night for weeks, I *will* pay back every dime he's spent to get me out of this mess.

"You can pay me back in trade."

CHAPTER 3

Carmen

I stare at him, my mouth hanging open in shock.

"Close your mouth, and get your mind out of the gutter." His chuckle is sexy and galling. "As appealing as your idea might be, that's not what I'm talking about."

I feel my face go hot and not from the bright sun beaming down on us. "You don't know what I was thinking!"

"Oh, please. Like your every thought doesn't show on your face."

"It does not!"

"Does too."

"I never knew neurosurgeons could be so immature."

That draws another laugh from him. "Our childlike brilliance makes us so charming and lovable."

I roll my eyes. "*Whatever.*" I'm surprised there's room left for me in the small car with all the space his overblown ego requires. Good thing the top is still down.

"What I *meant* was I need your help."

"*You* need *my* help? With what, exactly?" I can't wait to hear this.

"My reputation has taken a rather serious hit, and I need to fix it—fast."

I'm intrigued by the agony I hear in his voice. I know what agony feels like, and despite my best intention to stay removed from him, I find myself shifting in the seat so I can better see him. And, oh my . . . He's put on the Wayfarer sunglasses, has one hand casually looped over the wheel of the powerful car, and the sleeve of his starched dress shirt is rolled up to reveal the golden hair and an expensive watch on his forearm. *Yum.*

"What do you mean? What happened?"

"When we get back to the office, do a search for my name. The whole thing is out there for the world—and the board at Miami-Dade General—to see."

I gasp. "You met with the board?"

He releases a short laugh. "If you want to call it that."

"Oh *God.*" Is it possible to get thrown in jail *and* fired in the same day? I fear I'm about to find out. My stomach takes a sickening dive. Giordinos don't get fired, and they sure as hell don't get arrested. When I think about the huge party my family held at the restaurant to celebrate my new job . . . I just can't go back and tell them it all went to shit on the *first* day.

"What?"

"Mr. Augustino requested that I, um, keep you clear of the board meeting."

His hand tightens on the wheel. "Great," he mutters. "You might've mentioned that to me."

"As if you gave me the opportunity!" Remembering him tossing me his keys *and* his gal pal has me scowling. "Why don't you tell me what's going on?"

"Because I want you to see what I'm up against before you hear my side of it."

"Are we talking personal or professional?"

"Personal. Extremely personal."

There's something about the way he says that . . . I don't want to be interested. I do *not* want to know what personal matter has left his reputation in tatters. Yeah, sure. I want to know all right. I want to know so badly I have to resist the urge to ask to borrow his phone so I can start searching right away.

My mind spins with scenarios and possibilities, none of them pleasant. I'm almost afraid of what I might learn about him. For some odd reason, I don't want to read anything that will force me to dislike him forever. I much prefer the kind, thoughtful man Betty described to the arrogant, entitled jerk I expected him to be.

"Just remember," he says, glancing at me, "you can't believe everything you read. There's *always* another side to the story."

His words send a nervous flutter through my abdomen.

We arrive at the hospital, locate the staff lot and secure him a parking pass rather efficiently in light of how the rest of my day has gone. When we're parked in his assigned space, he stops me from getting out of the car. "It was wrong of me to ask you to take care of Betty, but I want to thank you for your help."

"Even if it cost you more than six hundred dollars and got your car impounded?"

"You'll pay me back, and the car is fine."

"It might take me a while to pay you back, especially if I get fired."

"Why would you get fired?"

"Hello? I failed to do the *only* thing my boss asked me to do and ended up in *jail* on my first day of work. If he doesn't fire me, it'll be a flipping miracle."

"He doesn't know about the jail thing," Jason assures me. "Mona promised me she wouldn't tell anyone."

"Mona?"

"The executive assistant who took your call from, um, jail. When she tracked me down and told me what'd happened, I asked for her discretion."

"And I'm sure she was more than happy to give you anything you requested." I can't help the disgust that drips from every word I say to him. Guys like him can get any female they encounter to march to their orders just by looking at them with their bedroom eyes.

"She assured me she wouldn't tell anyone, which I figured would be important to you." His shrug makes me feel small for questioning his methods. How does he manage to infuriate me and endear himself to me in the same second? He's giving me whiplash. "And by the way, I like your hair all curly like that."

I reach up to smooth the ratty disaster area. "Now you're just making fun of me." I get out of the car and slam the door, setting out for the nearest entrance, aware of the warm breeze rushing over the hole in my hose.

Jason catches up to me. "I'm not making fun of you. I like your hair curly. Why is that a felony offense?"

"Because it's not *curly*. It's *frizzy*. It looks horrible! I spent an hour straightening it this morning for nothing."

"Doesn't look frizzy to me. It looks *curly*. And sexy."

"You should probably have your eyes checked before you go digging around in anyone's brain if you think my hair looks *good* right now."

He cracks up, and of course laughter is a very nice look on him. "First of all, I don't 'dig around' in people's brains, and second of all, I think it looks nice like that, better than it did when it was all straight and severe looking earlier."

"You need to stop talking."

"And you need to learn to take a compliment."

If we weren't about to enter the hospital, I might've screamed in frustration or compounded my troubles by assaulting the hospital's new neurosurgeon. He drives me freaking bonkers—in more ways than one. In the lobby, we wait for the elevator. I push the number five and wait for him to choose his floor. When he doesn't, I look over at him. "Where're you going?"

"To meet with Mr. Augustino to find out what the board decided to do about me."

"Do about you? What does that mean?"

He leans against the back wall of the elevator in a relaxed pose that's in sharp contrast to the tension that has his jaw pulsing and his lips flat. "Apparently, there was some considerable debate about whether they're going to extend privileges for me to practice here."

"Aren't you supposedly some sort of world-class pediatric neurosurgeon?"

"Supposedly."

"So why would they deny you privileges?"

"Do that search. You'll find it highly illuminating."

In the executive suite, the woman I assume is Mona greets us with a sympathetic look for me and a lustful gaze at Jason. "I'm so sorry," she whispers. "I haven't told anyone."

"Thank you for that." It occurs to me that I owe Jason a debt of gratitude for anticipating the need to keep a lid on what happened to me. Without his quick thinking, the news of my stint in jail would be ripping through the corridors, and I'd be a laughingstock on my first day.

"Did that happen in jail?" Mona asks, pointing to the smear on my suit jacket.

I almost forgot about that. Funny how that disaster pales in comparison to the others that followed.

"It was an industrial accident," Jason offers in a grave tone.

"Oh." Mona's eyes go wide with dismay as she tries to figure out what kind of industrial accident I encountered. I figure she's in her early fifties and single, judging from the lack of a ring on her left hand. She has a sweet round face and an unfortunately choppy haircut. To Jason, she says, "Mr. Augustino is available whenever you're ready."

"Well," he replies with the charming smile that makes my insides go batty and my panties damp, "here goes nothing. Wish me luck."

"Good luck," Mona says, clearly enthralled.

"Yes." I clear the lust from my throat. "Good luck."

He leaves us with a deceptively jaunty wave and heads for the hospital president's spacious office on the far side of the suite.

"He's dreamy, isn't he?" Mona watches him until he's out of sight.

Since the last thing I want to talk about is Jason Northrup's dreaminess, I turn the focus toward work. "Is Taryn around?" She's my other boss, the director of public relations.

"You haven't heard? She had her baby early. She'll be out for the next six weeks." Mona lowers her voice. "I don't think she's coming back, but you didn't hear that from me."

This day goes from bad to worse, and I wouldn't have thought that was possible. I break into a fit of nervous laughter that I struggle to contain. I'm going to be either laughing hysterically or sobbing any second. The chance to work for Taryn was one of the things I was most excited about. She seriously impressed me with her savviness during my interviews. I was looking forward to learning a lot from her.

"She left instructions in your office and a thumb drive with some other documents she thought you'd find useful. She must've had a premonition that she was going early. Let me know if I can help with anything."

"Thank you."

I step into my office and sink into the desk chair. I'm hungry, thirsty, miserably sweaty and disheveled beyond repair. But before I attend to any of those pressing concerns, I fire up my computer and open the browser to type Jason's name into the search engine.

A quick scan of the headlines that pop instantly onto the screen shocks me to the core. "Oh my God. Oh my *God*."

Jason

After a grueling thirty minutes with Augustino, I return to Carmen's office, trying to prepare myself for her disappointment and disillusionment. I sensed her attraction to me even though I could tell she didn't want to be attracted. Interestingly, I had the same reaction to her—instant attraction at the worst possible time.

Arriving this morning to find her waiting for me outside the hospital, so prim and pretty and put together, reawakened something that's lain dormant in the long weeks since "the disaster." The urge to muss her up, to unbutton that sexy power suit and run my hands over her extravagant curves the suit tried—and failed—to hide, took me by surprise. I wasn't lying when I told her I like her hair curly and loose, as if she just rolled out of bed.

The thought of her naked in a bed catches the attention of the libido I feared was lost forever—until images of her in white cotton underwear assailed me earlier.

Forcing myself to put a damper on the salacious thoughts—for now anyway—I stand in the doorway to her office, arms propped on the doorjamb over my head, watching her dark eyes dart across the screen as she reads about what a scum-sucking slimeball I am. What she won't find anywhere in the vast coverage of what happened in New York is mention of how I was victimized by a woman with an agenda.

She's so absorbed in her reading she doesn't notice me there until I decide she's probably seen enough to get the gist. "Quite a story, huh?"

Jolting in surprise, she looks up at me, and in that brief instant of eye contact I see all the things I feared as well as a healthy dose of revulsion that makes me sadder than I've been since it first happened.

I drop into a chair, exhausted after weeks of sleepless nights tinged with heartache and serious fear over what's to become of my once-promising career. "Too bad most of it isn't true."

"What part isn't true? The fact that she was married to the chairman of the hospital's board, or the part where you slept with her for months before he caught the two of you together?"

I expected the indictment, but for some reason it hurts more than usual coming from her. "The part where she didn't tell me she was married and used me to get rid of a husband she'd grown tired of." I watch Carmen's expressive face as she processes the information, but unlike earlier when her every thought and emotion were on full display, now she's closed off, guarded.

"You're saying she set you up."

I nod. "And I fell for it hook, line and sinker. Her husband demanded my immediate resignation, but the board balked because of all the research money and grants tied to my work. So they voted to ship me off to their sister facility in sunny Florida. Turns out, though, sunny Florida isn't so sure it wants me, either. And in case you didn't know, it's damn tough to practice neurosurgery without hospital privileges."

"What did Mr. Augustino say?"

"He jumped at the chance to hire me when offered the opportunity. Unfortunately, he wasn't told about the scandal, only that I was looking for a transfer. So his neck is on the line now that I'm here, bringing all that crap with me. The board is apparently unhappy with him—and me—to have been put in this position and wants two weeks to thoroughly review the situation before they decide."

"What're you supposed to do in the meantime?"

"Cool my heels, play tourist, repair my reputation. You know, the usual stuff people do on vacations."

"Why don't you just quit and go somewhere else? Surely you'd have no trouble finding a position elsewhere. I read your CV, too."

She's referring to my curriculum vitae, which boasts an impressive list of accomplishments and cutting-edge surgical achievements, for all the good that does me now. "Because I have years of work tied up in research and grants that'll be lost if I leave. The only way I can continue my work is to stay within the East Coast Health Partners system. This was the only pediatric neurosurgical opening available in a state where I'm already licensed. East Coast requires us to be licensed in multiple states so we can be called in to consult on cases where needed. I've actually worked at Miami-Dade once before, when I was brought in to assist with a surgery."

Carmen rolls her lip between her teeth. "Why didn't you go public with how she set you up? You could've saved yourself a lot of grief if you'd told your side of it."

"Two reasons. One, it's damned hard to refute the fact that her husband caught us naked together in their Hamptons house."

Carmen winces at that.

"And two, she has teenage children who don't deserve to be dragged any further through the mud. It's not their fault their mother is a calculating bitch who was cast as the victim in the media that savaged the handsome, douchebag neurosurgeon. To hear them tell it, I seduced the unsuspecting wife and mother. She never said *anything* to discount those assertions." Even all these weeks later, it's still hard to reconcile the calculating bitch with the warm, giving woman I thought I was in love with.

"Her children matter more to you than repairing the damage to your reputation?"

This is where it gets sticky. "My father had a rather ambitious extracurricular track record." My dull, flat tone is the same one I've used anytime this subject has arisen over the last twenty years. "I remember far too well how it felt to learn he was cheating on my mother and to have the whole town talking about it. I can't be responsible for doing that to innocent kids who can't help what their mother is."

Is that admiration I see coming from her? And why does it matter so much to me? "Will you help me, Carmen?"

"You need a team of crisis communication experts, not someone right out of school with hardly any experience—"

"I want someone who needs a big win as much as I do. We've got two weeks to prove to the board that letting me join their staff won't be a mistake. Can I count on you?" I don't mention that her morning exploits cost me more than six hundred dollars—not that I care in the least about the money—but she owes me a favor. "Carmen?"

She makes me wait a long time before she replies. "I want the full story before I agree to anything."

"Fine." I stand to leave. "I'll tell you the whole sordid tale tonight over dinner."

"Wait. I never said anything about—"

"Please?" I give her my best imploring look.

After a long pause, she writes something on a piece of paper and hands it to me.

Her address.

I'm weak with relief. "Thank you."

"You're welcome."

"Pick you up at seven thirty?"

"That's fine."

Right at seven thirty, I park on the street outside her building and walk up two flights of stairs to Carmen's apartment. I feel guilty about the way I insisted she see me tonight. The fact is, I don't know what else to do. I need someone who knows the local area and can help me figure out a plan to ingratiate myself with the hospital board so they'll take a chance on me.

If they don't, my career and years of research will be in serious jeopardy.

I can't let that happen. I'm so close to a critical breakthrough that'll have a major impact on the treatment of pediatric brain tumors. It's important work that I've devoted tremendous time and resources toward, and I can't let one conniving woman ruin all that progress.

As I knock on the door, I refuse to give her that in addition to what Ginger has already taken from me, namely my reputation as well as my faith in humanity and womankind.

The door opens, and once again, I'm struck speechless by the sight of Carmen Giordino. She's wearing a black wrap dress that accentuates the curvy figure that makes me want to drool. Her dark hair is down around her shoulders, and I'm delighted she's left it curly rather than straightening it into submission.

When I say the last freaking thing I need is another romantic entanglement with someone associated with my work, I mean that with every fiber of my being, and yet . . . I'm incredibly attracted to this woman.

"Come in. I'm almost ready." She gestures to the kitchen. "I opened a bottle of wine if you want some. Glasses are over the dishwasher. I just need another minute."

I can't imagine what she still needs to do to improve on perfection, but I know better than to ask. I wander into the kitchen, pour half a glass of red wine and wander around her small but stylishly furnished apartment. My gaze is drawn to an array of framed photos on the wall. One is of Carmen with a handsome dark-haired man in a police uniform. Next to it is their wedding picture.

I suddenly remember what happened earlier at the police station while recalling my earlier observation that she doesn't wear a wedding ring. I realize with a sinking feeling that she must be the widow of a police officer. Before I can begin to process this new information, she returns, bringing a scent with her that makes me want to get closer to her.

She notices I'm looking at her photos.

I feel like I should say something. "Handsome guy."

"Yes, he was."

"What happened?"

"He was shot and killed on the job when he walked in on a robbery in progress at a convenience store." The words sound well practiced, as if she's said them a thousand times before.

"I'm so sorry for your loss."

"Thank you." She takes a sip of her wine. "We'd been together since our freshman year of high school and married almost a year."

I ache for her. "What was his name?"

"Antonio, but we called him Tony."

"You were a beautiful couple."

She smiles even though her dark eyes are sad. "We were happy together."

"How long ago did you lose him?"

"Five years. He was in his second year on the job."

"You must've been very young at the time."

"I was twenty-four."

"Oh damn. I really am so sorry."

"It was a long time ago."

Something about the way she says those words indicates that even though five years have passed, the loss is still fresh for her in many ways.

"Where should we go for dinner?" she asks.

"You're the local expert. You tell me."

"What do you like?"

You. I like you. The words pop into my brain, an involuntary reaction to an innocuous question and the sort of thought I have no business having toward my new colleague. "I'll eat anything."

She thinks about that for a second. "I know where we should go."

I follow her out of the apartment, changed by the information I learned inside her home. While I can't and won't deny I was instantly attracted to her, I need to respect what she's been through, dial back the attraction and focus on getting my life sorted.

If I keep my mind where it belongs—on fixing the disaster my promising career has become—then I won't do anything stupid like allow myself to fall for the beautiful young woman who may hold the key to my redemption.

CHAPTER 4

CARMEN

I'll confess to having had a bad case of preconceived notions about the good doctor. Such as—if he looks like a sexy surfer dude and is also a brain surgeon, he must be a tool. In other words, a man like him can have anyone he wants, so I expect him to be full of himself and constantly looking for a better offer.

"We're going to Coconut Grove. It'll take a while, but you'll figure out all the various parts of Miami."

"I had no idea it was such a sprawling city."

"It's massive, especially when you include Miami Beach. And traffic is a nightmare, always."

"I'm seeing that." He no sooner says those words than a car cuts in front of us and crosses three lanes of traffic to take an exit. "What the hell?"

"Get used to it. People are allergic to turn signals around here."

"I thought New York drivers were bad."

"They've got nothing on South Floridians."

Half an hour after we arrive at a Mexican restaurant one of my friends told me about, I've come to realize my preconceived notions about him were grossly unfair. He's not a tool, and he hasn't looked at anyone but me and the young man waiting on us.

That's not to say the other women in the room aren't looking at him, but he seemed completely oblivious to the attention he received as we followed the host into the dining room. One woman dining nearby with a man is practically panting as she stares at my companion.

Women are gross sometimes. I want to snap at her to keep her eyes where they belong, especially since she's old enough to be Jason's mother.

And yes, he told me to call him Jason and not Dr. Northrup. That happened on the ride to the restaurant in the same Porsche that landed me in jail earlier today. I still can't believe that actually happened, I think with a nervous laugh.

He looks at me over the top of his menu. "What's so funny?"

"I was just recalling my time in jail."

"I'm glad you're laughing about it."

"The alternative would be to cry hysterically."

"Nah, no need for that. You handled it like a champ."

"I'm glad you think so. On the inside, I was quaking." I lean in to whisper. "I've never even been to detention."

He laughs, and the sound washes over me like a soothing balm, surprising me with a familiar feeling of comfort. "You're a very good girl, aren't you?"

"Yes! I always have been."

"Here's a newsflash. You won't go to hell because you spent an hour in lockup."

"How do you know that?"

"Because. Hell is reserved for the truly bad people, and you're a truly good person."

"And how do you know *that*?"

He dips a chip into salsa. "Am I wrong?"

"I try to be a good person and help others."

"There you go. An hour in the clink isn't going to undo all that goodness."

"If my grandmothers find out about it, I'll never hear the end of it."

"There's no reason to tell them or anyone. It was a misunderstanding. That's all."

"It was an hour in *jail*."

"Think of it as life experience. Now you know what it's like to be arrested."

"That's the kind of life experience I could do without, so you can quit trying to make it into something positive."

"It's a good story you can tell your kids someday, about the time Mommy stole a Porsche and got herself arrested."

I'm in the middle of a sip of water when he says that, and I cough as water comes spewing out my nose and mouth.

He loses it laughing again, and every female head in the place—and a few of the male heads—swivels in his direction. "Do you need CPR over there?"

I wave him off and use the white cloth napkin to wipe the water off my face. "A, I did not *steal* a Porsche. I *borrowed* it to do your dirty work. And B, I didn't actually get arrested, because I was never arraigned."

His brows furrow with concern. "You know there was nothing dirty about what went down with Betty, right?"

"I heard what you did for her. It was very nice of you."

"It was no big deal. I felt so bad for her when we ran into each other at baggage claim yesterday, and she was crying because her guy blew her off. Then her bag never came, and I couldn't just leave her there by herself in a strange city."

"Most people would've walked away and left her to fend for herself."

"Well, I'm not most people."

"I'm beginning to realize that."

The waiter arrives with salads for both of us.

"Talk to me about what you want to see happen with this so-called campaign of yours."

"I'm looking for community service opportunities, things I can do to stay busy and make a difference at the same time."

"With publicity or without?"

"Preferably without, but I do need a way for the board to find out I'm doing it."

"We could make that happen."

"*We* could, could we?"

I'm unnerved by his amusement as well as the intrigued way in which he looks at me. Since I lost Tony, I've been on more first dates than I can count but have mostly avoided confronting the reality that the love of my life is gone and never coming back. Everyone who is anyone has told me that someday I'll find love again, and while I'm not opposed to that, I certainly haven't been looking for it.

Today and tonight with Jason . . . It's the first time I've felt anything for another man since Tony died. The feelings he arouses in me are unexpected and mostly unwelcome. I don't want to react to him the way I do. I want to help him with his problem and be on my way, with my debt to him paid.

But with every minute I spend in his magnetic presence, it becomes clear that nothing about my association with this man will be simple.

"Carmen? Are you okay?" He seems genuinely concerned as he watches me across the table.

"I'm fine, and to answer your question, I'm sure we can find a way to make sure the right people hear about your outreach efforts without making it into a media circus."

"That's good," he says, sounding relieved. "The last thing I'm looking for is any more media attention."

"You promised you'd tell me the whole story of what happened in New York."

"I know." He puts down his fork, wipes his mouth and sips his margarita, taking a full minute to gather himself before he speaks. "You should know one thing before you hear anything else."

"What's that?"

"I thought I loved her, and I assumed she loved me, too. I thought I'd finally found 'the one.'" His entire demeanor changes. "I'm sure you think you've got me pegged. Reasonably handsome dude, a doctor, must be a player, must have a different woman in his bed every night, and so on."

"Those thoughts never crossed my mind."

He smiles, but it's a sad version of the earlier smiles that lit up his entire face. "Sure they didn't. The truth is, I work like a fiend. Or I used to work like a fiend, back when I had a job and a research team and surgeries scheduled back to back. I'd work sixteen or eighteen hours straight without blinking an eye. I had no time to be a player, and besides, I'm just not wired that way."

"How're you wired?"

"I always imagined that once my training was finished, I'd find someone I liked well enough to spend forever with and get married and have some kids. I never had the desire or time to chase a different woman every night. That's not to say that some of my doctor friends don't do that, because they do. But it wasn't my thing."

He takes another sip of his drink and props his elbows on the table. "I met Ginger at a fundraiser for childhood cancer. A doctor I went to medical school with had invited me. He's a pediatric oncologist now and was one of the sponsors. Since my research focuses on malignant pediatric brain tumors, he thought I might be interested in the event. I was by myself at the bar when she approached me. We started talking. She was funny and beautiful, and it'd been a long time since I'd taken even five minutes for myself. When she asked if I wanted to get a nightcap after the event, I was all in."

The retelling of this story seems to pain him, and I feel for him, even if my goal is to help him without getting overly involved. That goal slips further out of reach with every minute I spend with him. I like him. I don't want to like him, but I do.

"So we went to the bar in the hotel where the fundraiser was held, and we continued to talk and laugh. Pretty soon it was last call, and we were the only ones left in the bar. When she produced a room key and asked if I wanted to join her upstairs, I didn't hesitate. I'd had more fun with her than I'd had with any woman in years. That was the start of it."

"How long were you with her before you learned the truth?"

"Three months. And I own the fact that I should've asked more questions, but I was busier than hell at work and with her if I wasn't working. It was the most fun I'd had since before med school. I fell completely in love with her, or so I thought."

"She never mentioned her husband or children in that time?"

"Not once. With hindsight, I can see that she was intentionally vague about her life away from me. She told me she was on several boards, including the organization that had the fundraiser the night we met, and her volunteer work kept her super busy. I also realized, after the fact, that she was intentional about us not being seen together in public after that first night. She told me she wanted to hibernate with me, and that was more than fine with me. After spending ten or twelve hours in an OR, I was fine with a home-cooked meal and a night in bed with her.

"By the time she invited me to her home in the Hamptons for the weekend, it never would've occurred to me that she was married or had children."

"The thing I don't get is if she wanted out of the marriage, why didn't she just ask for a divorce?"

"I didn't understand that, either, but later I learned that it was about humiliating him with a younger man who, in her words, was everything the husband wasn't—young, sexy, hot in bed, successful in a way the husband would never be. It had nothing at all to do with me and everything to do with paying her husband back for years of ignoring her as well as protecting her bank account. Or something like that. I may never know the full story of what went on between them. One thing I do know is she never intended for it to become public. That wasn't part of her plan. The fact that her kids were deeply hurt is what bothers me the most."

"Because of what happened in your own family."

"Yeah. It's the worst thing ever to have everyone in school find out that one of your parents has been having an affair. Kids have no ability to understand that shit, and it shouldn't be something they have to deal with."

The forceful way he says that tells me he's never gotten over what his philandering father did.

"It's really important to me that you know, that everyone knows, there's *no way* I would've been part of something like this if I'd known the truth. And yes, in this day and age, anyone with a cell phone has the ability to find out anything they need to know about anyone else. But it never occurred to me that I needed to be suspicious of her. I thought I'd finally found someone I could spend my life with. Instead I found myself embroiled in a scandal that screwed up my entire life and threatened a career I've given everything to. Sometimes I still can't believe it actually happened."

"I'm really sorry she did that to you."

He looks up at me, his expression madly vulnerable. "You believe me?"

"Of course I do."

He exhales a deep breath. "I'm sure some of the people I worked with in New York couldn't believe I had no idea who she was, but I really didn't. I had nothing to do with the hospital's board of directors. I worked so much that it was all I could do to find time to eat and sleep a few hours every day. What did I care who the chairman of the board of the hospital was? As long as he stayed out of my way and let me do my job, I had no reason to deal with him. My boss was the chief of surgery, not the chairman of the hospital board."

"I'll never understand why people do the things they do sometimes. After I lost Tony, a woman who was married to one of the other officers in his squad started a fundraising effort for me and then kept the money. I never asked her to do it, but people were so nice afterward. They wanted to help. I didn't even know she'd started the fund. I got caught up in that mess at a time when I had zero defenses."

"People suck."

"Sometimes. Thankfully not all the time. There was so much more good than bad after Tony died, but the idea that someone would actually take advantage of his death for their own gain was so impossible to believe."

"It's disgusting. Did you ever get the money?"

"A year or so later, and she ended up charged with a crime. It was awful on top of everything else I was dealing with."

"I'm sorry that happened to you. Losing your husband at twenty-four is more than enough trauma without it being compounded by greed."

"For sure."

Our entrées are served—chicken enchiladas for him and tacos al pastor for me. The food is blah compared to what I'm used to, but there's no way I could take him home to the family restaurant, even if the food is way better. I don't need them making this into something it isn't.

"Tell me about the night he caught you with her."

"Ugh, do I have to?"

"I want to make sure I know the whole story so I can help you figure out the best plan."

He pushes his half-eaten dinner aside, takes another sip of his drink and speaks in a dull, flat tone. "She planned everything about that night to ensure maximum carnage."

"How do you mean?"

"When he walked in on us, she was on her knees giving me a blow job."

I wince. "Damn."

"I heard the bedroom door open, and I looked down at her in time to see the calculating look she sent his way even as she continued to suck my dick with great enthusiasm." He glances at me. "Sorry for being so blunt."

I wave off his apology. "What happened then?"

"My first order of business was getting my dick out of her mouth, and then I was focused on defending myself because he came at me with fists flying. I had no idea what was happening, but she did. She knew exactly what was going on, because she'd planned the entire shit show."

"Where were their children?"

"I don't know. I only found out she had children the next day when I heard from my boss that my privileges at the hospital were suspended and I was to stay off the hospital campus until the board had a chance to meet and discuss the sordid mess. He's the one who told me that all this time I'd been screwing the married mother of two teenagers and that her husband was the chairman of the board of my freaking hospital."

"I can't imagine how shocking that had to be for you."

"It took days for me to realize our entire relationship was a setup on her part. I finally did what I should've done when I first met her and looked her up online. I found out that she'd been trying to get out of the marriage for years, but he refused to divorce her because all their money came from her family. If he divorced her, he'd lose everything, because they had a prenup. He was holding her hostage in the marriage, so she set out to humiliate him in the biggest way she could think of."

"That's so awful."

"It really was. It's one thing to go through a rough breakup when a relationship dies of natural causes, but this . . . This was on a whole other level. And then it got really fun when the New York media picked up the story and plastered it all over the city. The headlines were brutal. *Brain surgeon seduces hospital board chairman's wife.* I think the source on that story was one of my colleagues who was always trying to prove he's better than me when everyone knows he isn't. He took great pleasure in my downfall, especially when I got suspended."

"Have you considered a lawsuit against her?"

"I have, and I even went so far as to meet with an attorney who told me I'd have a very good case."

"So you're doing that?"

He shakes his head.

"Why not?"

"Her kids have been through enough. I just don't have it in me to drag them through the mud again."

"Jason . . . She ruined your life. She shouldn't be allowed to get away with that."

"She hasn't ruined my life yet."

"She ruined your life in New York."

"I just want to put it behind me, and a lawsuit would keep it alive for years. I had the lawyer reach out to let her know I was considering litigation, and he said she totally freaked out about that. It's enough for me that she's worried I might sue her. My only goal now is officially landing this job at Miami-Dade and having the chance to restore my reputation through the work. That's all that matters, and I can't do the work without hospital privileges. In many other specialties, I could fly solo, but not in neurosurgery."

"Does it have to be neurosurgery?"

CHAPTER 5

Carmen

He looks at me like I'm insane, and maybe I am. "It took *years* of training to get to where I was before this happened. I'm board certified, which is the holy grail. I'd be a fool to walk away from my specialty, not to mention the research I've worked on for years."

"I'm not suggesting you walk away. I'm just wondering if you have options."

"Of course I do, but I've been on this path for most of the last decade . . ." He shakes his head as his cheek pulses with tension. "I can't let her destroy my career, Carmen. I won't let her."

"Is your goal to find a way back to New York?"

"That'd be my preference, but I don't think that's going to happen. I'm persona non grata there after the board chairman personally saw to it that I was exiled to Miami. And now they're balking at being stuck with me."

"Is that what they said?"

"Mr. Augustino was rather blunt. He said the board isn't interested in dealing with me or my scandal, but they *are* interested in my research. Apparently, that's the only reason they're even considering granting me privileges at Miami-Dade."

"Did he say what happens at the end of the two weeks?"

"I assume they'll decide my research isn't worth the stink I bring with me. I think they're basically giving me lip service but have no intention of granting privileges."

"Is there any chance at all you'd consider doing an interview with someone here in Miami to set the record straight about what happened in New York?"

He ponders that for a minute. "I'd do it in a hot second if there was no chance of it being plastered all over the New York media. That's not going to happen, though, with the internet. And in order to clear my name, I'd have to trash hers."

"And you won't do that because of her kids."

"Right."

I totally respect him for doing what he can to protect her children from further humiliation. This day has been a good reminder about the danger of leaping to conclusions about people. "What about asking her to contact the Miami-Dade board directly?"

His grimace tells me what he thinks of that idea. "That would require me to speak to her, and I'm not willing to do that."

"Even to save your career?"

"I wouldn't do it to save my life."

"Could you text or email her so you wouldn't have to speak to her?"

"Ugh, I really don't want to have anything more to do with her if I can avoid that."

"Maybe have the lawyer do it in exchange for possibly not suing her?"

"I suppose I could do that, as long as we leave the option open to sue her. It gives me pleasure to imagine her sweating that. I'll hit up the lawyer tomorrow."

While I ponder other options, the waiter clears our plates and leaves dessert menus. Since Jason hardly touched his dinner, they box it up for him.

I order fried ice cream to buy myself time to think about a strategy that might work to change the board's mind about him. I have one idea that's been floating around since earlier.

"How would you feel about doing some pro bono work while you wait to meet with the board?"

"What do you have in mind?"

"There's a free clinic in Little Havana that does amazing work in the community. The doctor who works there was recently in a serious car accident and will be out of work for quite some time. The nurses are doing their best to keep up, but they could use some help."

"I'd have to check with my insurance carrier. I'm still an employee of East Coast and covered by their insurance, but I also have my own policy due to the high-risk nature of my specialty. I'm pretty sure I can get coverage for any volunteer work I do through that one."

"Let me make a few calls and see if we can make this happen." My cousin Maria is a nurse at the clinic, but I'll keep that to myself until I know whether I can pull this off. "In the meantime, check with your insurance and let me know."

"I'll call in the morning."

I push the fried ice cream toward him.

He uses the second spoon the waiter brought to take a bite.

"What about past patients?"

"What about them?"

"By now you must have a few satisfied customers who can attest to your skill and the care they received from you."

"More than a few." The note of cockiness reminds me of the man I met this morning. That seems like a lifetime ago in light of what I've learned about him since.

"Can you reach out and ask them to send testimonials we can share with the board? We need to show them the other side of the story."

"I can ask my former assistant in New York to handle that. She would have all the contact info."

"Do it. It certainly can't hurt anything. Have them write to me directly." I give him my new business card, which includes my email address. "Don't go through Augustino."

"You don't trust him?"

"I barely know him. I have no idea whether he can be trusted, which is all the more reason to funnel everything through me. After being misled, he may not want you any more than the board does, for all we know."

"True."

"I need you to know that I'm willing to do whatever I can to help you, but I don't want to lose my job over it."

"I understand."

The waiter brings the check, and we both lunge for it, knocking it off the table, which makes us laugh.

It's closer to Jason, so he grabs it. "This is on me."

"I'm the one who owes you money."

"Don't worry about that."

"I *am* worried about it. I pay my own bills."

"You're helping me figure a way out of this mess. That's all the payment I need." He pulls out the black American Express card again to pay the bill. "I'd be losing my mind if I didn't have your help in figuring out how to handle this situation."

"I still say you should have someone far more qualified than I am helping you."

"I don't know anyone else I can ask, and you know the area, so that gives me an inside track I could never get with someone else." He signs the credit card receipt and stands, waiting for me to go ahead of him as we leave the restaurant, which has thinned out since we arrived.

I glance at my phone, stunned to realize that it's after ten o'clock. How did two hours go by in a flash? Ever since I lost Tony, time has been my enemy. It either goes by too quickly, making me wonder how it's possible that life just marches on without him. Or it drags interminably, leaving me to question how I'll fill all the time I have left in a life that no longer includes him.

The valet driver has Jason's car parked right outside the door.

He hands the young man a twenty-dollar bill. "Sorry to keep you waiting."

"No worries. That car is *sweet.* Did you drive it here from New York?"

"I wish. I was short on time, so I had to have it shipped."

The valet hands a business card to Jason. "If you need someone to take it back for you, give me a call."

"Will do. Thanks." Jason holds the passenger door and waits for me to get settled before closing the door. He slides into the driver's seat and hands me his take-home bag to hold for him.

"What about social media?" I ask when we're on the way back to my place.

"What about it?"

"Have you thought about using your accounts to change the narrative?"

"What accounts?"

I look over at him. "You're not on social media? At all?"

"Nope. Never had the time for it."

"Well, that's a golden opportunity to take control of your own story. We should set you up with an Instagram account that shows you getting to know your new city, and if we can make the free clinic idea happen, that'd be even better."

"I don't know how I feel about volunteering at the clinic to get attention."

"That's the whole point."

"I know," he says, sighing. "I hate doing altruistic things for attention. It feels seedy."

"Under normal circumstances, it is seedy. These are not normal circumstances. If you want to save your career, you're going to have to suck it up and court some positive attention."

"I hate this."

We're about a mile from my place when blue lights flash behind us.

After glancing in the rearview mirror, Jason pulls the car over. "What the hell?"

"This can't be happening twice in one day."

"First time for me. Grab the registration for me, will you?"

I open the glove box, where the registration was the only thing in there this morning, and immediately realize it's not there. "Um, Jason?"

~

They put us in the same cell I was in this morning, the door closing with the same shocking clatter that jolted me the first time around. The cop said he pulled us over because the car had a taillight out, but when we couldn't produce the registration for the very expensive car, he had no choice but to bring us in until they could confirm that Jason owns the car.

And so, here I am. In jail. *Again.*

To my credit, I held it together the whole time we were told to stand with our hands on the hood of the car, our legs spread. I held it together when they told us we were being taken in until they could determine who owns the car. I held it together when they cuffed us and put us into the back seat of the squad car. But being back in that cell with the toilet sitting out in the open takes me right over the edge.

I disintegrate into helpless laughter.

"What the hell is so funny?" Jason asks.

I can't breathe or talk. I wave my hand to encompass the entire situation.

"This is not funny. It's the last goddamned thing I need right now."

Even knowing he's right, I can't stop laughing. Could this day be any more ridiculous? It takes me five full minutes to catch my breath, and by then Jason is truly pissed with me for laughing.

"It's a good thing they took our phones, or I might be tempted to get your Instagram account up and running with a photo from jail."

That draws a small smile from him, as if he can't help it, even if he finds nothing about this funny.

"Can't you use your connections to get us sprung?"

"I tried that. The patrolman said he was in high school when my husband was killed, can't just take my word for it and needs to confirm the info I told him. But he did say he was sorry for my loss. So here we are."

"Jesus."

I wince at the cavalier way he utters the Lord's name.

"What?"

"My grandmothers would cut out your tongue for saying that."

"Sorry. *Fuck.* Is that better?"

"Much."

He laughs, and the sound rolls through me like a hot bath, soothing and calming. I like making him laugh, especially since he's had nothing much to laugh about in the last few weeks.

An older officer comes to the door of the cell. "You're Tony D'Alessandro's wife?"

"Yes, I was."

"Come with me."

"May I bring my friend?"

"Yeah, sure."

We follow him through a series of corridors into a nondescript room with a table and chairs and not much else.

"You can wait here."

"The car is mine," Jason says. "It was impounded earlier after a misunderstanding, and the impound lot didn't return the registration. I didn't realize it until we got stopped."

"We're looking into it. As soon as we confirm what you've told us, you'll be free to go." The officer looks to me. "You're free to go now. I can have someone drive you home if you don't want to wait."

"That's fine. I'll wait for my friend."

"You want some coffee?"

"No, thanks. We're good."

"I'll do what I can to get this figured out for you."

"Thanks."

He leaves the room, closing the door behind him. I don't think it's locked, but I'd rather not know if it is, so I don't check.

Jason takes a seat at the table. "You should go."

"It's fine. I'll stay."

"You have to work in the morning."

"I know."

"It's getting late."

"I said I'd stay, and I will."

"Are you afraid to leave me to my own devices?"

"Terrified. I've got enough of a mess to clean up without you making it worse."

He's startled until he figures out that I'm kidding, and then he begins to laugh. He laughs as hard as I did earlier. Like my laughter, his has an edge of hysteria to it that I can certainly understand. Rule-following overachievers like us don't end up in jail, let alone twice in one day for me.

"You're a regular jailbird today," he says when he finally quits laughing.

"Only because of you! I was minding my own business when you and your Porsche showed up to cause trouble for me."

"Admit it. This is the most fun you've had in a long time."

I cross my arms defiantly. "I'll admit to no such thing."

The smile he directs my way sets off that flurry of reaction inside me that's been happening all day. I've never had an opinion on instant attraction, because it hasn't happened to me before. Tony and I were friends for two years before we started officially dating when we were juniors in high school. I've seen my friends and cousins come home dazzled by a man they just met, but most of the time the dazzle doesn't last.

"What're you thinking?"

His question startles me. "Huh?"

"You just got all serious, and your brows were furrowed." He does an impression of the face I was making.

"Oh, um, I wasn't thinking about anything in particular." I can't very well admit to the object of my instant attraction that I was pondering the phenomenon of instant attraction.

"Liar." He tips the chair back, balancing precariously. "Tell me what made you frown and furrow."

Is it hot in here, or is it me? "I was just wondering what's taking them so long to confirm the car is yours."

"They probably had to track down the impound guy."

"Are you going to have to pay *again* to get it out of there?"

"Probably."

And my debt to him just doubled since I'm the one who got the car impounded in the first place.

I flop into a chair across the table from him. "I'm really sorry about all of this. When Mr. Augustino told me to babysit you, I don't think he meant for me to do it in jail."

"He used the word *babysit*?"

I squirm under the heat of his glare. "Maybe?"

"That's just great. Glad I've spent my whole life in school so I could be *babysat* at my new job."

"Don't shoot the messenger."

"It's not your fault. It's mine. I let myself get sucked in by a woman—literally—for the first time in my life, and I'll be paying for that mistake forever."

"Not necessarily." The visual of him being literally "sucked in by a woman" has me breaking into a sweat. I feel betrayed by myself. Why do I have to be attracted to *him*, the subject of my first assignment at the job I busted my ass for years to get?

The irony isn't lost on me. I've been moving through life in a grief-fueled fog for five years, and the first time I feel *something* for another man, it has to be *this* man. My friends and family have been trying for a while now to find me someone new. Only a few of the many first dates they've arranged for me have led to a second, which has frustrated matchmakers determined to see me happy again.

They'd be thrilled to know that Dr. Jason Northrup makes my scalp, and other more important parts, tingle with awareness. But with my new boss determined to keep Jason and his scandal far from the hospital where I now work, he's the last man in the world my nipples should be interested in.

Try telling them that.

I cross my arms, hoping he won't see what's going on under my clothes. That's not something he needs to know. Besides, I'm sure it's just a fluke. He's a handsome, charismatic brain surgeon, for crying out loud. Any heterosexual woman with a pulse would react to him.

I'd like to think I'm not "typical," in the sense that I don't freak out about stuff that sends my friends and cousins into a tizzy. For instance, Justin Bieber once came into the restaurant with an entourage, and everyone else went dumb in the head while I waited on them.

Biebs puts his pants on one leg at a time, just like everyone else. I had absolutely no reaction whatsoever to a man whom other women throw panties at when he's onstage. Was it fun to meet him? Sure. Not to mention he left a massive tip that came in handy when it was time to put down the damage deposit on my new apartment.

"Now what're you thinking about?"

"Am I frowning and furrowing again?"

"Sort of."

"I'm thinking of the time I met Justin Bieber, actually." He also doesn't need to know I'm thinking of the Biebs in the context of having no reaction at all to him while Jason makes my nipples hard. Why is that exactly?

"What was that like?"

I shrug. "Nothing special. He came into my family's restaurant with a group of people. I waited on them while everyone else had a nuclear meltdown."

"I can picture you all calm, cool and collected while everyone else freaked out."

"I don't go crazy over famous people. I've been meeting them all my life."

"Is that right?"

Nodding, I get up to stretch and then sit on the table next to him. "Giordino's is very well known around here. People come from all over to eat there. Gloria Estefan and her husband celebrate their anniversary there every year. JLo comes in whenever she's in town. George Clooney and his parents were in last year."

"Wow, that's amazing. Has it always been in your family?"

"My father's Italian parents opened the restaurant when they first moved to South Florida from the Bronx in the fifties. Cubans moved into the neighborhood that became known as Little Havana in the sixties. Then my parents met and fell in love, and when they eloped, my father brought my mother into the business and insisted on making her part of it. From there, it's evolved into one side Cuban and one side Italian, with my grandmothers hosting their sides of the house. They bicker like crazy, and people come from all over to see their show."

"So they don't get along?"

"Actually, they're the best of friends behind the scenes, but you'd never know it. Their public persona is very comical. They say it's good for business, and they're right."

"That's amazing. I love it. I can't wait to see them in action."

I try to picture him amid the chaos at Giordino's. "The only way you can come there with me is if you're planning to marry me."

CHAPTER 6

JASON

I stare at her, shocked and unreasonably aroused by everything she says and does. "*Marry* you?"

She laughs at my reaction. "You have to know my grandmothers. They've been trying to find someone new for me since about two years after Tony died. If I bring you there, they'll pounce on you like the fresh meat you are and call in the priest before the main course is served."

"*Whoa.*"

"I know, which is why I can't take you anywhere near them unless you're prepared to say 'I do.'"

I know she's exaggerating, to a point, which is probably what spurs me to throw gas on the fire that's been simmering between us all day. "What if I'm not afraid of them?"

She lets out an inelegant snort. "Spoken like someone who's never met them or seen what they're capable of."

"Eh," I say, waving a hand. "After what I've been through, what can a couple of grandmothers do to me?"

Carmen stares at me with dark-brown eyes fringed with extravagant lashes that other women would kill for. Her flawless skin is a lovely golden brown, and her lips are what take her face from pretty to stunning. I've never seen a more kissable mouth in my entire life, not to mention she's curvy and lush and smells so good it's all I can do not to bury my face in her hair and breathe her in. "You haven't the first clue what you're talking about."

I'm well aware that I have absolutely no business categorizing Carmen Giordino's many attractive attributes. I'm in enough trouble as it is without having salacious thoughts about the young woman who's trying to help dig me out of the hellhole I've fallen into since I found out what Ginger really wanted with me.

"You'd protect me, wouldn't you?"

Before she can answer, the officer who brought us to this room returns. "You're both free to go. The impound lot found the registration to the Porsche. Might be a good idea to keep that handy going forward. We had to wake up the guy who runs the impound, which is why it took so long." To Carmen, he adds, "Sorry to keep you waiting. We asked him to wait for you so you can get the car tonight. He, um, wouldn't waive the fee, though. We tried."

"Thanks for trying," Carmen says.

Great. Another six hundred bucks out the window. Good thing I work so much that I hardly ever spend any money. The Porsche is my one major indulgence. My apartment in New York is a studio because I'm hardly ever there. I gesture for Carmen to lead the way out of the interrogation room.

The officer escorts us to the main door and sees us out.

We head in the direction of the impound lot.

"I'm having déjà vu."

Carmen laughs. "I know. Me too. I really am sorry about all of this. I should've just called an Uber for Betty."

"What fun would that've been?"

"Ah, well, I wouldn't have done two stints in the slammer today."

"You'll be dining out on this story for the rest of your life."

"No, I won't! I don't want anyone to know I was in jail. My God, my parents and grandmothers would *die* if they knew."

"It was all a misunderstanding—both times. If you tell them that—"

"It's *jail*, Jason. I can't tell them."

Something about her prim-and-proper tone turns me on like crazy, even as I tell myself to knock it off. I love that she's such a good girl, that she's never been in any kind of trouble before today.

We arrive at the impound lot, where the grumpy owner is waiting for us. "I think you should waive the fee since you forgot to give me back the registration the first time."

"Is that what you think, pretty boy?" He's a scary-looking dude with huge muscles and a tattoo on his face.

I meet his gaze and refuse to blink. "That's what I think."

"You should've asked for your registration when you picked it up before."

"Why would I assume you'd take the registration out of the car when you impounded it?"

"Look, it's one o'clock in the morning. I want to go home. I can either give you your car or keep it. Up to you."

I can't take the chance that this is going to get ugly or physical. I'd never risk damaging my hands for six hundred bucks, and I won't put Carmen in the middle of something like that, either. I hand him my American Express card. Again.

He takes it, runs it and hands me the receipt to sign.

"Be right back."

"It's total bullshit," Carmen says when we're alone.

"Not worth fighting over. That's for sure."

"Now I owe you twelve hundred bucks."

"No, you don't."

"Yes, I do."

We continue to bicker back and forth about the money until the Porsche comes to a skidding halt outside the office.

Grumpy is grinning from ear to ear. "This thing is *sweet*."

I ignore him and get in the driver's side while Carmen jumps into the passenger seat. I hit the gas and spew gravel at him as we leave the yard. I hope some of it hits him.

"Seriously, I will pay you back."

"You're helping to repair my image. That's more than enough repayment."

I pull up to her apartment building at just after one thirty.

"I'm going to be a wreck tomorrow," Carmen says, yawning.

"I'll walk you up."

"You don't have to. It's late. Go get some sleep."

She fumbles with the door handle, so I reach across her to help. The press of my arm against her abdomen sets off another one of those fireworks shows that've been happening inside me since the first time I saw her. Was that really only twenty or so hours ago?

"I've got it."

I retreat from her, but I wish I didn't have to. That's not a thought that someone sitting in my boat ought to be having about any woman. "Check in with me tomorrow?" Part of me is afraid I'll never hear from her again after this disastrous day. Just when I think things can't get worse, I cause an innocent young woman to end up in jail *twice* in one day.

"I will. I've got a few ideas we can get going on."

"I'm ready when you are. I have an appointment with a Realtor to look at condos. I should probably keep that in case I get to stay."

"I can help with that, too."

"Perfect."

"It's the least I can do after costing you more than a thousand dollars in one day."

"Not your fault. Go to bed, Carmen. Have sweet dreams about something other than jail."

"Too soon, Jason. Far too soon."

She leaves me laughing as she gets out of the car and walks inside. I wait to make sure she's safely in before I take off, heading for the hotel the hospital put me up in.

Before bed, I make the mistake of checking my email and find a message from Mr. Augustino asking me to refrain from stepping foot onto the hospital campus until the board has time to review my situation.

Awesome.

I want to throw the phone across the room. I'd do it except for the hassle it would be to replace it. I've got enough hassles in my life right now.

I really hope Carmen can help me, because the way things are looking now, I'm totally fucked if she can't.

Carmen

I dream of jail. I blame Jason for putting that idea in my head. Despite the rough night, I'm determined to make my second day on the job less eventful than the first one. With that in mind, I'm at my desk by eight thirty with a cortadito, otherwise known as Cuban coffee, from my girl Juanita's ventanita. I'm counting on it to clear the cobwebs from my sleep-deprived brain.

Mornings aren't my thing, even when I have a full night of sleep.

Jason texted to tell me what Mr. Augustino said about staying away from the hospital until the board comes to a decision. I can tell that has him more dejected than he was last night. That fires my determination to help him, though I still think he should be hiring crisis communication experts.

Mona arrives shortly after I do and comes to my door. "Did you go out with Dr. Northrup last night?" The question is asked with a girlfriend giggle that reminds me of nails on a chalkboard.

"We had a business dinner."

"Is that right?"

"I don't do gossip, Mona, and I don't appreciate when others do, either, especially at work."

As if I didn't say anything, she comes into my office and sits. "Have you heard about him? About what happened in New York?"

"Yes, he told me about how he was set up by a woman who wanted out of a bad marriage and how the career he's worked toward for more than a decade is in jeopardy because of what she did."

That seems to take some of the air out of her sails. "She set him up?"

I'm not sure he'd want me sharing this with her, but we're going to have to tell his side of the story if we're to put his career back on track. "She used him shamelessly to advance her own agenda and broke his heart in the process."

"Why hasn't he said so?"

"Because she has children, and he doesn't want to drag them through their mother's mess."

"Huh."

"You can't believe everything you see and hear, Mona. There're always two sides to a story." Why do I feel as if I'm the older of the two of us when she has decades on me?

"What's he going to do?"

"He's trying to repair his reputation so he'll be offered privileges here."

"How does he plan to do that?" Mr. Augustino asks from the doorway, startling us both.

Crap.

Mona, that rat, gets up and hightails it out of there.

Mr. Augustino comes in, shuts the door and takes a seat in my visitor chair. I figure he's in his late fifties, with salt-and-pepper hair and a matching goatee. He's immaculately dressed in a navy pin-striped suit with a light-blue pocket square that complements his tie.

I'm hit with a serious case of nerves. The hospital president is *in my office*. I have no idea how to play this. Does he want Jason, er, Dr. Northrup, to redeem himself, or is he opposed to the idea?

I decide to go with the truth. "You should know there's another side to the story of what happened in New York."

"Dr. Northrup told me that and indicated he's unwilling to go public with his side because the woman in question has children."

"That's right."

"I've passed the information along to the board."

"Oh. You did?"

Mr. Augustino nods. "I'm not looking to further damage the man's career, Ms. Giordino. He's a world-class physician. I've felt all along that we'd be lucky to have him—and his very promising research—on our medical staff. That said, I do understand the board's hesitation in light of the scandal in New York and the lack of candor about that at the outset."

"I have some ideas of things we can do to help restore his reputation."

"Such as?"

"My cousin works as a nurse at the Our Lady of Charity free clinic in Little Havana. Their doctor was injured in an accident, which has left them shorthanded. Dr. Northrup might be able to fill in while their doctor is out on medical leave. For free, of course."

"And he's willing to do this?"

"Provided he has insurance coverage. He's checking on that today."

Mr. Augustino tilts his head and gives me an odd look. "So you've already discussed this possibility with Dr. Northrup?"

Dammit. I've painted myself into a tight corner. "Yes, sir. I offered to help him with his situation. On my own time, of course."

"Why would you do that?"

"I, um, he helped me with something yesterday, and I owe him a favor." *Please don't ask what, please don't ask what . . .*

"What did he help you with?"

I think fast. "He asked me to take care of getting him an employee parking space, which turned out to be more complicated than I anticipated. When he came to assist me, we got to talking about what brought him to Miami. One thing led to another, and I offered to help him to thank him for helping me." *God, I hope he believes me.*

He mulls that over for what feels like a full five minutes, even though it's probably only thirty seconds. It's long enough to send me into full-blown deodorant failure. "I like the idea of a PR campaign to redeem his image. That could be very effective in convincing the board to give him a chance to work here, which is my ultimate goal. If his research pays off the way we think it will, that could be a huge coup for us."

He looks me in the eye. "I want you on this project full-time for the next two weeks, with a report to me at the end of each day on what's being done. The more you can document through photos and videos, the better. We can put together a presentation for the board that shows him embracing his new community. I really like this idea. Good work, Ms. Giordino."

"Oh, um, thank you." It's all I can do to refrain from giggling like a deranged lunatic. If only he knew the full story. But thank you, Jesus, he doesn't and hopefully never will. "What about covering the department while I'm out?"

"Don't worry about that for now. This is the priority. I want this guy—and his research—on our team. I want to see our hospital get the credit when his work pays off. If you can help to make that happen,

I'll consider you for the director position that's recently come available. Taryn has decided to stay home with her baby for the first few years."

My mouth falls open in shock. On day two, I'm being considered for a massive promotion? Day two is definitely shaping up to be a vast improvement over day one. "That'd be amazing. I'll do my very best for you and for Dr. Northrup."

"I have no doubt. You seem like a very responsible young woman, and we're lucky to have you on our team."

If only you knew where I was around this time yesterday . . . "Thank you. I won't let you down, sir."

"Excellent. Feel free to come and go from the office as needed to accomplish the assignment. I'll let Mona know you're working off-campus so she's aware. Just make sure she has your cell number so she can reach you if need be."

"I will."

He stands to leave and reaches my door before he turns back, seeming slightly chagrined. "When I told Mrs. Augustino that you joined our team, she mentioned how difficult it is to get a reservation at Giordino's. Our anniversary is coming up. I thought it might be nice to surprise her."

"I'll take care of that for you. Just let me know when you'd like to go."

"Thank you so much. It's nice to know people with influence. I'll let you know."

"Sounds good."

He walks out of my office, leaving me momentarily stunned by our conversation. Not only did he encourage me to help Jason, but he made it my only assignment for the next two weeks and dangled a dream promotion should I succeed in rehabilitating the good doctor's reputation.

"Holy moly," I whisper before I reach for my cell phone to text Jason. *Big news. Mr. Augustino has made you my only assignment for the next two weeks. He wants me to help you make a case to the board at their next meeting.*

He responds right away. *Whoa. That is big news. I sort of got the feeling he didn't want me around any more than the board did.*

Not the case. After hearing your side of the story, he seems to have changed his opinion. He's very interested in you and your cutting-edge research and having a world-class pediatric neurosurgeon on his team.

Okay, so maybe I'm building him up a bit, but after the reception he received yesterday, he has to be feeling pretty low. I don't mention the possible promotion that's at stake for me, because that's not something he needs to know. I was prepared to help him before there was a promotion on the table, so that hasn't changed anything.

What's our first order of business, boss?

I want to speak to the free clinic. Can you check on your insurance?

Will do right away.

I'll hit you up shortly.

Sounds good.

I grab my purse, keys, phone and coffee and head out of my office. "I'll be out for the rest of the day."

"Mr. Augustino said you're working on a special project."

"That's right."

"Is he tall, blond and handsome?"

"Bye, Mona."

"I won't tell anyone. Don't worry."

I roll my eyes and walk out of the executive office suite into the hallway that leads to the elevator. As I walk to my car, I place a call to my cousin Maria.

"Hey, prima. How's the new job?"

"It's been rather interesting so far."

"In a good way, I hope."

"Jury's still out. I have a question for you. Are you guys still looking for a doctor at the clinic?"

"God, yes. We're so slammed, and with only a part-time nurse practitioner who can write scripts, we're dying over here."

"I may have someone who can help."

"Fantastic."

I tell her about Jason.

"What the hell does a pediatric neurosurgeon want with a free clinic in Little Havana? He knows we can't pay him much, right?"

"Here's the thing. He's willing to volunteer."

"What's the catch?"

"He's had some challenges in his personal life that have the board at Miami-Dade questioning whether they want him on their staff."

"What kind of challenges?"

I lean against my car, close my eyes and say a silent prayer to my late grandfathers, hoping they can help me out here. If the clinic doesn't work out for whatever reason, I don't exactly have a plan B waiting on deck. "He had an affair with the board chair's wife in New York."

"Ugh, Carmen . . ."

"Wait, there's more." I tell her the rest about how the woman used him and that Jason didn't know she was married, least of all to the chairman of the board of his hospital. "He had real feelings for her and was crushed by the whole thing."

"Why doesn't he just say so?"

"Because she has kids, and he's being sensitive to what it would do to them if he came out and said their mother used him for sex so she could get rid of their father."

"I guess it's true what they say," she says with a sigh.

I'm not following her. "What is?"

"There's no such thing as a free neurosurgeon."

"He wouldn't be doing it for the money, Mari. He's determined to make a new life for himself down here. He wants to get to know the community and make an impact."

"And if the end result is that Miami-Dade grants privileges, all the better, right?"

"Will you meet him and give him a chance?"

"Let me talk to my boss and see what she thinks. It's her call. The good news for your guy is we might be desperate enough to overlook the scandal."

"Call me when you know?"

"Will do."

"Thanks for this. I appreciate it."

"How'd you get involved?"

"That's a story for another day and requires vodka."

"I can't wait to hear it. I'll get back to you shortly."

"Thank you again."

"Yeah, yeah. You owe me big for this."

"Whatever you want."

Maria is laughing as the connection goes dead. God, I hope she can make this work. If not, I've got to come up with something else he can do in the community that would have the same impact.

CHAPTER 7

Carmen

I put the key in the ignition of my car, an old Honda that Tony and I bought when we were first married. I'm suddenly overcome by an unexpected flood of emotions that take me by surprise. Why am I so invested in Dr. Jason Northrup and his career? Why has his cause become mine? It's not just because of the money I owe him. I wish it were that simple.

It's also because of the integrity he's showing in not wanting to harm his ex-lover's children. That really gets to me, especially after he shared what he endured growing up with a cheating father.

The scorching South Florida sunshine quickly makes it necessary for me to turn on the car and the AC, but I sit there for a long time, staring out the window, trying to make sense of everything that's happened over the last twenty-four hours.

When I arrived for the first day of my new job this time yesterday, I was still blissfully unaware that Dr. Jason Northrup was about to upset my well-ordered existence in every possible way. While driving a Porsche and my two trips to jail would be banner headlines at any other time in my life, the fact that I feel a genuine connection to a man for the first time in five long years is the truly remarkable development.

I've often wondered if it would happen again, if I would meet someone who made me feel *something*. But until yesterday morning, it hadn't happened, despite the enthusiastic efforts of everyone who loves me to find me someone new to love. While I was reluctant to be fixed up on more blind dates than any girl should be forced to endure in a lifetime, I made a genuine effort to connect with each of them, only to be disappointed time and again.

After having had the real thing, I know the difference between *something* and nothing. How many times have I said just that to my grandmothers, parents, cousins, friends and even customers at the restaurant who've become invested in the quest to find Carmen a new man?

Abuela told me a year or so ago that all the foolishness and fixups are really about making sure I'm ready when the right one comes along. I hadn't thought about it that way before, and those words come back to me now, proving once again how wise Abuela really is.

She, too, was widowed young, although she was almost twenty years older than me when it happened to her. My grandfather died of a massive heart attack at forty-two. Abuela was forty then, with three young children still at home and a broken heart that never healed.

"I don't want you to end up like me, mi amor," she said when I complained to her that I was getting tired of all the first dates I'd been on. "I refused to even consider another man after my sweet Jorge died. Now, I'm growing old alone, and I wish I'd taken another chance on love."

"You're never alone, Abuela."

"I'm thankful for you and our family all the time. But I don't have to tell you that the love of a beautiful family and friends isn't the same as the love you felt for Tony or that I felt for Jorge. It's just not the same."

No, it isn't the same. Nothing is ever the same after you lose the person you love the most. For a long time after Tony died, I wondered if

I would survive the loss. The first year was a haze of grief and numbness and nonstop events honoring him and his ultimate sacrifice.

Through it all, my goal was to keep breathing, to keep putting one foot in front of the other, to cope with grief so deep and pervasive I feared it might suffocate me. But it didn't. To my astonishment, I actually survived losing him and was forced to figure out what I was going to do with the rest of my life. That's when I ended up in an undergrad program that later led to a master's in communications.

Thinking about that time, right after we lost Tony so suddenly, can still bring tears to my eyes, even after five years. I've learned that you never really get "used to" being without the one you love. But you do learn to live without him, as preposterous as that seemed at the beginning. My love for Tony is as present to me today as it was the day he died. It's as much a part of me as the heart that's beat only for him since I was fourteen.

I grip the steering wheel, caught in the web of grief once again as I acknowledge that yesterday, for the first time ever, I felt *something* for a man who isn't Tony. The emotions are complex—confusion, relief, despair, sadness.

Part of me never wanted to move on from him, even if I always knew it would happen eventually. Of course, it probably shouldn't happen with a colleague, but it's comforting to know I still have the capacity to be attracted to a man.

In widow circles, they talk about the "Chapter 2," which is when a widow finds new love. I've read a lot of stories of how people move on to their next love while honoring the one they lost and admire the courage it takes to risk everything once again. Especially knowing what can happen. I haven't given much consideration to whether I would ever have a Chapter 2, or if I even want that.

I snap out of my thoughts sometime later to find that I'm still gripping the steering wheel as I process a fresh wave of the grief and confusion that were my constant companions for so long after that dreadful first day. Not only was I heartbroken for myself and his family, but I was wrecked for *him*. At twenty-four, he walked into a convenience store, probably to buy gum or Gatorade, and had the rest of his life stolen from him in a random act of violence.

We found out later that the man who shot him had scuffled with police in the past. It was believed that the shooting had nothing to do with Tony and everything to do with the uniform he wore. After two years of court appearances and a trial that reopened the healing wound, the man was convicted of murdering a police officer and sentenced to life in prison with no chance of parole.

That was another surreal moment in this never-ending journey, and while we were thankful to see justice done, it was a fresh reminder that nothing would bring Tony back.

My phone rings, and I take the call from Jason. "Hi."

"Hey. Everything okay?"

"Yes, why?"

"You sound weird."

"I only said hi."

"You sound weird."

It astounds me that one word has tuned him in to the fact that I'm not okay. "I'm, uh . . ."

"Do you need me to come get you?"

"No, I don't need you to come get me."

"Why do you sound weird? Did something happen?"

"I'll tell you when I see you."

"Okay," he says hesitantly. "I called to tell you I talked to the insurance company and bought the rider I needed to volunteer, so I'm good to go if the clinic approves our plan."

"That's great news. I pitched it to my cousin, who works there, and I'm waiting to hear back."

"Since Mr. Augustino assigned you to me, you can help me look at a couple of condos while we wait to hear from your cousin, right?"

I'm not sure that spending any more time with him than absolutely necessary to do the job is a good idea, but my boss told me to work with him. "Sure, we can do that. Where should we meet?"

"Come by my hotel?" He gives me an address I recognize near the hospital. "We can park your car, and I'll drive."

I'm afraid to go anywhere near the car that landed me—twice—in jail, but I don't tell him that. "I'll be there in ten minutes."

"Great, see you then. And Carmen?"

"Yes?"

"Thanks for all you're doing to help me out."

"Just working off my debt."

He laughs. "I really appreciate it."

"No problem." The sound of his laughter gives me goose bumps. Everything about this man is a problem to me, but I have a job to do, and as long as I stay focused on that, I can keep this situation under control.

At least I hope so.

Jason

I wait for Carmen in the car outside the main door to my hotel. I'm excited to see her again, which is baffling. Three weeks ago, I had my heart crushed by a conniving, manipulative woman who shamelessly used me to advance her own agenda. I have absolutely no business being attracted to or looking forward to seeing any woman, let alone one I work with, but I don't know this city at all and I want to make sure I end up somewhere that makes sense.

While my medical colleagues dated each other like crazy, I stayed away from those complications, even though it's difficult to meet anyone who isn't somehow related to work due to the hours we keep.

Hospitals are full of interpersonal drama—doctors and nurses getting busy with each other is almost a cliché, frowned upon but actively happening. Although I've never known of people having sex in the on-call rooms or storerooms like they do on TV. That's not to say it doesn't happen, but I haven't been aware of it.

Since med school, dating and sex and all the nonsense that goes with them were an afterthought for me, mostly consisting of one-night hookups that never went beyond first names and basic attraction until I met Ginger. Weeks after the disaster, I can't think of her without seething. I've gone beyond the heartbroken stage and am settling into the furious part of the program now.

I've had ample examples in my life of the many ways people can suck, but until she had her wicked way with me, I had no idea how painful it is to be screwed over by a woman. She fucked with my head, my heart and my body, taking full advantage of me while she had me in her clutches. We hooked up at least three times a week for months, most of the time at my place in the city, which I now realize was strategic on her part. Until that fateful night on Long Island when her husband caught us, which was her plan all along.

Why am I still thinking about her and what she did to me? Why can't I just forget about her and move on? Because I loved her. I hate that, but it's true. I totally fell for her. I didn't plan to let that happen. At first, it was about the sex, which was awesome, and later, it became about so much more than that. I could talk to her, and she really listened. A difficult case at work consumed me for months, a child with a brain tumor that resisted all conventional treatment. When I lost that child after a Hail Mary surgery failed, I was despondent.

Ginger came to my place that night, after I told her I wasn't up for getting together. She held me when I bawled from the frustration and despair I felt after not being able to save that little boy's life. She didn't ask me for anything and gave me everything.

How could she do that, knowing our entire relationship was nothing more than a scam? Did she ever care about me at all, or did she only pretend to care so I'd stick around long enough to get caught? I hate that I still wonder if she ever actually gave a shit about me or if the whole thing was nothing more than a big game to her.

I want to stop thinking about her. I want to stop reliving every minute I spent with her and picking it apart, looking for clues that simply weren't there. Or if they were, I never saw them. All I saw was a witty, beautiful, smart, sexy woman who briefly made me a believer in true love and fairy tales.

Such bullshit, which is exactly why I shouldn't be looking forward to seeing Carmen Giordino or any woman. I don't have the bandwidth at the moment for anything other than doing what I can to salvage the career that is my life. Nothing else but getting that back on track matters, and I need to remember my ultimate goal here.

Carmen arrives a few minutes later, driving a navy-blue Honda. I wave to her and point to the free parking area.

A few minutes later, she makes her way toward me. Today she's wearing a black suit with a floral-print silk blouse. Her hair is long and curly, and I'm riveted.

Didn't you just have a talk with yourself about why you can't be riveted by Carmen or anyone else?

I did just have that conversation with myself, for all the good it did me. She's beautiful and vibrant and smart as hell. Her story about losing her young husband so tragically moved me last night. I thought about it long after we parted company, wondering what it was like for her to become a widow at twenty-four.

It's horrible to even imagine, way worse than what Ginger did to me. That's nothing compared to what Carmen endured.

She gets into the passenger seat, bringing an alluring scent with her that has the attention of every part of me, despite my determination to steer clear of anything to do with romantic entanglements.

Don't forget, my inner voice reminds me, *she's only helping you because she owes you money and her boss told her to.*

It's a good reminder that this, whatever this is with her, needs to remain strictly professional.

She puts her seat belt on. "Where to?"

"I'm meeting a Realtor in South Beach."

Out of the corner of my eye, I catch her frowning.

"What?"

"I didn't take you for a cliché."

"What's that supposed to mean?"

"*South Beach?* Really?" Every word drips with disdain.

"I asked around. People said that's where the action is."

"If you're twenty-five and looking to party, sure. Do you have any idea what the commute from South Beach to Kendall would be like on an average workday?"

"Uh, not really."

She shrugged. "If you want to spend an hour bumper to bumper each way, it's your life to waste."

"I usually go to work crazy early and come home super late. I rarely hit rush hour."

"I'm telling you. You don't want to live there."

"And you know me well enough to say that?"

"I do."

I laugh, delighted by her even if I don't want to be. "Where do you think I should live?"

"You should check out Brickell. It's a great part of town, closer to the hospital and not a total zoo like South Beach is."

"I'll ask my Realtor to look there, too, but I can't cancel on her now."

"Then let's go to South Beach, but don't tell me I didn't warn you."

"Duly noted."

It takes two seconds after our arrival for me to realize she's one thousand percent right about South Beach—and the traffic. Even on a Tuesday, it's hopping. I can't imagine what the weekends must be like. The bars are doing land-office business, and the beach area is bustling with people, cars, bikes and joggers. *Zoo* is definitely a good word to describe it.

In a past life, I would've loved to live here, but not now. When I'm not working, I need a place where I can decompress and relax. That can't happen here.

The condo is located in a high-rise with an incredible ocean view and great amenities. But on the ninth floor, I can hear the street noise, even with the doors and windows closed.

Deb, the Realtor, is peppy, enthusiastic and probably already calculating her commission on the nine-hundred-thousand-dollar condo that's all glass and hard edges and modern features. I hate to disappoint her. "I'm not feeling this place."

"Oh, thank God," Carmen says, breath leaving her in a whoosh of relief.

"You hate it."

"I hate it."

Deb is clearly offended but keeps that to herself.

"What've you got in Brickell?" I ask her.

"Oh, well, I'd have to look and see what's available."

"I think that'd be better for me. It's closer to work."

"Give me a minute to check the listings."

After Deb steps into the kitchen to work on her phone, Carmen shoots me a smug smile that I find ridiculously adorable—and funny. I love that she's not afraid to tell me how she really feels. That's a refreshing change from women I've known in the past who would say what they thought I'd want to hear rather than sharing their true opinion. I dated one woman in college who never seemed to have an original thought the entire time we were together. She was all about pleasing me, and while that has its advantages, it got boring after a while.

I have a feeling I'd never be bored with Carmen, not that I'm planning to date her. I'm just saying . . . She's unique. And so, so pretty in a natural, unaffected way that really appeals to me. She doesn't need layers of makeup to enhance what she was born with.

Why am I thinking about how pretty Carmen is, or whether she needs makeup? I'm supposed to be focused on finding a place to live—if I end up with a job here—and restoring my reputation. Once again, I need the reminder that *this is not the time* to be dazzled by Carmen.

"I've got quite a few in your price range, one with excellent views of the Rickenbacker and Biscayne Bay," Deb says from the kitchen, where she's scrolling on an iPad.

Carmen gives me a thumbs-up.

So I won't be at the beach. That's fine. I'd hardly ever have time to take advantage of the proximity anyway. "Sounds good."

"Let me check in with some of the listing agents and see what I can do."

CHAPTER 8

Jason

After she walks away, I glance at Carmen. "I'm probably jinxing myself even looking at places. The board is a long way from approving me."

"They'll approve you. We'll make sure of it."

"You're far more confident than I am."

"We have to make it so they'd look stupid to say no to you."

"And how do you propose we do that?"

She thinks about that for a second. "Where are we with the testimonials from former patients? I was thinking we could use them to tell your story for the presentation. If there're photos of you with the patients, that's even better."

I forgot I was supposed to ask my former colleague in New York about that. "I'll reach out to Terri now." I fire off a text to the nurse administrator, who's the glue that holds the neurosurgery department together, and tell her what I need. I list a few of the patients I'm thinking of who might be grateful enough to share their stories of working with me. I saved their lives. Perhaps they can help save my career. "Done." I glance at Carmen. "It's a really good idea and one I never would've thought of on my own."

"That's because your job is brain surgery. Mine is publicity, promotion and marketing."

I laugh at the cocky way she says that. "Touché."

"Stay in your lane, Doc. I gotcha covered on the rest."

I'm so thankful to have her on my side. She gives me hope that it may be actually possible to repair my tattered reputation.

"We have to tell your story as a world-class physician. You're far more than one measly scandal."

"The scandal wasn't measly."

"No, but it's yesterday's news. I did a deep dive online last night, and there's been no mention of it anywhere in more than a week. While it's the biggest thing in your life, everyone else has moved on. Well, except for the Miami-Dade board, that is. But by the time we're done with them, they'll be so inundated with the positive they won't remember the measly little scandal in New York. That's the plan, anyway."

"I like that plan."

"I figured you would."

"When did you have time last night to do a deep dive online between dinner and your second trip to jail?"

She grimaces at the mention of jail. "I did it before we went to dinner, but I didn't mention it because I was still formulating my plan of attack."

"Well, it's good to know it's not big news in New York anymore."

"You can thank the twenty-four-hour news cycle for that. It moves on faster than it used to."

I'm unreasonably relieved to hear the scandal isn't headline news anymore, but the damage is certainly done. I hate that for the rest of my life—and beyond—anytime someone searches for my name, the crap with Ginger will come up.

Deb returns to where we're waiting for her in the condo. "We're in luck. I was able to line up a showing in Brickell. I'll text you the address. Shall we meet there in an hour?"

I glance at Carmen, and she nods. "We'll be there," I tell Deb.

"Great."

We walk out together, and when we get to my car, I hold the passenger door for Carmen, who winces when her backside connects with hot leather. As I get in the car, my phone chimes with a text from Terri. *Hey, it's good to hear from you. Everyone is still wound up about what they did to you. Hope things are working out for you in Miami. We sure do miss you here! I'll definitely reach out to the patients you mentioned and see what we can do. This whole thing is utter BULLSHIT, and the entire department is pissed about how you were treated. How can YOU be scrambling to find another job?!?!*

I read and reread Terri's text, soaking in words that are like a balm on my broken heart, before passing the phone to Carmen. "From my former colleague."

She quickly reads Terri's message. "That must be nice to hear."

"It is. I always worked hard, respected my colleagues, filled in for them when needed and treated the nurses like the superheroes they are."

"Let's get statements from Terri and the others in your former department."

"For what?"

"For the PowerPoint presentation we're going to put together for your next meeting with the board."

"I'm not sure how I feel about asking my former colleagues to do that."

"You want to fix this, right?"

"Very much so."

"Then you're going to have to do some things that may not sit well with you, such as getting testimonials from former colleagues and publicity for pro bono work at the clinic, if we can make that happen."

I grimace at the thought of generating attention for volunteer work. Under normal circumstances, I'd never go for that. But these circumstances certainly aren't normal. "Fine. I'll ask her." I respond to Terri's text. *Thanks for the help. Much appreciated. My associate down here is telling me it wouldn't hurt to have some endorsements from the people I worked with there. Do you think they'd be willing to provide them?*

I'm pained as I send a text that would've been inconceivable a few weeks ago. It still amazes me that a life and a career can be blown apart in a single day.

Terri responds right away, putting me out of my misery. *Absolutely. I'll get on that, too. Don't worry, we've got you covered, Doc.*

I breathe a sigh of relief. *Thank you. Means a lot to me.*

She sends back the smooching emoji.

"She's on it," I tell Carmen.

"That's great. I know it sucks to have to ask, but anything we can do to paint a complete picture will help. Right now, all they see is scandal. We have to give them a different narrative."

"You told me yesterday I need a seasoned crisis communication team. I'd say I have exactly what I need with you."

"Thanks. I'm hardly seasoned, but it's fun to use the stuff I learned in years of school."

The traffic leaving South Beach is proof of what she told me I'd face if I lived there. I'm glad to have someone with local knowledge helping me figure out this new place. "You must've been in college when you lost your husband, right?"

"I was attending community college, working at the restaurant and trying to get pregnant. We planned to be young parents. I was going to stay home with them and go to school when they did. After Tony died, I got a big insurance payout that I put toward school. It gave me something to do once the initial shock of his death wore off."

"I'm so sorry that happened to you."

"Thanks."

"Have you . . ." I shake my head. It's none of my fucking business whether she's dated anyone else since she lost her husband.

"Have I what?"

"I was about to ask you a deeply personal question."

"It's fine. I'm used to it. Everyone I meet wants to know if I've dated again since I lost him, and the answer is I've had a lot of first dates, a couple of second dates and very few third dates. My grandmothers love to fix me up with guys they know, their friends' grandsons, customers at the restaurant. At first I wanted nothing to do with it, but after a while, it was easier to go on the dates than have to constantly tell them why I didn't want to."

"It was their way of trying to help you move on, I suppose."

"Yes," she says with a sigh, "and I love them for it. We all suffered over the loss of Tony. He'd been part of our family for ten years by the time we lost him."

"I can't imagine what it would be like to meet 'the one' when you're as young as you guys were." I've never met anyone I could picture spending the rest of my life with. I'd begun to wonder if Ginger might be my "one" when I found out what she really wanted with me—and it had nothing to do with forever except for the stain she put on my good name.

"It's funny that I can't remember meeting him. We used to talk about that a lot. He remembered every detail of that day, but I don't. I was with friends at an arcade in the mall, and he said the Selena song 'I Could Fall in Love' was playing the first time he saw me. I used to say he was making that up, but he swore it was true."

"That's very sweet."

"We lived near each other but went to different schools, which is why we hadn't met before. He had friends who went to my school, and they approached me to ask if I'd consider meeting their friend, who'd decided he was going to marry me."

"No way. They did not say that."

"They did!"

"What did you say?"

"I said, 'I'm fourteen, and I'm not marrying your friend.' They begged and pleaded with me to at least talk to him, which I said I'd do, mostly because I sensed they weren't going to let up until I did. I figured I'd talk to him once, tell him to get real and move on."

"But that's not what happened."

"That's not what happened."

I'm completely captivated by her story and more than a little heartbroken to know how it ended. "Don't stop now! I have to know the rest. But only if you want to tell me."

"It's one of my favorite stories to tell. He called me that night and every night for a month. My parents were all over me about who I was on the phone with every night. I can't really recall the specifics of what we talked about, but I do remember laughing—a lot. He was really funny. I think that was the first thing I loved about him, that he could make me laugh even when I was annoyed with him."

"An important quality, for sure."

"It took two years of us being best friends before my parents would officially allow us to date."

"Holy crap. That must've been a *long* two years."

"It was, and believe me, I was so pissed about it. I thought my parents were impossibly old-fashioned. But when I look back at it now, I can see how important that friendship was for everything that came later."

"It set the foundation."

"Yes, exactly."

"No one waits two years to date anymore."

"Right? It's all about instant gratification."

"It's a very sweet story. I'm so sorry you lost him the way you did. I can't imagine what that must've been like."

"Worst day of my life."

Without thinking much about it, I reach over and cover her hand with mine, giving a gentle squeeze. The second my skin connects with hers, I realize I've made a critical error by touching her.

The subtle gasp that escapes from her lets me know she feels the same thing I do.

Even knowing all the reasons why it's a bad idea to leave it there, I don't remove my hand. "You don't have to talk about it if it's too painful."

"It was a long time ago."

"Still . . . Some things never get easier with time."

"True." After a long pause, she releases a long deep breath. "I was working at the restaurant when the cops came. At first, I thought it was him. He would pop by to say hello sometimes when he was on duty. He worked second shift, three to eleven, so our work hours were the same. There were two cops, and I remember looking around them to see if he was with them. They said something to my dad, and he . . . He just crumbled." After another pause, she continues. "I think I knew Tony was gone the second I saw my dad's reaction from across the big room."

"God, Carmen. I can't imagine."

"It was pretty horrible, but we were very well supported. The department was amazing. They took care of everything. That first week was just a blur of people and food and so much heartbreak. The restaurant became the gathering place for everyone, and it went on for days. It seemed like half the city passed through before the actual wake and funeral were held. Thousands of police officers came from all over the country. It was so amazing and overwhelming."

"I don't know what to say."

"There's not much to be said. My grandmothers, who are both widows, were incredible. They helped me find a way through the grief. It took a while, but I bounced back. I thought he'd approve of me going to school since I wasn't going to be a stay-at-home mother after all, and I didn't want to waitress for the rest of my life. Although, I made a very decent living at the restaurant."

"He'd be so proud of you. I'm proud of you, and I just met you."

"Thanks. I like to think he'd be proud that I survived it. He loved me so much. I never had any doubt about that."

"He was lucky, and he knew it. Smart man."

"We were both lucky."

"Did he always want to be a cop?"

"From the time he was twelve and did a ride-along with a friend's dad who was a cop. He never deviated from that plan. We even waited to get married until he'd completed his training. It's comforting to know he was doing exactly what he loved when he died."

"I'm glad you are able to see it that way."

"There's no other way to look at it, really."

The GPS directs us to the address Deb gave me, and I finally release my hold on Carmen's hand as I find a visitor parking space. "We don't have to do this now if you're not up to it."

She smiles warmly at me, making the breath catch in my lungs. Affection of any kind from her feels like a rare, special gift. "You're just hearing about this. For me, it's old news."

"I suppose it is."

"Not that it has ever reached the point where it doesn't still hurt. It just doesn't hurt like it did at first, when it was an open wound making me wonder if my life was over, too."

Is it weird that I hurt *for* her? Probably. The ache stays with me as we go inside and take the elevator to the seventh floor where Deb is waiting for us. My emotions are all over the place after hearing Carmen's story. She's certainly helped to give me perspective on my current predicament.

So what if my career is a mess at the moment? No one is dead. It's sobering to realize the full magnitude of what she went through at the tender age of twenty-four. I try to picture her surrounded by people and police officers and compassion and endless sympathy. After having known her for only two days, I have little doubt she was strong and resolute through it all, determined to make her young husband proud of her.

As we step into the condo, I can tell this place is special. It's modern and fresh but still warm and inviting. The view of the bay is dazzling. We're high enough that we can see the boats and activity, but not so high that it seems like we're looking down on a tiny village. In New York, I lived on the twenty-eighth floor of my building, far removed from the goings-on below. That was a good thing there. Here, being a little closer to the action below seems good.

"I love it," I tell Deb.

"I do, too," Carmen says. "This kitchen is to die for. You have two ovens and the best fridge money can buy. We have three of these at the restaurant."

"I'm not sure how I feel about glass doors on the fridge."

"Abuela says it's incentive to keep it clean."

"Abuela is a wise woman."

"Take a look at the bedroom," Deb says. "I think you'll like it."

The condo has just one bedroom, which is fine with me. I don't expect to have a lot of visitors, so I don't need a guest room. My mom prefers a hotel to my guest room when she visits. She jokes that I don't have room service at my place.

The master lives up to the hype, with high ceilings, full-length windows that maximize the view and space for a small office area.

Carmen goes to check out the bathroom. "Come see this shower!"

I wander into the bathroom to check out the glass shower with the intricate tile work and multiple showerheads. "Wow."

"I think you need a PhD to work that thing."

"Crap. I only have an MD."

She snorts with laughter. "*Only* an MD. Bet you've never said that before."

I pretend to give that considerable thought. "I don't think I have."

"Hopefully, the shower comes with instructions."

"You approve of this place?"

"I do. Although it makes mine look rather sad in comparison."

"Yours is great."

She rolls her eyes. "Mine is okay. This is great."

"You can come visit anytime you want." I peruse the handout Deb gave me. "The building has a gym, indoor and outdoor pools, a hot tub and a spa."

"I have a pathetic gym in my complex and laundry *in* my apartment."

I laugh at the way she says that. "I'm willing to share my amenities with friends."

"You may live to regret that offer. I love a good spa."

I'll file that info away for later. If she succeeds in helping me land this job, the least I'll owe her is a day at a high-end spa.

We return to the open-concept living area, where Deb is waiting for us. "What do you think?"

"I love it," I tell her.

"Me too," Carmen says.

"If you'd like to make an offer, I'd be happy to write it up for you."

"I'm sort of in a weird spot since I first reached out to you."

"Oh?"

"I'm not yet sure I'm going to be working at Miami-Dade."

"There was an administrative snafu." Carmen steps up when I find myself at a loss for words. "We're trying to work it out, but it's apt to be a week or two before Dr. Northrup receives word that his employment is approved. Are you able to make an offer, contingent upon his job working out?"

"I could talk to the seller's agent and see what they say. The unit has been on the market for sixty-three days, so they may welcome the interest enough to consider that caveat. I'll reach out and let you know."

"Thank you."

"No problem. I'll be in touch."

I guide Carmen out of the condo ahead of me. When we're in the elevator, I glance at her. "Thanks for jumping in there. I didn't know what to say to her. I made this appointment when I thought I had a job lined up."

"I'm sure she deals with special circumstances all the time. Like she said, the place has been on the market for a while, so they're probably willing to deal. I wouldn't worry. If this doesn't work out, there're a million others just like it."

"True, but I like this one."

"I do, too."

How is it possible that in two days her opinion has become so important to me? I have no idea how that happened, but it has, and I need to rein that in before it gets out of hand.

If it hasn't already.

CHAPTER 9

Carmen

I like being with him. I like talking to him and hearing his thoughts. I like the way he didn't fall all over himself comforting me when I told him about the day Tony was killed. Some of the guys I've dated haven't known what to say when they heard how I lost my husband, so they either said too much or not enough.

Jason got it just right.

It's not easy to talk about that day, but it felt right to tell him.

I like how he looks in casual attire—flip-flops, khaki shorts, a navy-blue T-shirt from a surf shop in Maui and those sexy Ray-Ban Wayfarers.

"What's next on our agenda, boss lady?" he asks as we drive away from the condo complex.

"We're basically on hold until I hear back from Maria about the clinic, so how about I give you the two-dollar tour? We can take some photos for Instagram that show you getting to know your new home."

"Sure, we can do that."

It's a perfect South Florida day, if you like it hazy, hot and humid, which I do. "Can we run by my place so I can change?"

"Of course."

I can't believe I'm actually getting paid for this. The thought makes me giggle.

"What's so funny?"

"I was just thinking that it's weird I'm getting paid to play tourist in my hometown."

"That's not all you're doing. You're helping me, which is what Mr. Augustino told you to do."

"True, but this hardly feels like work." After a stop at my place, where I change into a casual dress and sandals, we get back on the highway. A short time later, I point to an exit. "Take this one. I want to show you where I come from." I point to the planes descending into Miami International. "We're very close to MIA."

He takes the exit, and I direct him. "I want you to see 8th Street, otherwise known as Calle Ocho, the main drag through Little Havana." On the way in, we pass signs for the Miami Marlins' ballpark. "Of the nearly three million people in Miami, roughly half of them are Cuban or of Cuban descent. You can live here your whole life and speak only Spanish and be totally fine."

"I'm going to have to work on that. My Spanish is rusty."

"I can help with that, too."

As we creep along busy streets, I try to see the neighborhood from an outsider's viewpoint and immediately feel proud of every part of it, including the coin-operated laundromats, massive new-car dealerships adjacent to used-car lots, graffiti, car washes and restaurants offering Cuban and every other kind of cuisine, including Taco Bell, where the drive-through line blocks the street.

Jason navigates around the cars. "Why would anyone go to Taco Bell when there's all this authentic Cuban food to be had?"

"Great question. Some people were appalled when Taco Bell came to the neighborhood, but as you can see, they do good business."

"Baffling. I'd want the real deal if it was as close by as it is here."

"We've got the real deal at Giordino's. It's the best Cuban in town, in my humble opinion."

The streets are full of stores and restaurants. There's everything from a brand new CVS pharmacy to a Goodwill thrift store to a Cuban coffee shop to nightclubs. Cubans love their nightlife.

We pass a park where a group of men are gathered around a table, intensely engaged.

"What're they doing?" Jason asks when we're stopped at a light.

"Playing dominoes. It's very popular in Cuba—and here."

Little Havana is a juxtaposition of the past and present, sleek and decrepit, coexisting in a mishmash of culture and vibrancy. I love every inch of this place that made me. "When my cousins and I were young, our only goal was to leave this neighborhood, but most of my cousins and friends came back here."

"There's no place like home."

"That's for sure."

We drive by high-rise apartment buildings with balconies and down streets full of pastel-colored houses with stucco exteriors and metal security gates. He takes a left turn onto Calle Ocho. "There's a massive block party here in March every year called Carnaval Miami. It's so much fun. It stretches from 12th to 27th Avenue."

"That sounds fun. I love all the music."

"It's always loud on this street. You'll hear everything from traditional Cuban music to Pitbull. Did you know he grew up around here?"

"I didn't."

"He got his start playing on stages in this neighborhood. See that place over there?" I point to a yellow building with a counter open to the sidewalk. "That's Los Pinareños Fruteria, one of the oldest fruit stands in the country. The lady who works there has been pressing the sugarcane for more than fifty years. They're known for a drink called guarapo. It's pure sugar, so some people call it diabetes in a cup."

Jason laughs. "I'll pass on that."

"It's *so* good. They roll cigars over there. Best cigars you'll ever find."

"I'll pass on them, too. I know too much about what smoking does to the body."

"Keep that to yourself around here if you value your life. We're very serious about our cigars."

"Will do," he says, chuckling.

I direct him to take a few turns that lead to a two-story pink stucco house. Out front are colorful flowers in the window boxes and an ornate white security gate with gold accents.

"Home sweet home." I note that my father's Ford pickup truck and my mother's Mercedes coupe are in the driveway. Any minute, however, they'll be heading to the restaurant for the rest of the day and night. A trickle of sensation works its way down my spine as I imagine them catching me here with Jason and his Porsche.

"This is where you grew up?"

"Uh-huh." I'm relieved when he slows the car but keeps inching forward past the house. "We moved here when I was two. Tony's family lives three blocks that way."

"What are the trees in the yard?"

"Coconut palms and mangoes. You see them everywhere in South Florida."

He starts to speed up.

"Wait. Stop." I point to the chickens and rooster starting across the street, oblivious to the possibility of certain death. "You have to watch out for them around here. They're all over the place."

"Good to know."

"You'll see chicken art and statues everywhere in Little Havana."

I show him the Shenandoah Elementary School I attended as well as the dance studio that was like a second home to me through high school, and the Presidente Supermarket. "I briefly stocked shelves there when I was so fed up with my parents that I didn't want to work at the restaurant anymore."

"That must've gone over well."

"Yeah, not so much. They were more hurt about me quitting the restaurant than they were about me not speaking to them."

"What'd they do to deserve the silent treatment?"

"They refused to let me officially date Tony until I was sixteen."

"Oh right, the waiting period."

"It was torture! We were in love!" I laugh at my own foolishness. "The drama was exceptionally high during those years."

"I can only imagine," he says with a low chuckle.

"My parents have old-fashioned values that didn't sync with my teenage mentality. We butted heads a *lot*, but I always did what they told me to do. As much as I wanted to rebel, I couldn't bring myself to actually do it."

"Such a good girl," he says, smiling. "Was it just you? No siblings?"

"Just me. My mother had nine miscarriages before I arrived."

"Oh my goodness!"

"I know. From what I've been told by others, it was dreadful for them. They don't talk about it at all, though. That's probably why I didn't go totally wild and defy them when I really, *really* wanted to. So there I was, their miracle baby who became a less-than-miraculous teenager. I look back at it now and cringe at how awful I was to them."

"We're all awful teenagers."

"You were, too?"

"Oh God, yes. I was horrible. If my parents had any inkling of the crap I used to do . . ."

I'm immediately intrigued. "Like what?"

"I smoked all the pot, drank all the beer, slept with all the girls. And I was a total jerk to my parents."

Hearing he slept with all the girls, I want to claw their eyes out. That's a totally normal reaction, right? Yeah, I know. Ridiculous. "You were a typical bad boy."

"In every way except for one—I got straight As without really trying."

"Ugh, you were *that* guy? I hated that guy! He ruined it for the rest of us."

"That was me," he says, laughing. "A total fuckup in the rest of my life, but because my grades were perfect, my parents couldn't do much about the rest."

"That's a good position to be in."

"I quite enjoyed it."

"Where'd you go to college?"

"Full ride to Cornell undergrad and Duke medical school."

"Wow, that's impressive, but I suppose you don't get to be a brain surgeon without having a pretty good brain of your own."

His lips quiver with amusement. "It does tend to help. School was always easy for me, until I got to med school and discovered my lack of study skills was going to be a major problem. It was like hitting a brick wall going ninety miles an hour."

"It makes me feel better to know you got your comeuppance."

He laughs. "I totally did. In a big way. I nearly flunked out after my first semester. I was a disaster until one of my classmates took me under her wing and made a real student out of me."

"Is that *all* she did with you?"

"Oh no, we fucked like rabbits between marathon study sessions."

I laugh so hard I end up with tears in my eyes. "The way you say things . . ." I wonder what it would be like to *fuck like rabbits* with him. The thought makes my face flush with heat and embarrassment as a tight knot of desire settles between my legs. I cross them, hoping to quell the sensation, but that only makes it worse.

He flashes a sexy grin that has my skin prickling with awareness of him. "I'm told I have a way with words. But seriously, she saved my ass. We were together through med school, until we got residencies at programs on opposite sides of the country and went our separate ways. Long-distance relationships are hard enough, but throw in two residencies, and it became impossible. We're still friends, though. She reached out to me after the disaster in New York. A mutual friend told her what was going on."

"That was nice of her."

Nodding, he changes the radio and lands on a Cuban station. "News travels fast in medical circles."

I sing along to the song in Spanish, adding some hand gestures from my dance training.

"Are you fluent in Spanish?"

"Sí. You can't grow up here and not speak the language."

"I took years of Spanish, but I suck at comprehension."

"Glad to know you suck at something."

"I suck at a lot of things." He waggles his brows suggestively. "And other things, I'm really, *really* good at."

Dear God, I want to know about those things. I want to experience those things. I want to—

Stop it. Be professional and stop lusting after your colleague. Do your job.

I have a sudden moment of inspiration. "Turn the car around and go back."

"Go back where?"

"I'll show you when we get there."

"You're the boss." He finds a place to turn around, and we retrace our path to the park where the men are playing dominoes.

"Park there." I point to a rare open spot on the street. "Come with me." Jason follows me to the gathering of men. "Excuse me." I recognize some of them from Giordino's, especially Mr. Perez, who brings his wife, Eva, in on Saturday nights. They range in age from sixty to ninety, and all of them know who I am and who I lost. Such is my life after working at the restaurant since I was old enough to roll silverware into napkins.

In Spanish, I tell them, "My friend Jason is new in town and doesn't know how to play dominoes. Would you mind if he watches?"

"Not at all," one of the men replies, moving over to make room for Jason on the picnic bench. "Have a seat."

Jason sends me a questioning look.

I give him a nudge forward. "Roll with me."

He walks around the table to take the open seat.

Speaking in both English and Spanish, the men start giving him pointers, rules and advice, arguing about the best strategies and generally confusing the hell out of him. Thankfully, Mr. Perez translates for Jason.

Despite his initial reluctance, Jason gets sucked in, asking questions and fully participating as I suspected he would. The game is loud and spirited, dominoes clicking against the table with rapid movements that have Jason struggling to keep up. I suspect that doesn't happen to him very often, and the faces he makes are comical.

I pull out my phone and start taking photos, moving around the table for better lighting and angles.

He throws his head back and laughs at something one of the men says about another's idiocy, giving me the money shot.

Many minutes later, he resurfaces from the game, looking around until he finds me with the phone. I'm aware of the exact second he figures out what I'm doing and why.

He flashes a warm, private smile that lights me up from within. Every part of me is aware of him and how he makes me feel just by smiling at me. Despite the fact that we're surrounded by people, the connection between us seems intimate somehow.

"We'd love to share the photos I took on Dr. Northrup's Instagram account. Would any of you object to being in the photos?"

"You're a doctor?" one of the men asks.

"I am."

"What kind?"

"A pediatric neurosurgeon."

They're obviously impressed. They tease him about doctors they've seen on TV and begin to ask about their own medical issues, one of them showing him a mole on his arm.

"You should get that looked at," Jason says.

"See?" the man says to one of his friends in Spanish. "I told you it was bad!"

"No objections to posting the photos?" I ask again, needing to be certain.

"Nope," Mr. Perez says as the others shake their heads.

Jason stands to leave. "Gentlemen, this has been very educational. Would you mind if I stopped by to play with you again sometime?"

"Anytime you want. We're here most days."

Jason shakes hands with each of the men, which impresses them. For some reason, it matters to me that they like him. "I'll be back."

"We'll be here," Mr. Perez says. "Someone's got to keep an eye on the place." He looks at me and winks. "Me agrada tu amigo, mija."

"Sí, gracias." I keep my response low-key, hoping it won't be all over the neighborhood that I brought a man home.

"That was fun."

"Glad you enjoyed it."

"What did he say to you in Spanish?"

"That he likes you."

"Will he tell everyone you brought me here?"

"I really hope not."

"Would that be so awful?"

"It would make things complicated, and I'm not sure either of us is in a good place for complicated right now."

"True." He sounds disappointed, and I'm not sure how to take that. I'm thankful he doesn't pursue it any further.

When we're back in the car, I open Instagram and log out of my account. "We need to start an account for you. What do you want your username to be?"

"Whatever you suggest."

"How about MiamiDoc?"

He pulls a face full of distaste. "That's kinda douchey."

"It's taken by another douchey doctor. What if we do JNorthMiamiDoc? We want to make the connection between you and your career."

"If we must."

"We must." I set up the account using Priscilla@0624, the date we met, as the password. For his profile photo, I use one of the pictures I took of him looking contemplative while he listened to the men explain the rules of the game. I post photos of Jason with the men, using the caption, "Getting to know my new city. Thanks to my new friends in Little Havana for showing me how to play dominoes. Can't wait to go back to play again. #newhome #miami #littlehavana #doctor #pediatricneurosurgeon."

Then I create a story that encourages people to follow him as he discovers his new city. I do all this in a matter of minutes. Not only do I love Instagram personally, but I took an entire class in grad school about using it for marketing purposes.

"When do I get to see this restaurant I've heard so much about?" Jason asks.

"Oh, um, take a left at the light."

He follows my directions until we arrive at the restaurant on West Flagler Street.

"There she is in all her glory." The stucco building is painted a pale yellow with green shutters and window boxes. Both the Cuban and Italian flags fly from either side of the doorway. Above the door, GIORDINO'S is carved and painted in gold leaf that my mother touches up on the first of January every year. She also personally sees to the window boxes that change with the seasons. Right now they're filled with purple petunias and pansies.

"It looks really nice," Jason says.

"They're quite proud of it."

"You should be, too."

"Oh, I am, for sure. They've worked so hard to make it what it is."

"Do they expect you to take it over someday?"

"They do, which is why I'm determined to have a career separate from the restaurant while I can."

"You don't want it?"

"It's not that so much as I don't like the idea of having no choice about it."

"None of your cousins are interested?"

"They might be, but my parents are the owners, so it would be weird for them to skip over me in favor of my cousins, or so my father says."

"I can see that. You could always hire a manager, you know."

"I've thought of that. I hope I won't have to think about that for many years yet. My grandmothers will seriously live forever, and my parents are in their mid-fifties. They all scoff at the idea of retiring. Nona says she wouldn't know what to do with herself if she retired."

"They must really love it if they have no desire to leave it."

"They do love it."

"Do they serve lunch?"

"Yes . . ."

"I'm kinda hungry."

"Jason . . ." My entire system goes haywire at the thought of walking into the lion's den with him.

There are never parking spaces available on the street, except for right now. He skillfully parallel parks and kills the engine. "I can take whatever they're dishing out."

I'm not sure *I* can take it. As he reaches for the door handle, I'm frozen in place.

He glances over at me. "It'll be okay. Don't worry."

I laugh. "How can you possibly know that when you've never met them?"

"I've met you. They raised you, right?"

"Yes . . ."

"Then they must be great people, because you're amazing."

I hold his gaze for a long, charged moment before I look down, overwhelmed by his words and the way I feel around him—dizzy, off my game, aroused, intrigued, afraid. The last time I gave my heart to a man, it was broken into a million pieces. I just don't know if I have it in me to go there again. I don't want to spend the rest of my life alone, but sometimes I think that might be easier than risking the safety net I've built around myself since I lost Tony.

"Tell me what I need to know about them."

CHAPTER 10

Carmen

I'm not at all prepared to take him in there. They know me so well. They'll take one look at me with him and *know* I'm attracted to him.

I swallow hard, as nervous flutters in my abdomen make me feel like a teenager in the throes of first lust. That's exactly how this feels, as if the ground beneath me has suddenly disappeared, sending me spiraling into the unknown.

"If you don't want me to meet them, that's fine, too. It's completely up to you."

I do want them to meet him, so I dig deep for the courage it'll take for me to bring him in there, knowing full well what they'll make of it. "When you meet my grandmothers, be sure to make eye contact. That's important to them. And it's often loud and boisterous in the restaurant. You might think something awful must be happening, but it's just business as usual. If someone wrinkles their nose at you, they're just asking you to elaborate on whatever you just said. They're not saying you stink."

He laughs at that. "Good to know."

"Abuela, my Cuban grandmother, will invade your personal space. She's not trying to be intimidating. That's just how she rolls. They're apt to kiss you, so be prepared for that, and there's always lots of touching and whatnot. People who aren't used to it tend to be surprised by that. My grandmothers and my parents love to complain about *everything*, but in reality they hate drama of any kind. They're all talk and no action when it comes to controversial topics. What may sound like a knock-down, drag-out fight to you is just a conversation to them. Left side is Cuban. Right side is Italian. There's a bar in the middle, and we'll sit there to avoid showing favoritism to either side."

His eyes light up with amusement. "I can't wait to meet them."

"You say that now."

He covers my hand with his and looks at me with affection and humor in his gaze. "I heard what you said before about timing and complications and whatnot. But I want you to know . . . When I got to the hospital yesterday and found out they weren't exactly rolling out the red carpet for me, I nearly had a heart attack. I've put years of hard work into my career, sacrificed so much, and the possibility that it could be taken from me because of a vindictive woman . . ."

He shakes his head in disbelief. "But then I got the message that the lovely young woman who greeted me when I arrived was in trouble with my car and needed me to come to the police station. I was so thankful to have an excuse to get the hell out of that hospital. The minute I saw you sitting in that cell, I felt better. The turbulence inside me calmed when we started talking about how we might turn this thing around. *You* did that for me. After everything that happened with Ginger, I would've thought it impossible to feel anything for another woman, especially so soon after that disaster. But you . . ." He shrugs. "I feel something for you, Carmen, and I think you might feel it, too."

I want to deny it. I want to go back to who I was yesterday morning when I didn't know this man existed. I was safe then. Nothing bad can happen if you don't put yourself out there. I can hear Abuela reminding me that nothing *good* can happen, either. Life is a risk, she says. Love is a risk. It's all a risk, and the people who have the courage to take the leap are the ones who're most richly rewarded.

And devastated when it ends. I can't ever forget about that.

I lick lips that went dry as I listened to him and tried to process what he was saying. "I do." I take a deep breath. *Courage, Carmen.* "Feel something."

"And you aren't sure you want that, am I right?"

I nod.

"I'm not sure I want it, either. I need to be one thousand percent focused on my career and fixing the disaster. And yet I find myself enjoying every minute I get to spend with you." He gives my hand a squeeze. "All I want is to spend more time with you."

"They'll take one look at us, and they'll know . . ." I lick my lips again. "That there's something . . ."

"Okay." He looks at me for a long moment that ends when his gaze shifts to my mouth.

I realize he wants to kiss me and that I want him to. I want that very much. But not here and not now. I clear my throat and look away from him, unnerved by the intensity of the connection I feel with him. It's not the same as it was with Tony. That connection began with close friendship and grew into something wonderful and comfortable over a period of years. This is something altogether different. It has the potential to be cataclysmic if I allow it to be.

His stomach growls, breaking the tension as we laugh.

"I'm starving."

"So I heard." I glance at Giordino's and then at him. "Let's get you fed to within an inch of your life."

"I'm down with that."

We get out of the car and wait for a break in the traffic to cross the street. This place is as familiar to me as anywhere in the world, and as I walk through the doors into the rich scents and usual chaos, it feels like something big has changed. But the change hasn't occurred in the restaurant, which is the same as it's always been. The change is happening within me, and it's all due to the gorgeous man who follows me inside.

As usual, we're doing a bustling lunch business on both sides of the restaurant, but I'm relieved to see that the bar in the middle is mostly empty.

"Carmen!" My mother lets out a shriek and comes to hug me, as if she hasn't seen me in months when in fact I was here two days ago for brunch, during which everyone toasted me and my new job.

She steps back from me, taking a measuring look at my face. "Why are you here in the middle of the workday? Did something happen?"

"Did you get fired?" my father asks when he joins us.

"I did not get fired." I probably would've gotten fired if my boss knew about what really happened yesterday, but thankfully he doesn't. I hug them both and then gesture to Jason. "This is Dr. Jason Northrup. He's new to the staff at Miami-Dade, and I was asked to help him find a place to live and to show him around."

My parents look at him and then at me and then at him again. I swear to God they can see everything that's happened between us from the second we met, or so it seems to me.

"It's very nice to meet you, Dr. Northrup." My mother shakes his hand with the reverence she usually reserves for celebrities. "Welcome to our humble establishment."

I want to roll my eyes at her ridiculousness. At just over five feet tall—and the "just over" part is very important to her—she's about six inches shorter than me. In every other way, I'm her all over again.

"Please, call me Jason, Mrs. Giordino."

"Then you must call me Vivian, and my husband is Vincent. We both answer to just V as well." She loops her hands through his arm and tries to walk him toward the Cuban side of the house.

"We're eating at the counter, Mami."

My father looks at me and shakes his head at the shameless way she tries to take him to her side of the restaurant. He's six foot two, with broad shoulders, dark hair and a handsome face that brings in the female clientele who blatantly flirt with him.

My mother encourages it because, as she says, it's good for business and because she knows he's hopelessly devoted to her.

"Where're Abuela and Nona?" It's almost unheard of that they're not working the hostess stations during business hours.

"At the hairdresser. They'll be back soon."

"They went *together*?" That, too, is nearly unheard of.

"Nona told Abuela that her hair is blue and that she needed to go to Nona's girl to get it fixed. They had a big fight about it until Nona wore her down."

"Nona *wore her down*? Is Abuela sick? Did you take her to the doctor, Mami?"

"She's fine. I told her Nona was right. Her hair *is* blue, and her lady is too old to be doing hair. The woman has cataracts the size of dinner plates that she refuses to do anything about. It's no wonder she can't get the color right."

Next to me, Jason shakes with silent laughter.

"This is my life," I tell him.

"It's awesome."

"Come, sit." Dad gestures for us to take seats at the bar. He pours an ice water with a lemon wedge for me. "What can I get for you, Jason?"

"Soda water with a lime would be great."

"Coming right up." He gives Jason a large black leather-bound menu and pours his drink while my mother hovers nearby so she won't miss anything.

"We thought we'd hear from you last night after your first day," Dad says.

"I'm so sorry. I meant to call, but I got home late, and by the time I got my clothes ready for today, it was after eleven."

His brows furrow. "Why're they making you work so late?"

"It was Jason's first day, too, and they wanted me to show him around. Mr. Augustino told me I'd be asked to work occasional nights when he hired me."

"But your first day." Mami clucks with disapproval that doesn't surprise me. If they had their way, I never would've gone to college or done anything other than work at the family business. I know they're proud of all I've accomplished, but disappointed at the same time that I chose a different path from the one they planned for me.

"What looks good to you, Jason?" Dad asks.

"All of it. What do you recommend?"

"How about a sampler with a little of everything?"

"Including Cuban?" I ask him, raising a brow.

"Of course." He feigns offense that I'd even ask. I roll my eyes at him, letting him know I don't buy his act. I wouldn't put it past him to bring only Italian food, the way my mother would bring only Cuban. Like their mothers, they're nothing if not territorial that way.

"A sampler sounds perfect," Jason says. "Thank you."

Dad goes into the kitchen to give orders to both chefs, and yes, we have executive chefs for both sides of the house, while Jason takes in the signed photos of my parents with various celebrities that line the walls. Everyone from Frank Sinatra to Taylor Swift has come through our doors at one time or another. The restaurant is listed as a "must-see" on most of the Miami-area tour sites, and we see a steady stream of tourists along with our local regulars.

"Eva Perez said you were playing dominoes in the park this morning," Mami says with a nonchalance that's totally fake. She's gone behind the bar to wipe the gleaming surface that doesn't need wiping.

Honestly. I can't make this shit up. This really is my life. "We stopped by because Jason wants to get to know his new town, and I thought he'd enjoy learning to play."

"She said you took photos."

"Yes, for his social media."

"Maria said you asked about him working at the free clinic."

I sigh to myself, because God forbid she should hear me sigh at something she says.

"Allow me to explain," Jason says.

I want to throw myself in front of that, but before I can stop him, he's telling her the full story of what happened in New York as well as how I'm helping him restore his reputation and get approved by the board at Miami-Dade.

My mother hangs on his every word, her mouth hanging open in shock when he gets to the part about how Ginger betrayed him. About halfway through the retelling, my father returns and is equally interested. I'm not sure if I'm watching a slow-moving disaster or a smart move on his part.

"What kind of woman does that to someone?" Mami is filled with outrage on his behalf.

Her outrage is a relief to me. I don't want her to dislike him because of what happened. And besides, it's probably best that he told them himself since they'd be googling him two seconds after we leave. The four of them are in love with their iPhones and their emojis.

"This is a very important assignment you've been given, Dulcita."

Jason glances at me, eyebrow raised. "Dulcita?"

"Sweetie," my mother tells him. "It's what I've always called her."

"She is very sweet."

I'm mortified, and he knows it, but he laughs anyway. And here I thought I liked him. When I look up, my mother is giving me a curious look, as if she just put together a thousand-piece jigsaw puzzle in the span of a second. That's my mother for you. Nothing gets by her.

"Where are you from originally, Jason?" Mami asks.

"Outside of Milwaukee."

"Where do your people come from?"

Jason glances at me.

"Nationality." My family is always interested in where other people are from.

"Oh, um, English, Irish and Dutch, or so I was told."

"Do you have siblings?"

"I have a younger brother."

"And what do your parents do?"

"Mami! This is lunch, not an inquisition." I feel like I should put a stop to this, even though she's posing questions I'd like to ask.

"It's fine, Dulcita." Jason winks at me as I scowl at him. He's not allowed to call me that, but he doesn't seem to care. "My mom is a doctor and my dad is an attorney."

"Oh my." My mother has always been impressed by people with fancy educations, although as my dad frequently tells her, fancy educations don't necessarily equal fancy people. He likes to give her examples of people we know who have all the education in the world but don't know enough to come in out of the rain, as he puts it. "They must be very proud of you."

"They were until things blew up in New York."

"That wasn't your fault."

He shrugs, seeming a little defeated. "People don't believe I didn't know who she was. She didn't change her name when she got married, so how was I supposed to connect her to the board chair? And it never occurred to me that I should google this fabulous new woman I met who seemed so genuine. That's on me."

"It's not your fault." Mami reaches across the bar to place her hand over his. "It's her fault. She set out to use you without a care in the world about the damage it would do to you, probably figuring you were a typical self-involved rock star surgeon who wouldn't care if she used you to break up her family. I'm very sorry that happened to you."

"Thank you."

He's wallowing in the maternal vibes my mother is putting out. She mothers everyone, like a woman who was meant to have ten children, not just one. And like so many others before him, Jason is powerless to resist her. Tony *adored* her and told her all his problems to the point that I had to plead with him not to share everything that went on between us with *my mother*!

Let me tell you—it wasn't easy being a rebellious teen when all my friends were telling me how *amazing* my mother was and that I ought to be nicer to her. Talk about frustrating.

The pager on my dad's belt vibrates to let him know food is ready in the kitchen. He goes to get it and returns with two platters that he puts down in front of us. "Cuban on the left. Italian on the right."

"It's never the opposite here," I tell Jason. "Ever."

"Good to know. I wouldn't want to mess that up."

"Don't worry," Mami says, "we won't let you make that mistake."

"Give me a tour of what we've got here."

I point to the basket of confections that Dad brought along with our food. "Croquetas, pastelitos and bocaditos. On the platter, there's arroz con pollo, which is rice and chicken, and arroz con frijoles negros, or rice and black beans. That's ropa vieja, shredded beef in tomato sauce. *Ropa vieja* actually translates to 'old clothes,' but don't let that stop you from trying it. It's one of my favorites. We've also got tostones, which are plantains, and yuca hervida con mojo, or boiled yuca. On the Italian side, there's manicotti, which is what we're known for, as well as eggplant parm, fritto misto and a sausage and broccoli rabe frittata."

"I hope you provide to-go containers, because this is enough for three meals."

"We'll pack it up for you, mijo," Mami says. "Don't you worry."

I'm stricken by her use of the word *mijo*. That's what she called Tony, the slang term for *mi hijo*, or "my child."

She immediately realizes what she did and sends me an imploring look, as if she's asking me to forgive her. I do. Of course I do, but hearing that term for the first time in five years hits me like a shot to the heart.

Jason doesn't notice, which is just as well. He's too busy trying bites of everything. His moans of pleasure zing through me like live wires attached to all my most important parts as I try to get a few bites down.

Needing something to do, I get out my phone, go around the bar and take photos of him sampling—and obviously enjoying—traditional Cuban and Italian food.

"This is the best meal I've ever had in my entire life," he declares when he's put a sizable dent in both platters.

My parents beam with happiness. He couldn't pay them a higher compliment. They love nothing more than feeding people to the point of explosion.

"How about dessert?" Dad asks.

Before we can reply, the front door swings open with a crash as my grandmothers come in, fighting like angry cats, per usual.

Abuela is fussing with her hair, which looks lovely as always. "It's too short. I told her not to cut it so short, but she didn't listen. Leave it to you, coño, to take me to a hairdresser who doesn't speak English *or* Español."

"She speaks perfect English and Spanish, and unlike your blind-as-a-bat lady, she can actually *see* what she's doing!"

"If I didn't know better, I'd think you told her—"

Everything stops when Abuela notices me sitting at the bar.

With a man.

Nona glances our way to see what Abuela is looking at, and that quickly, their argument is forgotten.

They have much better things to do than fight about hair when I'm sitting at the bar. *With a man.*

"Incoming," I mutter to Jason.

CHAPTER 11

Carmen

Descending upon us like locusts, they hug and kiss me like they haven't seen me in weeks, bringing clouds of Chanel and Dior perfume with them. They're the scents of home to me. Abuela is petite and delicate, her snow-white hair perfectly coifed after her trip to the salon, during which the blue hues were thankfully washed out. Though she's nearly seventy-five, her face is unlined and her makeup is flawless. I've never once seen her looking anything other than stunning, even first thing in the morning.

Nona towers over her and is twice as wide, and much to Abuela's dismay, Nona's hair has remained stubbornly dark with only a few gray hairs to indicate she will soon be seventy-six. Nona doesn't give a rat's ass about makeup or what she's wearing or any of the things Abuela obsesses over. They couldn't be more opposite if they tried to be, and they put a hell of an effort into being as different from each other as they can possibly be.

They have one huge, all-consuming thing in common, however . . .

Me.

I jump in before they can start asking questions. "Nona, Abuela, this is Dr. Jason Northrup, one of my new colleagues at Miami-Dade. Jason, these lovely ladies are my grandmothers, Marlene and Livia, but almost everyone calls them Abuela and Nona."

He stands and shakes both their hands, looking them in the eye when he tells them it's so nice to meet them both.

I'm unreasonably proud of him.

"A *doctor*," Nona says. "How lovely. What kind of doctor are you?"

"A pediatric neurosurgeon."

Abuela gasps. "A neurosurgeon! Like Patrick—"

"—Dempsey." Nona completes Abuela's sentence as usual. Abuela can never remember names. Faces, yes, but she's awful with names. That's why she calls our customers Mami and Papi. It's easier than remembering their names.

"Yes, just like him," I reply, "only Jason is an *actual* brain surgeon."

Abuela directs a shrewd glance my way. "Jason is, is he?"

I realized my mistake the second I made it, but it's too late to take it back.

"I'm so happy you're already making such *amiguitos* at work, Carmen." What she lacks in memory, she doesn't make up for in tact. *Amiguitos* means good friends in a sort of flirtatious sense, and she put the extra oomph behind it to make her point. Like I wouldn't have gotten her meaning otherwise.

Abuela is bowled over by his handsome face as much as his curriculum vitae, not to mention he's here with me. She's going to dine out on this for weeks. Her granddaughter brought a *neurosurgeon* into the restaurant, a real live *neurosurgeon*.

"My boss asked me to show Dr. Northrup around since he's new to the area and needed help getting acclimated."

"You've come to the right place, Dr. Northrup," Nona says. "We can teach you everything you need to know about the Miami area."

"That's very kind of you, ma'am. Carmen is doing an excellent job of showing me around."

"Is she now?" Abuela's laser-beam gaze delves inside me to root around for the real story.

I put up my mental block and give her nothing. "We should get going." I hope I'll be able to extricate him from their clutches.

Before we can make a move, my cousin Maria comes in, wearing pink scrubs with cartoon babies all over them. She has my build, height and coloring, but her hair is longer and curlier than mine. People often mistake us for sisters. She smoothly navigates the grandmothers to kiss my cheek. "Heard you were here."

"How is that possible?" Jason asks under his breath.

"It's better not to ask. Dr. Jason Northrup, my cousin Maria Giordino. Maria, Dr. Northrup."

"Jason," he says.

My grandmothers begrudgingly step aside so Jason and Maria can shake hands.

"Good to meet you." Maria gives me a side-eyed glance that conveys an entire conversation that would go something like this if we were alone: *Her: Are you for real right now? This guy is freaking hot. Me: Is he? I hadn't noticed. Her: Whatever. My ass you didn't notice.* "I hear you might be looking for a volunteer gig."

"You heard correctly, and it's nice to meet you, too."

"I come bearing good news. The clinic would love to have your services tomorrow if you're available."

He glances at me.

"He's available on one condition."

"What's that?"

"We can take photographs of him at work."

"No patient faces online without signed releases."

"Done."

Maria smiles at Jason. "You're hired."

"That's great. Thank you so much."

"We're very happy to have you."

"I thought you said you're a neurosurgeon," Abuela says. "What're you doing working in Maria's free clinic?"

"Community outreach," I quickly reply for him. "The hospital requires it."

"That's a wonderful gesture," Nona says.

He's won her over forever by giving his time to the needy. My dad gripes about how much food she donates to the numerous causes she's involved with, but even he respects how much of themselves she and Abuela give to others.

"You want lunch, sweetheart?" Dad asks Maria.

"A house salad with chicken to go would be great, Uncle V."

"Coming right up."

"What time and where tomorrow?" Jason asks Maria.

"Is nine okay?"

"Works for me."

"I'll bring you so I can take photos," I tell him.

"Sounds good. Thanks to both of you."

"Thank *you*. My boss couldn't say yes fast enough when I told her about your offer. I would've had an answer for you sooner, but she was in meetings all morning with the finance people, which usually puts her in a foul mood."

"Does the clinic need money again, honey?" Nona asks.

"I'm not sure what's going on, but I'll let you know."

"We can do another spaghetti dinner," Nona says. "Just say the word."

"Thank you." Maria kisses Nona's cheek and then Abuela's. She's like a third grandmother to Maria. That's one thing to adore about my grandmothers' unique relationship. They love each other's grandchildren like their own.

My dad has packed up all the leftovers for Jason, and judging by the size of the bag he presents, I assume he's added enough for a few additional meals, too.

"Thank you, Daddy."

"Anything for you, love."

Jason reaches for his wallet.

"You'll insult us if you try to pay." Dad affects a comically stern tone. "It's our pleasure to welcome our daughter's colleague to Miami and our humble establishment."

Jason leans across the bar to shake my father's hand. "Thank you so much for your hospitality, Vincent. It's been such a pleasure to meet you all."

"Likewise," Abuela says. "I hope we'll see you back here very soon. In fact, you should come for Sunday brunch." The calculating look she gives me lets me know she's trying to help me, whether I want her help or not.

"I'd love to."

"Wonderful. Carmen will give you the details, and we'll see you Sunday." She crooks her finger to get him to come down to her so she can kiss his cheek.

Then Nona hugs and kisses him while my mother waits for her turn.

I nudge him to get him moving for the door before they think of something else they need to tell him or ask him.

"Call me later, Carmen," Mami calls to me as the door closes behind us.

"So. That's my family."

"I have so many questions."

As we walk toward his car, I laugh as hard as I've laughed in years.

Jason

She has no idea how incredibly lovely she is, which only makes her more so. Seeing her with her family has added an intriguing layer to my impression of her and filled me with curiosity about the family dynamics.

"Abuela is your mother's mother, right?" I ask when we're back in the car.

"Yes, she left Cuba when she was about ten. Nona's family came from Italy to New York, originally, when she was two, so too young to remember much about it. Abuela, on the other hand, remembers everything about leaving Cuba. It was very traumatic for her and her entire family, especially after they lost her father."

"What happened to him?"

"My great-grandfather infiltrated Batista's administration as part of the revolutionary effort to overthrow his corrupt government. Batista was the president in the chaotic time before Castro came to power. When my great-grandfather was found out, he was executed."

"Oh my God."

"Sadly, this happened a month before Batista was forced to flee the country. One of my great-grandfather's friends came to the house and told Abuela's mother they had to get out immediately. He got them on a flight leaving for Miami that afternoon. Her mother escaped with five children and nothing more than the clothes on their backs. They went from being wealthy, prominent citizens of Havana to living in a new country where they didn't speak the language, with few resources available to them."

"What a shock that must've been."

"From what I've heard, my great-grandmother never truly recovered from losing her husband, home and country all in the same day. Abuela and her older sister helped to raise their younger siblings while their mother worked long hours at a dry cleaner to put food on the table in the cramped apartment where they all lived. The saving grace, if you can call it that, was the community of exiled Cubans who ended up here."

"It must've helped to have others from Cuba close by."

"It was a mixed bag for them. There were so many competing interests at the time. Some people revered them for what their husband and father had done, and others were less appreciative. Fun fact—I was named after my great-grandmother Carmen."

"What an amazing story."

"When the travel restrictions were eased a few years back, my parents took Abuela and her older sister to Havana. My parents said Havana is like the place time forgot. They're still driving cars from the fifties and have hardly any of the modern conveniences we take for granted here. They were supposed to be there for a week but came back after only two days. Abuela and her sister couldn't bear to be there. The memories were too painful."

"That's so sad."

"She said the trip provided closure for them. That's all she's ever said about it. Since then, she's asked us to speak to her in English more than Spanish so she can continue to improve her English. It's like she's finally accepted she's never going home."

"You'd never know she's experienced such heartache."

"She hides it well. Despite all she's endured, she's still one of the most optimistic, joyful people I've ever known."

"I'll confess to not knowing much about Cuban history, beyond what we hear in the news about people trying to escape to the US by boat."

"We only hear about that when it goes badly and people die. The history of the revolution is fascinating. We studied it in school."

"Whereas we studied the Cuban Missile Crisis in high school, but otherwise, I don't remember learning much else. You said your Nona is from New York?"

"Right. Her family moved to Miami from Brooklyn when she was a teenager, so she's a New Yorker at heart. She gets back there as often as she can, especially now that two of my cousins live there. We joke that she gives them twenty-four-hour notice that she's coming to town, and they have to spend the entire time cleaning their apartment to make it ready for her."

I laugh at the image she paints of two young New Yorkers scrambling to prepare for their beloved but exacting grandmother's arrival. "Thank you for sharing them with me. That was the most enjoyable and delicious meal I've had in a long time." I glance at the restaurant. "Are they talking about us in there?"

"Oh hell yes," she says, laughing. "I made a critical error when I called you Jason in front of them."

"How so?"

"You must've missed the calculating look that Abuela gave me. I swear that woman can see inside me sometimes. Me calling you by your first name indicates familiarity, and she homed right in on that."

"Our generation is far less formal than theirs."

"True, but she *sees* far more than I want her to. She always has. My mother is the same way."

I turn toward her, more intrigued by her with every minute I spend with her. "What do you suppose they saw today?"

Carmen rolls her lip between her teeth as she studies me intently.

I begin to worry that I have sauce on my face or spinach in my teeth, but I can't look away from her to check.

"They saw that I'm interested in a man for the first time since I lost Tony."

Her confession touches the deepest part of me, and I lean toward her, needing to kiss those sweet lips.

She casts a wary glance at the restaurant. "Not here."

I bite back a groan. "Where do you want to go?"

"Let's take a ride out to the beach."

I pull into traffic while she directs me to the southbound freeway toward Miami Beach. While I drive, she fiddles with the radio until she lands on a station playing classic rock.

She turns up the volume on "Hot Blooded," and when she catches me watching her, she smiles. "I grew up on classic rock. It was all my dad wanted to listen to at home and in the car."

"I'm a classic-rock kinda guy myself. What's your favorite band?" If we talk about music, I won't think about how I almost kissed her, right? Will she let me kiss her when we get to the beach? God, I hope so. I'm dying to kiss her.

"It's a toss-up between Fleetwood Mac and the Eagles."

"Two of my top three."

"What's the third?" she asks.

"The Stones. I saw them last year in New York. It was a dream come true."

"I can't believe the way Mick prances around the stage in his seventies."

"I know, and even after having heart surgery, he's still at it. Have you seen them?"

"Not yet, but I'd love to."

I file away that information for future reference. "Who else have you seen?"

"The Eagles came to Miami last year. They were *so* good. Glenn Frey's son Deacon is touring with them now, and he was awesome."

"I heard about that. Who else are you dying to see?"

We talk about music and bands and shows we've seen as we navigate heavy traffic on the way to the beach. It's a welcome distraction after what she confessed to me. I want to kiss her and hold her and spend more time with her. If you'd have told me I'd be having those thoughts so soon after the disaster with Ginger, I would've laughed. But that was before I knew Carmen Giordino existed in this world.

While I drive, she works on her phone, posting the photos she took of me at the restaurant, enjoying authentic Cuban and Italian food at Giordino's. Traffic is slow, which is how I manage to catch her frowning as her fingers fly over the screen. "What's wrong?"

"Nothing."

Her tense posture and expression say otherwise. "Tell me."

"Just some asshole comments on the photos from earlier."

My heart sinks. "What kind of comments?"

"Bringing up the shit from New York, but don't worry about it. I deleted the comments and blocked the accounts."

I'm disheartened to hear that the bullshit followed me south, but what did I expect? "In the digital age, you can run, but you cannot hide."

"Don't sweat it. We'll keep adding to the narrative, and over time we'll make them forget all about what happened in New York."

I wish I was as convinced as she is that people will forget such a juicy scandal.

Carmen takes a call from her cousin Maria that she puts on speaker. "Hey, what's up?"

"I had a thought about your project," Maria says.

I assume that means me.

"What's that?"

"Remember my friend Desiree from high school?"

"Oh, she works for NBC 6 now, right?"

"Yep. I could hit her up about doing a feature story on the pediatric neurosurgeon who offered to work pro bono at the clinic so he could get to know his new city."

Carmen glances at me, and even though courting attention is contrary to my nature, I'm well aware it's going to be necessary if I have any prayer of repairing my reputation. I nod, giving her my reluctant approval.

"That'd be awesome, Mari. Have her call me if she's interested?"

"Will do."

"Thank you for this."

"Thank you for pimping out your doctor to us."

We both laugh at her use of the word *pimp* to describe Carmen's role.

"My pleasure," Carmen says. "Let me know what Desiree says."

"Will do. Later."

"If we can pull off TV coverage," Carmen says to me, "that'd be amazing."

"Yeah." I grip the wheel tighter, my gaze fixed on the road.

"You don't think so?"

"I do. Of course I do. It's just . . . In my normal life, courting that kind of attention for a volunteer gig would be unheard of."

"I have no doubt your humility will come through in an interview, or I'd never agree to let you do it. People will love you for stepping up for the less fortunate in the community you hope to call home. It's a great story."

"It's a better story when it's someone else on the camera."

"You'll be a star."

"Great," he says, grimacing. "Will they dig up the crap in New York?"

"I'll come clean about what happened, and do my best to keep the focus on what you're doing here."

"Is it always going to follow me? Will it be the opening line in my obit?"

"You've got a lot of years left to do amazing things that'll push that further down on the list."

She makes me feel optimistic when I've had no reason to for weeks.

"If you get to do the interview, you should talk about your tumor research and how close you are to a major breakthrough. That's the kind of thing that'll resonate with regular people. Everyone knows someone who's battling a serious illness. Being reminded there're dedicated doctors out there working on these challenges is comforting."

I hang on her every word, soaking up her insight and wisdom. "You make me believe we might just pull this off."

"Stick with me, kid."

CHAPTER 12

Jason

I love the adorably cocky grin she flashes my way. I love that she's fully embraced my situation and made it hers. She makes me feel less alone with my problems than I was before I met her.

"Park over there." She points to a public lot as she gets busy on her phone again.

After I pull into a space, I start to read the sign about how to pay through an app.

"What's the deal with paying at this lot?"

"It's all done on an app. I took care of it. I'll set you up with the app on your phone. You'll need it to park around here."

"You're very good to have around."

"Why, thank you. Let's walk."

We stash her purse in the trunk before she leads the way to a boardwalk that runs the length of Miami Beach.

"My parents honeymooned here in the early eighties," I tell her.

"Where did they stay? Do you know?"

"The Fontainebleau, I think."

"Let's go check it out. It's changed a lot since they remodeled it. Personally, I don't love it. I liked how it looked before when it was more in keeping with the art deco feel of Miami and Miami Beach. Now it just looks like every other modern, sophisticated hotel. But it's still a cool spot to grab a drink and people-watch."

To our left are dunes and lush vegetation that block our view of the beach on the other side. I catch sight of bits and pieces of the ocean as we make our way to the pool deck of the Fontainebleau, which is hopping with mostly young people. Skimpy bikinis are everywhere I look, not that I want to look at any woman other than the one I'm with.

She's got me completely captivated, especially since she admitted to being as attracted to me as I am to her. The disaster with Ginger might've never happened for all it matters to me now that I've met Carmen and managed to catch her interest.

I understand it's a big deal for her to admit that she's attracted to me. I'm honored and humbled to be spending this time with her. We take seats at a bar called Glow, located in the middle of the action at the vast network of pools and bars. Dance music plays loudly—too loudly for my liking—over speakers positioned for maximum coverage.

One of six bartenders puts drink and food menus in front of us. I peruse the offerings, noting the prices are in line with what I'd expect to see in Manhattan. "I can't picture my parents here."

"It was nothing like this when they were here. When I was younger, my parents would take one Sunday a month off from work, and we'd play tourist in our hometown. We'd take turns picking what we were going to do, and my mother always wanted to come out to the beach. We'd have lunch here and play in the pool. They had this cool winding slide that was one of my favorite things to do. After a while, we'd end up at the beach, playing in the surf. Those were some of my favorite days."

She catches herself and offers the shy smile I'm becoming addicted to. "Sorry. Don't mean to ramble on."

"You're not rambling. I like hearing your stories."

She orders a Miami Heat, which is Bacardí Limón, passion fruit puree, Tropical Red Bull and jalapeño, while I go with a Preacher Man, made with Four Roses bourbon, lime juice, simple syrup and ginger beer.

"Let me get a picture of you enjoying the local flavor." She holds up her phone and takes several pictures of me mugging with the fancy drink and then taps away at her phone to post it.

"What did you say with that one?"

"Enjoying the local flavor at the Fontainebleau."

"Any more snarky comments?"

She scans her screen for a minute, her brows furrowing as she taps away at her screen. "Nothing to worry about."

That means yes, so I decide to change the subject. "If I drank Tropical Red Bull, I'd be up for two days."

She laughs. "Nothing keeps me awake. When I'm done, I'm done. I fall over and crash. My cousins make fun of me because I can't 'hang' with the rest of them at night. I make it until about eleven on a good night. I've always been that way. They call me Abuela."

"That's cute."

"No, it isn't! At my age, I'm supposed to be partying the night away, not acting like an old lady in a recliner falling asleep watching *Golden Girls* reruns."

I lose it laughing at the indignant way she says that. She's so damned adorable. Everything new I learn about her only makes me like her more. And the more I learn, the more I want to know. I stir my drink with the paper straw and take a sip of the tasty concoction. "I can't stop thinking about the story you told me about your great-grandmother escaping Cuba with five children and nothing but the clothes on their backs."

"I've heard that story all my life, and it still gives me goose bumps."

"I can see why. Did she ever remarry?"

"She did, about ten years later. She married a man fifteen years older who'd never been married. He owned a chain of car dealerships in South Florida and adored her and her children. Treated them like his own."

"That's really great." I'm incredibly moved by this story, for reasons I can't begin to fathom.

"By all accounts, it was a good marriage, but Abuela would tell you her mother never got over the sudden, violent loss of her first husband."

"How would you get over something like that?"

"You don't. You learn to live with it, but you never get over it."

I tip my head to study her more intently. "Are we still talking about your great-grandmother?"

Her small smile conveys a world of understanding. "Grief is a very strange journey, and no two people follow the same path. I'd heard the story of what happened to my great-grandfather all my life, but until I lost Tony, I didn't really *get it*, you know?"

"No, I don't know, but I hear what you're saying. It gave you perspective."

"Yes, exactly. Then compound the loss by having to leave your home and your country while consoling five grief-stricken children in a country where you don't speak the language or have a source of income or a place to live, and you wonder how she survived. Her struggles make mine look simple by comparison."

"And yet there was nothing simple about it."

"No, there wasn't. There still isn't. It's like this ache that just stays with you. Even on really good days, like this one has been, the ache is always there. It becomes a part of who you are now."

I take her hand, link our fingers and look into her beautiful brown eyes. "I think who you are now is every bit as admirable as who your great-grandmother was."

"That's nice of you to say, but I'd never compare my loss to hers."

"I have to believe she'd be proud of the way you've put your life back together and figured out a new path for yourself, the same way she did."

"I'd like to think she would be."

"How could she not be? You're a very impressive young woman, Carmen."

"That's high praise coming from a brain surgeon."

"Don't do that. Don't use my accomplishments to diminish yours. I've never been through anything remotely close to what happened to you, not to mention at such a young age. I'm allowed to think you're impressive for the way you've survived it."

"Thanks," she says softly as amusement overtakes her expression. "It does mean a lot coming from a brain surgeon."

I smile and roll my eyes at her. "This music is annoying me. Let's go find somewhere quieter." I hand my credit card to the bartender, who runs it through and returns it to me. After I sign the slip, we take a walk into the hotel. She shows me photos of how it looked when my parents were here.

"That seems more their speed than the jet-set vibe it has now. I saw a sign for luxury car rentals. Want to rent a Lambo?"

"Nah, my friend has a Porsche. What do I need with a Lambo?"

Laughing, I put my arm around her as we walk through the fancy, upscale, contemporary hotel to the exit that leads to the beach. We kick off our shoes and walk along the water's edge. It's a warm, sunny late afternoon, and I feel a sense of peace come over me that reminds me of before scandal exploded my life. Not that I had a lot of peace or quiet in that fast-paced life, but it suited me.

Carmen's hand brushes against mine, and I take hold of it, wanting to touch her now that she's let me know I'm welcome to. After a long walk down the beach, we find a place to sit and watch the sunset.

"Let me get a picture of you on the beach," she says. "Give me pensive and contemplative."

I make faces that have her laughing before I get serious and give her what she needs.

When she's seated beside me on the sand, I can't wait any longer to address what she shared with me outside her family's restaurant. "What you said before . . . I want you to know, it means so much to me."

"Ever since Tony died, I've wondered if that was it for me. If he was it, and after a couple of years, I decided if that was it, I was lucky, you know? Some people never get what I had with him."

"I've never had it."

"I thought I was being greedy to hope it might happen again. But the downside is that once you've experienced the real thing, it's hard to settle for anything less." She laughs and looks out at the vast ocean. "I don't mean to be making this into some big heavy thing the day after we met. It's just that there hasn't been anyone else who truly interested me, so I'm glad to know I can still feel that. I don't want you to think I'm turning this into something—"

I kiss her because I can't wait another second to do what I've wanted to do almost since I first saw her. I take it slow and easy, holding back to give her time to catch up, fully aware that this may be the most important first kiss of my life. Raising my hand to her face, I wait for her to join the party, and when she does . . .

Holy shit.

The kiss goes from sweet to hot as hell in the span of a second when her hand curls around my neck and her tongue connects with mine. Dear God, she's adorable and sexy and smart and . . . I can't find the words I need to describe what it's like to kiss her, to touch her, to breathe in the rich, fragrant scent of her hair as the warm breeze washes over us.

We kiss for a long time, our bodies straining to get closer. I pull back from her only when I begin to worry about us getting arrested—again. Kissing her is almost worth the risk, but I don't think she'd agree.

"I feel it, too," I whisper against her lips. "In case you were wondering."

Her nervous laughter is the best thing I've ever heard. "I don't do stuff like this."

"Stuff like what?" I shift my attention to her neck, which is every bit as appealing as her lips.

She shivers and buries her fingers in my hair. "Make out like a teenager on Miami Beach."

I'm unbearably aroused by her, so much so that I feel even the most innocent of caresses everywhere. "You should do it more often."

"Spoken like the devil himself, leading me astray."

Smiling, I lean my forehead against hers, counting backward from one hundred as I remind myself to go slow with her, to respect what she's been through and to understand that it's a far bigger deal for her to be starting whatever this is between us than it will ever be for me.

She blinks and seems to realize quite a bit of time has gone by since we first sat in the sand. "We should go. It's not the best idea to be out here after dark."

I stand, brush the sand off my shorts and reach out a hand to help her up, releasing it only long enough for her to deal with the sand on her clothes.

We reach for each other at the same moment and then share a smile at how silly we are, two grown adults acting like teenagers in the throes of first romance. But that's how it feels, to me at least. There's an innocence about it, a throwback to a simpler time, maybe because I have to be so careful with her.

With any other woman, I might be suggesting we find the nearest horizontal surface after a make-out session of such epic proportions. But this woman is special. She's had her heart broken and managed to put her life back together. Nothing more will happen between us until she says so.

We ride back to my hotel in companionable silence. I'm not ready for our day together to end, but I'm resolved to proceed with caution so I don't scare her off by wanting her too much. It's amazing to me that Ginger might never have happened for all I care about her since meeting Carmen, who has more substance and integrity in her little finger than Ginger has in her whole body.

With hindsight, I'm ashamed of the way I was taken in by Ginger, bowled over by how she looked and the way she seemed to want me so fiercely in bed. I wonder now if even that was part of her ploy, to pretend to be so wildly attracted to me that I'd lose my mind over her, which is exactly what happened. I was so deeply in her thrall that I didn't even realize someone else was in the room watching us until it was far too late.

I shudder remembering the horror of that moment and all the ones that followed, as the story blew up into a scandal within hours of the husband I didn't know she had discovering us naked in his bedroom. That he was also the chairman of the board of the hospital where I worked only made it that much more horrific, especially when I was called into the president's office and asked to relocate.

"What're you thinking about?"

Carmen's question interrupts the disturbing path my thoughts have taken. "Nothing, really."

"If it's nothing, then why is your whole body tense?"

"I was thinking about things I'd be better off forgetting."

"Ah, I see. Don't you wish you could flip a switch and not think about that anymore?"

"More than anything."

"You're the brain surgeon. You should know where the switch is located."

When I find myself laughing, I realize how quickly she defused my tension and got me thinking about other things, such as when I might get to kiss her again. "Maybe you're the switch."

"What do you mean?"

"You're doing a very good job of making me forget something I thought I'd never stop thinking about."

"Clearly, I'm not doing that good of a job if you were thinking about it just now."

"You're doing a very good job. I was only thinking about how if that hadn't happened, I wouldn't have met you. That would've been truly unfortunate."

"I'm sorry you went through what you did, but I'm glad you landed in my city and that we had the chance to meet."

I reach for her hand and hold on to her all the way back to my hotel, where I'm forced to let go. For now.

When we're standing beside my car, I notice she seems reluctant to leave. "I'll be by around eight, okay?"

"I'll be here. Take some of these leftovers."

She takes a few of the containers her parents packed up for us. They'd included one of those plastic ice packs to keep them cool.

"Don't get coffee in the morning. I'll take you to my ventanita for cortadito, which is Cuban espresso topped with steamed milk."

"Okay . . ."

"Trust me. You'll love it."

I place my hands on her hips, bringing her closer to me. "I have no doubt. Today was fantastic. Thank you for sharing your family, your restaurant, your hometown, yourself with me." I kiss her gently, or that's the plan anyway, until she winds her arms around my neck and kisses me back with all the desire and need I feel for her.

Pulling away from her is one of the hardest things I've ever done. I want to take her by the hand and bring her with me when I go inside. But more than that, I want to do the right thing by her. So I walk her to her car and hold the door while she gets in. When she's settled, I lean in and kiss her one more time.

"Text me to let me know you got home okay."

"I'll be fine."

"Text me."

"If you insist."

"I do." One more kiss and then another. I can't get enough. I force myself to step back, to let her go, to wave her off as she drives away. I take several deep breaths of the warm, humid air before heading into the icebox lobby and up to my room, where I immediately turn down the air. There doesn't seem to be a happy medium when it comes to temperature in South Florida. I'm either sweltering or freezing.

Of course, it doesn't help that Carmen has my blood boiling from her sweet kisses.

As I'm stashing leftovers in my minifridge, my phone rings. My heart skips a happy beat, as I hope it might be Carmen, and then falls just as quickly when I see MOM on the caller ID. I take the call, dreading what I have to tell her. "Hey."

"Hey, yourself. What's happening?"

Everything. Everything is happening. "Not much. Just getting acclimated to Miami while I wait to see if the board at Miami-Dade is going to extend privileges." I cringe as I say those words, knowing what her reaction will be.

"What do you mean *waiting for privileges*?" My mom is a general practitioner in the Milwaukee area. The proudest day of her life, or so she always says, was my graduation from medical school.

"Just what I said. They aren't sure they want me after what happened in New York."

"You've *got* to be kidding me."

"I wish I was." One of the most difficult moments in a nightmarish month was calling my mother to tell her what happened with Ginger so she wouldn't hear about it somewhere else. The two of us and my younger brother, Ben, have been a team since my dad left. Disappointing her crushed me. "The board has asked for two weeks to consider the request, and in the meantime I'm working with one of the hospital's public relations professionals to change the narrative. She's helped me land a pro bono gig at a local free clinic and is working on other publicity that we hope will help to sway the board."

"Dear God, Jason. How can this be happening? You're a board-certified pediatric neurosurgeon. They ought to be rolling out the red carpet."

"Well, they're not. I guess they're afraid I'll sleep with their wives—or their husbands."

"How can you joke about this? Your entire career is on the line."

"If I don't joke, I'll lose my mind. I know what's on the line, Mom, believe me. I'm doing everything I can to win them over. I'm not sure what else I can do besides hope for the best."

"You could apply elsewhere."

"And abandon my research? I can't do that. It's not just about me but everyone else who's been involved."

"This PR professional who's helping you? She knows what she's doing?"

"She's outstanding." And brave and smart and so beautiful she makes me ache. I can't say anything like that to my mother, who'll think I'm insane for getting involved with another woman so soon after what the last one did to me. Hell, *I* think I'm a little insane, but damned if I can stop this thing that's happening with Carmen. I don't want to stop it. Nothing has ever felt as good as being with her does.

"Check out my new Instagram account." I give my mom the account name. "Carmen is posting pictures of me getting to know

Miami. We've got permission from the clinic to post pics of me working there, with patient consent, of course, and there's a possibility of a local TV interview, too."

"The pictures are great. You look happy."

"It was a good day. It's nice to think about something else besides the disaster in New York."

"I'm sure it is."

"We're doing everything we can. I have to believe if it doesn't work out here, something else will pop."

"I hope that bitch in New York is proud of herself. All your years of hard work . . ."

"My credentials haven't changed, Mom. She can't take that away from me. Someone will want me, scandal or not."

"I hope you're right about that."

"Try not to worry. This, too, shall pass."

"I'm glad to hear you sounding better and more optimistic anyway."

I have Carmen to thank for the attitude adjustment. She's giving me reason to feel optimistic, among other things. "I'm doing what I can to get the train back on the tracks. That's all I can do."

"Keep me posted?"

"I will. Watch the Instagram account for updates."

"I'll do that. Call me if you need to talk."

"Will do. Love you."

"Love you, too."

I grab a beer from the stash I put in the fridge last night and twist the cap off before sitting down to do something I've been avoiding—check my email. I've got messages from a number of people I worked with in New York, many of them deriding the "raw deal" I got from the board and asking me what I'm going to do now.

"Good question."

I write back to each of them, thanking them for their support and telling them the truth—I'm waiting to see if Miami-Dade will extend privileges so I can continue my research. If not, I'll be looking to start over elsewhere.

One of the residents who's been working on the tumor project with me writes that she sent messages to each of the board members, telling them they're crazy to let me get away, especially when we're on the brink of a major breakthrough that could bring international prestige to the hospital.

I can't thank you enough for the support, Daniela, I write in my response to her. *Please don't risk your own neck on my behalf. It is what it is, or at least that's what I tell myself. I have to believe it'll work out and we'll be back on track before too long. In the meantime, keep monitoring our patients and inputting the data.*

I scroll through other messages from friends and colleagues before stopping dead on one from Ginger.

Jason,

I don't know what to say other than I'm sorry. I know you won't believe me when I tell you I have genuine feelings for you or I enjoyed every minute we spent together, but both those things are true. I've appealed to Howard not to retaliate against you for my sins. I told him you had no idea who I am to him. Everything that happened was my fault, and I hope someday you can forgive me for the mess I made of something so wonderful. I would love nothing more than to have another chance with you, to pick up where we left off and to move forward from here. You have my number. Call me anytime.

With love,

Ginger

I read the message twice, the first time in complete disbelief and the second time with rage boiling inside me. She fucked up my entire life, and she wants me to *forgive her* for that and pick up where we left off? We "left off" when her *husband* caught her giving me a blow job. Is she for real? I block her, delete the message and empty the trash so there's no chance I have to see that bullshit again.

Disgusted, I get up and step away before I'm tempted to hurl my laptop against a wall. I take the beer with me to the small balcony that adjoins my room and look down over the hotel's pool area, which is still busy even at almost nine o'clock.

Goddamned Ginger. She had to make it even worse than it already is. After making a total fool of me and costing me my job and sterling reputation, she actually thinks I might want to *get back together*? Is she *insane*?

If there's one kernel of good news, it's that she appealed to her husband on my behalf, or so she says, not that I think that'll actually help. He's not going to have the man who screwed his wife and humiliated him on his staff. What's funny, if you want to call it that, is how she fucked with both of us. He and I ought to get together, have a beer and talk about the many ways she did us both wrong. We might even be friends after that, a thought that makes me laugh.

As if.

I'd never claim to have been a saint in my dealings with women, but married women are a hard limit for me. Not that good old Howard would ever believe that in light of what I did with his wife. I think about what he saw that night in his bedroom in the Hamptons and cringe. Sex with Ginger was always "energetic," and that night was no exception. He walked in to see my bare ass and his moaning wife on her knees as she sucked me off.

"Ugh." I down the last of the beer and go get another one, wishing I knew the location of that switch Carmen mentioned, the one that could turn off thoughts we no longer wish to have. Maybe I should focus my research on figuring out that mystery. It'd be worth billions to people who'd give anything to be able to selectively forget upsetting or painful things.

I wish I'd never checked my email, even if it was mostly uplifting, with supportive messages from colleagues and friends. I didn't need to see the nonsense from Ginger, not when I've been making progress in trying to move on from that shit show.

Grabbing my phone, I sit on the bed and open a text to Carmen. Talking to her makes me feel better. Why? Who knows? It just does.

I stare for a long time at the text that says she's safely home before I type a reply.

I wish you hadn't left.

Send.

CHAPTER 13

Carmen

I've just stepped out of the shower when my phone chimes with a text. I wrap my hair in a towel and grab the phone off the bathroom counter.

Jason.

My heart does a funny flip-flopping thing that leaves me breathless.

I wish you hadn't left.

What does that mean? Is he saying he wishes I'd stayed and spent the night in his bed? And if so, why does the thought of that make everything inside me go haywire? My chest feels too small for my heart and lungs. My belly is fluttering, and the hot, tight feeling of desire that's been missing from my life for five long, lonely years has come roaring back to remind me that while Tony is gone forever, I'm still very much alive.

And I want this man.

My phone chimes with another text from him.

Sorry if that's too blunt. He includes the smiley face and red-face emojis. *But it's true. I wish you were still here.*

Before I can give in to my propensity to overthink *everything*, I respond to him. *I wish I was still there, too.*

Really? You do? <dies>

I laugh out loud at his silly reply and send the laughing and crown emojis followed by a text. *Drama queen.*

No, seriously. Today was just so . . . perfect. It was an absolutely perfect day, and that's because of you.

And you. I enjoyed it, too. So much.

My phone rings, and it's him, asking to FaceTime with me. I run my fingers through my wet hair and take the call. "If I look frightening, it's because I had no time to brush my hair."

"You couldn't look frightening if you tried."

I swallow hard at the sight of him sitting up in bed, his chest bare and the sheet gathered around his waist. Is he naked under there? I zero in on the golden hair that covers his chest and abdomen, arrowing down toward the sheet. I lick lips that've gone dry as I check him out. "You should see me first thing in the morning." The words are out before I take a second to contemplate what exactly I'm saying.

He responds with a wolfish grin that melts my panties. Oh wait, I'm not wearing any. Crap. "I'd love to see you first thing in the morning. When would you like to do that?"

I giggle like a silly girl, which is exactly how he makes me feel. Like I'm once again young with my heart still intact the way it was before tragedy shattered my world and crushed me. I've forgotten how it feels to be lighthearted, whole, happy, excited for the future. These emotions wash over me in a tidal wave of elation that meeting Jason has brought back into my life.

"I apologize for being inappropriate," he says, bringing me back to reality.

"You were joking. I know that."

"Um, well, no, not really. I can't stop thinking about being with you and kissing you and how amazing that was."

"It was pretty amazing."

"I'm glad you think so, too."

"I do."

"So yeah, not joking about wishing I could see you first thing in the morning, and all the rest of the time, too."

He's so cute and so sexy and so . . . I have to stop myself from diving straight off the cliff into whatever this is with him. I have to remember the *years* I spent in school preparing for my new job. *He* is my job for the time being, and as much as I want to take that dive, I probably shouldn't do that right now. Although, after kissing his face off, it's a little late to be warning myself off him.

"I know what you're going to say."

I eye him skeptically. "So now you're a mind reader *and* a brain surgeon?"

He laughs, which makes him even sexier, if that's possible. "Yes, they teach us how to read minds in neurosurgery school. It's part of the first-year curriculum. And what you were going to say is that we're working together, and this isn't the time for it to become anything more than that."

"They taught you well in neurosurgery school."

"Thank you. I am good at what I do. When I'm allowed to do it, that is."

The sadness I see and hear from him has my heart going out to him. "Are you getting crazy being cut off from work?"

"A little. It's been years since I went this long without drilling into someone's skull."

I sputter with laughter. "You're sick."

"I know it must seem that way to someone who doesn't do what I do, but to me, skull-drilling is just another day at the office."

"It's a really amazing thing to be good at."

"I always thought so, too, until it was taken from me." He sips from a beer bottle. "I got an email from Ginger."

Hearing that, I sit up straighter. "You did? What'd she say?"

"How sorry she is for everything that happened, that she never intended for my career to be impacted. That she'd like another chance with me. Yada, yada."

"That's such bullshit! What did she think would happen when she set you up to be caught naked with her by her husband, who was also your biggest boss?"

"Easy, tiger." He flashes that sexy grin that makes me feel powerful and powerless at the same time, and yes, I know that's as crazy as it sounds. But there you have it.

"I'm sorry, but I hope you aren't feeling forgiving toward her."

"Not at all. I deleted the email and blocked her so I never have to hear from her again."

"Good."

"It felt good."

"She never intended to mess up your career. *Whatever.* She knew exactly what she was doing, and she didn't give your promising career the first thought when she launched her insane scheme to get rid of her husband."

"You're very sexy when you're pissed. Remind me to rile you up more often."

"Jason! Stop. I'm dead serious."

"I know you are, and it means so much to me to have your support and your friendship and your professional expertise. You have no idea how much."

"My professional expertise, such as it is."

"You're doing great, Carmen. Your ideas feel right to me, and even if it doesn't work to sway the board, it'll all have been worth it to have met you and to have spent this time with you."

I'm so bowled over by him that I respond with humor rather than the emotion that's coursing through my veins like an out-of-control freight train that can't be pushed back into the station no matter how hard I try. Not that I'm trying all that hard. "Especially that time we went to jail."

He smiles. "Especially that. We'll always have jail. In other good news, some of the residents who've been working with me on the research have reached out to the board in New York to let them know they're crazy to let me go, especially when we're so close to a real breakthrough."

"That's amazing. Someday in the not-too-distant future, all of this will be a bad dream that you finally woke up from."

"Not all of it has been bad," he says in a meaningful tone that leaves no doubt he's referring to me.

I run my fingers through my hair, trying to bring order to it. "We have something in common, you and me."

"What's that?"

"We both thought we had it all figured out until it went to shit."

"True. Although your thing was a thousand times worse than mine."

"Heartbreak is heartbreak, no matter how it happens."

"We'll have to agree to disagree on that. Losing your young husband the way you did is far worse than what's happening to me."

"I still hate that she did that to you when you've worked so hard for the career that's now hanging in the balance."

"I have to believe it's going to work out. Even if I can't practice at Miami-Dade, I'm still a well-qualified physician. It's not like I'm going to suddenly be unable to make a living anywhere."

"I'm glad you're feeling more positive about it."

"I'm trying. You've been a huge help to me, Carmen. Seriously."

"It's been fun. My first week on the new job has been far more interesting than expected."

"Especially the time in jail."

"The beach was pretty nice, too."

"Way better than jail."

"Stop talking about jail!"

"Never," he says, laughing.

I'm tired, but I don't want this conversation to end. I could talk to him all night and never get enough of the sound of his voice or the amusing things he says.

"Hey, Carmen?"

"Yes?"

"I want to take you on a real date. Can we do that soon?"

I ought to say no. I ought to try harder to keep the boundaries in place between personal and professional, but in light of what's already happened between us, it's too late for such concerns. "Sure, that'd be fun."

"You had to think about it for a long moment there."

"It's not because I don't want to go out with you. I'm just concerned about the personal versus professional thing."

"I get that. I should be far more concerned about it after Ginger, but this is nothing like that was even before it went bad."

"How is it different?"

"Because you're you, and that makes everything about this special and unique."

"You know how to make a girl all fluttery inside."

"Yeah?"

"Mm-hmm."

"Are you tired?" he asks.

"A little. You?"

"I could sleep, but talking to you is more fun."

My phone chimes with a new text from Abuela that I quickly read. *Loved meeting your friend Jason today. He seems like a special young man. You don't like when I interfere, so I'll only say that you light up around him. Sweet dreams, mi amor. Xoxo*

"What're you smiling about?"

"A text from Abuela. She liked meeting you."

"I liked meeting her and the others. You have a great family."

"Wait until you meet the rest of them. You may not think so."

"I'm sure I will."

"Do you come from a big family?"

"I have a few cousins, but they're mostly older than me. I don't know them very well. It's pretty much been me, my brother and my mom since my dad left."

"You don't see him at all?"

"Maybe once or twice a year when he gets to New York. I'd prefer not to see him, but my mom encourages me to do it. She doesn't want me to have regrets."

"She sounds like an amazing person if she can think that way after he was unfaithful to her."

"She's all about forgiveness, even if we don't necessarily forget. But it took her a long time to get there after everything happened."

"I understand that. I decided to forgive the man who killed Tony because it hurt me more to hate him than it did to forgive him. I won't forget what he did, but I forgive him."

"That's really admirable. I'm not sure I could do that. I've barely been able to consider forgiving my father for what he did."

"I found out the man's family was evicted from their apartment. He was robbing the store because they were out of formula for his infant daughter, and he was desperate. He'd had issues with police in the past. When he saw Tony in uniform, he panicked. I honestly don't believe he intended to shoot or kill him."

"Wow."

"Two lives were ruined in the span of a second. When I heard the whole story, I asked the prosecutor to request life in prison for the shooter rather than the death penalty. I didn't think Tony would approve of me seeking a life for a life in this case."

"I give you so much credit for being able to think that clearly, at twenty-four, after losing your husband and best friend so senselessly."

"It helped to focus on the details of the case rather than wallowing in grief, not that I didn't do plenty of that, too."

"I'm so, so sorry you went through that."

His kind words leave a lump in my throat. "Thank you. I miss him, but I accepted a long time ago that I'll always miss him and love him. That'll never change."

"Of course it won't. Can I ask you . . ."

"What?"

"It's none of my business."

"It's okay. You can ask. Aren't we past the point where my business isn't your business and vice versa?"

His low chuckle makes me feel warm all over, my skin prickling with nearly painful awareness of how much I want this man.

"Carmen, sweetheart . . ." He sounds agonized, and I can't imagine why. "I like you so much. You have to know that."

"Why do I hear a 'but' coming?"

"No buts. I like you. I like you so fucking much it's not even funny. I like everything about you."

"That's a lot of like." He's adorable and sweet and sexy as all hell. "I like you, too."

"It's just . . . My life is such a ridiculous mess right now, and you . . . You haven't been with anyone since Tony died, and . . ."

"What's wrong, Jason? Just say it."

"I don't want to hurt you."

I lick my lips and note the way his gaze homes in on the movement of my tongue. He doesn't try to hide the fact that he wants me fiercely, and knowing that empowers me. "I'm a big girl. I can take care of myself."

"I know that. You're the strongest, most courageous person I've met in a long time. The last thing in the world I want to do is come sweeping through your life like a brush fire and leave ashes in my wake. I have no idea where I'm going to be two weeks or a month from now. It would kill me if, you know . . ."

My tremendous affection for him grows and multiplies as he shows his concern for me. That puts him light-years ahead of the other men I've dated since I lost my husband. "I have every reason in the world to stay far away from you. I worked my ass off to land this job, and I'm determined to have this career for as long as I can before I'll have to take over the restaurant."

"I don't want to do anything to fuck that up for you, sweetheart."

"I appreciate that you care. That matters to me. But if I've learned anything from what I've been through, it's that life is short and right now is all we're promised. I like you. I like how I feel when I'm with you—and even when I'm not. For the first time since I lost Tony, I want to know where it might go from here. If you end up somewhere else, I'll deal with that when it happens."

"And your job?"

"I'm not going to tell anyone that this has become something more than a job. Are you?"

"Hell no."

"Then it ought to be fine."

"'Ought to be' doesn't always go the way it *ought* to."

"Trust me, I know." I try to organize my thoughts into some semblance of sense. "You said today was a great day for you."

"It was the best day. Maybe the best day I've ever had."

"It was the best day I've had in five years, Jason. I'm well aware of all the reasons why I need to be careful, but I'm so tired of being careful, of sticking to the sidelines while life goes on without me. I want to *live* again, not just exist."

"Honey, you're killing me. I want to be there with you so badly it's taking everything I've got to stay put."

"I wish you were here, too, but I think we should both take a pause, think about all of this and make a logical decision about where we go from here."

"I already know where I want to go from here."

I lose my composure and giggle again. I love that he makes me laugh the way I used to, before life backhanded me across the face. "I'm serious, Jason."

"So am I. I'm as serious about this as I've been about anything."

"You're just coming off a major disappointment—"

"I've left her so far behind it's like she never happened. Finding out she set me up the way she did ruined any feelings I had for her. I swear to God this isn't a rebound, Carmen. Not even kinda."

"My head is spinning a little."

"Mine is, too, but it's the best feeling. Isn't it?"

"Yeah."

"Get some sleep. Tomorrow is another day. We'll figure this out."

"I'm looking forward to seeing you in doctor mode at the clinic."

"I'm looking forward to it, too. See you in the morning?"

"Yes, you will. Go to sleep."

"You too."

"Don't want to let you go."

I turn off the light and settle in under the covers, the glow from my phone bright in the darkness of my bedroom.

He does the same on his end, plunging us both into darkness. "I wish I was in bed with you, holding you and kissing you and other stuff."

"What other stuff?" I ask, breathless once again.

"The good stuff."

"It's been so long for me that I can barely remember the good stuff."

He groans loudly. *"Stop."*

"Don't want to."

"Carmen."

When I close my eyes, all I can see is the image of him sitting up in bed, the covers pooled at his waist, sexy man chest on full display. I was better off before I knew his chest looked that good.

I fall asleep with a smile on my face. When I wake hours later, the first thing I notice is that the connection is still live. I watch him sleep for a long time, wishing he were here next to me.

I should probably be concerned that I've lost all perspective when it comes to Jason. I couldn't care less about all the reasons why it might be a bad idea to get involved with him from personal or professional standpoints.

I don't care about anything other than being with him, and that's so far out of character for me as to be laughable. I always care. I always do the right thing and stay in my lane. I never do anything that would be considered risky, especially since I lost Tony.

Two days after meeting Jason, I feel like a new version of myself, and I like this new version a whole lot. If I've learned anything from what I've been through, it's that life isn't a dress rehearsal. It can be taken from us at any time, and we need to fully embrace every minute we have. I haven't done that the way I should've since my world was turned upside down.

I'll be damned if I'm going to miss out on this chance to fully live.

Dr. Jason Northrup had better look out. He has no idea that New Carmen will be greeting him in a few short hours, and New Carmen wants him.

Badly.

CHAPTER 14

Carmen

I dress with him in mind, choosing a sexy wrap dress that reveals more of my cleavage than I normally show. It's perfectly appropriate for what we have planned today, and if it makes me feel sexy, even better. I leave my hair curly and spend extra time on my makeup. In the shower, I shaved everything, just in case.

I laugh to myself at how ridiculous my thoughts have gotten.

Only a few days ago, the idea of shaving everything "just in case" would've led me to ask, *In case of what?*

I'm acutely aware of my own heartbeat as well as the sensitive surface of my skin. My nipples are tight, and between my legs . . .

"Ugh," I tell my reflection in the mirror. "This is going to be a long freaking day."

I receive a text from Maria. *Hope your guy is ready for this. There's a line out the door.*

He's ready and willing. See you soon.

I gather my things and am out the door with time to spare so I won't be late to meet him. Traffic is, as always, a beast. It probably seems worse to me today because it's standing between me and seeing him, and I'm dying to see him.

"This is bad." Maybe if I say it out loud, I can get a handle on this situation before it spins any further out of control. If I had to pinpoint the exact moment I lost control, it would be last night on Miami Beach when I made out with the man my boss assigned me to work with.

My boss. *Shit!* I forgot to report to Mr. Augustino last night. I summon Siri and tell her to call the hospital. When I reach the switchboard, I ask for the president's office.

"Office of the president, Mona speaking."

"Mona, hi, it's Carmen."

"Hello there! How're you doing?"

"Doing well."

"I *love* Dr. Northrup's Instagram account. Have you seen how many followers he already has? The photos of him playing dominoes were so perfect. He's—"

"Mona!"

"Oh, so sorry. What can I do for you, hon?"

"Could I please speak to Mr. Augustino?"

"Of course. Just a moment."

While I wait on hold and listen to the light rock music playing in the background, I dart through the traffic that stands between me and the source of my obsession. And yes, that's what he's become. What other word should I use to describe the man who occupies ninety-eight percent of my thoughts forty-eight hours after I first saw him?

I've about given up on Mona and Mr. Augustino when he comes on the line. "Carmen, good to hear from you. I expected an email from you this morning."

"I know, that's why I'm calling. I got caught up in making plans for today and forgot to send the email. I'm so sorry, but that's why I'm calling now." I cringe as the story rolls off my tongue with glib exaggerations. I'm headed straight to hell. "I figured I'd call you with my report, if that's all right."

"Sure, what've you got?"

I tell him about the Instagram account, about Jason playing dominoes with the men in Little Havana, eating at Giordino's and touring Miami Beach. "Today, he's seeing patients at the Our Lady of Charity free clinic in Little Havana, and according to my contact there, people are already waiting in line for the chance to see him. We've secured permission from the clinic to take photos with any patients who agree to be photographed, and I'll make sure they sign releases."

"This is excellent, Carmen. Very well done."

I breathe a sigh of relief.

"I've had some promising conversations with various board members who'd expressed concerns, and I'll be sure to make them aware of the Instagram account as well as Dr. Northrup's work at the clinic."

"That would be excellent."

"Keep up the good work."

"Yes, sir, and I'll be sure to get the written report for today to you tonight."

"I'll look forward to hearing how it goes. Have a good day."

"You too."

I end the call feeling optimistic after hearing Mr. Augustino has had some positive conversations with board members. The tide seems to be turning in Jason's favor, and I can only hope that his day at the clinic will help to seal the deal.

I seem to have a vested interest in keeping him in Miami.

When I pull into the parking lot, he's leaning against Priscilla, scrolling through his phone. He's wearing the Wayfarer sunglasses, a pressed button-down shirt that covers that sinfully sexy chest I got a look at last night and khaki pants. It's quite possible I'm drooling as I stare at him before he realizes I've arrived.

A horn sounds behind me, snapping me out of my stare-fest and catching his attention.

He smiles at me, and I die. I'm done. I can't think or function.

Until that damned driver in the car behind me lays on the horn again.

Jason cracks up laughing as I inch forward into a parking space. *Well, that was rather mortifying.* I'm flustered as I gather my things, and then my door opens and he's there, squatting next to me, still smiling.

"I'd hate to have to bail you out, *again*."

"But you would, wouldn't you?"

Nodding, he leans in, clearly intending to kiss me. "Every time."

I meet him halfway, our lips connecting with urgency that takes us right back to where we left off yesterday.

His hand encircles my neck, I grasp his shirt, and his tongue brushes against mine, making me moan from the power of the desire that touches every part of me. He smells so good. *So, so good.* Like soap and sporty cologne and heaven.

"Christ have mercy," he mutters when we come up for air. "I want to take you inside and spend the whole day feasting on you."

I try to say something, but what comes out sounds like "ungwh."

"Yes, my thoughts exactly."

"You've scrambled my brain."

"Back atcha, babe."

I use my thumb to wipe my lipstick off his mouth. "Maria says there's a line out the door at the clinic."

His tongue touches my thumb, and I gasp from the need that makes me want to forget all about the clinic, my job, his job, the hospital board. All of it. I just want to say *eff it* and follow him inside to his room to start a whole new scandal.

"There's good news and bad news," I tell him.

He pushes my hair aside and kisses my neck. "Hmm?"

I melt. I'm a puddle of want and need so sharp it clouds my better judgment and nearly makes me forget everything that isn't his lips on my neck. "The good news is I worried if it would be weird or awkward between us today."

"Not even kinda weird *or* awkward. So what's the bad news?"

"We need to be somewhere."

"That's very bad news, indeed. Might be the worst news I've ever heard."

"You already knew this."

"True, but I hadn't kissed you yet today, and now that I have . . ."

"What?" Have I ever been as breathless as I get around him? No, never.

"I'm going to need some time to settle down before we go anywhere."

I tell myself not to look, but I'm not listening to myself when it comes to him. I look. I stare. I want.

"Stop. That's not helping."

My phone rings, and I take the call from a local number I don't recognize. "Carmen Giordino."

"Hey, this is Desiree Rivera with NBC 6."

I give Jason, who's still in a crouch next to my car, a big-eyed look and put the phone on speaker so he can hear, too. "Hi, Desiree. Thanks so much for calling."

"Maria told me about your colleague, the pediatric neurosurgeon who's offering pro bono work at her clinic in Little Havana. My bosses love the idea of a feature story, if he's game."

Jason nods, but I can see the reluctance all over his face.

"He is, but there's a catch."

"What kind of catch?"

"The reason he's courting publicity is he was part of a scandal at his former hospital in New York. He met a woman, began a relationship with her and the whole time she was setting him up to help her out of a bad marriage—with the chairman of the board of his hospital."

"Whoa."

"He had no idea she was married, let alone to the chairman of the board. They transferred him to Miami-Dade without mentioning the scandal. Apparently, the board in Miami heard about it and isn't sure they want to extend privileges. Our goal is to show that he's someone we want and need in our community."

"So that's why he's doing the pro bono work?"

"Yes, but he's really looking forward to it. He would tell you he doesn't get to do a lot of routine medical stuff anymore since his regular patients come to him when they're in some sort of crisis. He welcomes the opportunity to make a contribution to his new community."

He smiles and gives me a thumbs-up, which is a relief, because I'm totally winging this.

"If we do the interview, I'd have to ask him about what happened in New York."

He grimaces.

I meet his gaze. "Understood."

"Let me test the waters here and get back to you in an hour or so. Maria said he'd be there all day today?"

"That's right."

"Okay, I'm on it. Talk soon."

She's gone before I can reply. "This is an amazing opportunity," I tell him.

"I know." He stands to his full height and stretches, all signs of arousal killed by the reminder of what we're doing today and why we're doing it. "You promised me Cuban coffee."

"So I did."

Extending his hand, he helps me out of the car.

"Jason."

"Yeah?"

"Are you okay?"

"I'm good."

"You're upset about the interview?"

"I'm upset that I *need* the interview."

"It'll help for people to hear the story from your point of view. I think you can talk in high-level terms about what happened without naming names."

He nods, but the tight clench of his jaw is indicative of his true feelings. The last thing in the world he wants to talk about is the scandal he left behind, but the coverage of his work at the clinic will be a major "get" for our project.

Our drive to my favorite ventanita in Priscilla is filled with uneasy silence. Tension comes from him in waves that I can feel in the deepest part of me. I hate this for him, as much as I would if it'd happened to me. I've dived headfirst into whatever this is with him, and I don't care about any of the possible consequences. And that's *so* not me.

New Carmen wants this with every fiber of her being, and far be it from Boring Old Carmen to stand in her way. I direct him to the Citgo gas station that's out of our way, but a necessary detour.

"I don't need gas."

"I know, but you *do* need a cortadito. Trust me. Juanita makes the best in town." I get out of the car and meet him with a smile, hoping to cheer him up before we get to the clinic. About five people are ahead of us in the line that forms outside a nondescript window.

"They really sell coffee here?" Jason asks, seeming skeptical.

"Calling it 'coffee' doesn't do it justice. You'll be ruined for anything else after this."

"You're the boss."

I explain to him the four types of Cuban coffee—cafecito, colada, café con leche and my favorite, cortadito. "Around here, if you visit someone's home, the first thing you're offered is coffee. It's a major part of our culture."

"I'm a big fan of coffee. Can't wait to try it."

"Hola, mi vida. ¿Quién es el guapo?" Juanita is in her early forties and has dark hair and eyes as well as a contagious personality that keeps people lined up outside her shop all day. She flirts shamelessly with her male customers but is hopelessly in love with her husband. He owns the car service company that took me and my friends to prom. Of course she wants to know about the handsome man I've brought with me today.

"This is Jason." I hold up two fingers, and she gets busy making two of my usual.

"Is he single and looking to mingle?"

"No, he isn't." Jason gives me that panty-melting look he ought to trademark because it's that effective.

"So it's like that, is it?" Juanita smiles at me over her shoulder as she works her levers and valves. Like everyone around here, she knows my story and takes an interest in anything I do. Such is my lot in life. In our community, when a young widow starts dating again, it's big news. Hell, everything is big news in our community. My mother jokes that we're outstanding at minding each other's business.

Juanita brings two steaming cups to the counter and goes back for two of the buttery pieces of heaven that've contributed to my curves. I give her a ten and two ones.

In Spanish, she says, "Bring him back again soon. He's easy on the eyes."

"Is he? I haven't noticed."

She snorts with laughter. "Sure, you haven't. You go, girl. It's time."

I offer her a small smile and a nod and then join Jason back at the car. We get in to drink the coffee.

He takes a bite of the pastelito. "Oh my God. What is this pastry?"

"First, you never call it 'pastry.' It's pastelito."

"It's the best thing I've ever tasted in my entire life."

"Try the cortadito."

He takes a sip and moans.

I flash a smug smile. "Told ya."

We eat and drink in companionable silence.

"I can't believe we bought this at a gas station window. Starbucks has nothing on this place."

"I know, right?"

"You're going to have to teach me how to make this coffee so I can have it every day for the rest of my life."

"I can show you, but mine is nowhere near as good as Juanita's. I don't know what the hell she does inside that little shack of hers, but it's magical."

"I'm a convert."

"Her grandparents fled Cuba in fifty-nine, too. My grandmother knew her grandmother in Havana. They were in school together."

"Does everyone know everyone else around here?"

"The long-established families in Little Havana tend to know each other, at least the grandparents do, but the rest of us don't know *everyone*. Although my family knows almost everyone because of the restaurant." I glance at the clock, which is edging closer to eight thirty. "We should get to the clinic. You're due to start in half an hour."

He turns the key, and Priscilla roars to life. Before he puts the car in reverse, he looks over at me. "In case I forget to tell you, I appreciate all of this. Even if it doesn't work—"

"It'll work. They'd be crazy not to want you on our staff. We've still got twelve days to show them that. Try not to worry. We're going to make this happen."

"You make me believe it."

"You can believe it. We're doing everything we can and then some."

He shifts the car into gear and follows my directions. "I'd be losing my shit without you helping me. Thank you. I truly mean it."

"I'm enjoying it. All of it."

"Don't talk about 'all of it' until later when we can do something about it."

"Do something about what?" I ask with pretend nonchalance.

The look he gives me is nothing short of incendiary. It scorches every inch of me and leaves me with no doubt whatsoever of what'll happen the next time we're alone together.

A twinge of apprehension works its way through me. What if I've forgotten how? What if I panic at the last minute or—

His hand covers mine, infusing me with his warmth. "Stop fretting. Nothing will happen between us unless or until you want it to. You're the boss in every way."

I melt into the leather seat, moved nearly to tears by his insightful comment. He gets it. He really gets it. Other men I've dated didn't have the first inkling of what it's like to suffer a loss like mine. They tried to be sensitive, but most of them were ham-handed clods when it came to navigating the emotional minefield that comes with dating a widow.

In the online support group of widows I belong to, people post stories about their dating disasters and some of the hilarity that ensues. Every so often, someone will post about their first significant relationship after the big loss.

Will Jason be that for me? Or will this be a passing fling, something to do until we both move on to more permanent relationships? I honestly have no idea, and that's okay. Either way, it's what I want right now. *He's* what I want, and wanting him feels pretty damned good. In fact, it's safe to say I feel better than I have in years.

We pull onto the street where the clinic is located, and the first thing I see is the crowd gathered outside. "Holy shit." I glance at Jason, who's taking it all in but doesn't seem rattled by the size of the line. "If it's too much . . ."

"It's fine. I like being busy."

We park behind the clinic and go in through the back door. Inside, we meet up with Maria.

"This is like when One Direction came to town," she says with a teasing smile for Jason.

"I don't know about that," he replies, seeming embarrassed.

"Well, to us, you're One Direction, Biebs and TaySwift all wrapped into one very welcome package. We haven't had a doctor here in two very long weeks."

"I'm happy to help in any way I can."

"We've set you up in here." She leads the way to a cramped exam room where a crisp white coat has been placed on the exam table. Maria shows him where everything is and hands him a prescription pad. "Can you think of anything else you might need?"

"Not at the moment, but I'll let you know."

"Okay, we're going to open the doors, then."

"I have release forms for anyone who wouldn't mind being photographed with Dr. Northrup." I hand the stack I printed at home to Maria. "If anyone is interested in sharing a story about their visit with me, I'd love to talk to them."

"I'll mention that as they come in. Here we go!"

CHAPTER 15

CARMEN

The day becomes a flurry of insane activity from then on. Jason sees fifteen patients in two hours. Most of them pose for photos with him, and three share their stories with me. Jason diagnoses one child with a severe case of strep throat, another with scarlet fever and a third with conjunctivitis.

The stressed-out mother of the three children told me how much it meant to her to be able to see such a highly qualified doctor for free and to receive much-needed medication. Another patient, a diabetic seventy-five-year-old man, received a referral to a wound clinic for an ulcer on his foot that refuses to heal.

Maria and two of the other women who work as admins translate for patients who don't speak English.

At one o'clock, my parents arrive with trays of sandwiches and bottles of cold water for the staff and the patients who're still lined up in the midday heat.

Dad comes over to kiss my forehead.

I lean into him. "You're the best, Daddy."

"Anything for you, honey. The whole neighborhood is buzzing about your doctor and what he's doing here."

"It's been a crazy morning. The people just keep coming."

"They're so thankful for the opportunity. Mrs. Lopez has had the worst time with gout, and the first appointment she could get with her doctor is in *three months*. Do you *know* how painful gout is?"

"I've heard."

"She came into the restaurant earlier singing his praises—and yours. We need more doctors like your Jason willing to give their time to help those with less access. It's a very good thing he's doing here."

I don't bother to correct him. He's not *my Jason*. But I agree it's a very good thing he's doing. Everyone who leaves the exam room comes out smiling, many of them clutching prescription slips.

After my parents leave to go back to the restaurant, I down a few bites of sandwich between taking photos, interviewing patients and posting stories to Instagram. The reaction to the stories is all positive, but I take the time to make sure there aren't any trolls weighing in on the posts.

So far, so good.

At two, my phone rings with a call from Desiree. "We're on for a feature story on tonight's eleven o'clock news. I'm on my way with a crew."

"Thank you so much, Desiree. I appreciate this."

"It's a great story. I'm happy to get the chance to tell it. See you soon."

I wave Maria over. "Desiree is coming with a film crew. How do we manage the line and consent?"

"Let's go outside, tell them what's happening and get the forms signed before Desiree arrives."

We spend thirty minutes in the broiling sun, explaining the form in English and Spanish and asking for permission for the prospective patients to be filmed by the TV crew. Most of them are excited by the idea of being on TV. A few volunteer to be interviewed, and I make note of who they are.

I'm giddy with excitement about what a great opportunity it is for Jason to have this interview. I can only hope it doesn't blow up in our faces. If they focus more on the scandal in New York than they do on what he's doing here in Miami . . . That can't happen. With all the people at the clinic prepared to attest to how thankful they are for the time he's giving them, that should be the point of the story.

I'm wilting in the heat when the NBC 6 truck arrives. I recognize Desiree from TV and from meeting her at a party I went to with Maria several years ago. She seems to remember me, too. In full makeup, with every one of her shiny dark hairs in place, Desiree extends a manicured hand to me. "It's so nice to see you again, Carmen."

"You as well. Thank you so much for coming."

"So you're working for Miami-Dade General now?"

"Yes, in the public relations department. My first assignment is helping Dr. Northrup acclimate to the community."

"I checked with a few sources and found out the board is reluctant to have him on the staff."

I hesitate, trying to find the words I need to handle this delicate situation. "Listen, Desiree. I understand you have a job to do, and the scandal in New York is salacious and titillating and all of that, but the truth of the matter is, he got a really raw deal from a woman he thought cared about him."

"I read up on it, and I have a question. If he didn't know she was married with children, why hasn't he said so since the whole thing went public?"

"Because she has kids, and he refuses to sling mud at their mother. Apparently, that happened to him when he was a kid, and he's determined not to repeat the cycle."

"Wow, well, that's a whole new angle on what I read online."

"I'm not going to tell you how to do your job. I can only ask you to look at the full picture and not get distracted by the tawdry bits."

"I appreciate the insight. Is he available for an interview?"

"I'll tell him you're here. We can catch him between patients."

"Sounds good. Is there an empty room we can use?"

"I'll ask Maria to set you up." I go inside, where even the tepid air-conditioning is a welcome relief. I find Maria working on a computer behind the reception desk and pass along Desiree's request.

"She can use our break room. It's the biggest room in the place." She gets up to greet her friend and see to getting the camera crew set up, while I wait for Jason to finish up with his current patient. I can hear the low tenor of his voice but not what he's saying, which is just as well. It's none of my business. We're walking a fine line in getting the publicity we need while protecting patient privacy.

The door swings open five minutes later, and an older woman emerges, clutching a piece of paper. She's smiling widely, her brown eyes sparkling with unshed tears. "Bless you," she whispers to me. "Bless you all for this." She squeezes my arm as she walks by me.

I duck inside the exam room to talk to Jason and catch him making notes on a chart. He's so handsome all the time, but seeing him in doctor mode takes his attractiveness to the next level for me. "Sorry to bother you."

He gifts me with a sexy, private smile that makes my insides go batshit crazy. "You're not bothering me. I've been missing my constant companion from the last few days."

"Me too. You're making people so happy."

"It's been very enjoyable. They're so sweet and thankful. I hate that they haven't had access to a doctor in weeks. So many of them are afraid to go to the ER because they know they can't afford it, and some are immigrants fearful of deportation. Our whole system is so jacked."

"It really is."

"Most of the time, I see people when they're in crisis and in need of emergency surgery. I don't get to spend a lot of time getting to know them. I really like this. I already told Maria I'll come back tomorrow."

He's so sweet and earnest that I feel myself slipping off the edge of the slippery slope I've been clinging to, trying to hang on to some semblance of sanity as I fall deeper into something significant with him. "They'll be thrilled to have you back." I try to remember why I came in here, but then he crooks his finger.

"Come see me."

I glance over my shoulder at the door, which isn't closed all the way. My heart beats fast as a jolt of excitement zips through me when I realize he wants to kiss me.

Though it's possible we could get caught by any number of people, I don't care. I cross the small room to where he sits. "You beckoned, Dr. Northrup?"

He stands, puts his arm around my waist and studies my face for a long, breathless moment before he gives me the softest, sweetest kiss. "I can't wait for tonight so we can be alone."

"Mmm, me too." And then I remember Desiree and the film crew and the reason we're here. "The NBC 6 team is here, and they'd like a few minutes."

His expression immediately hardens.

"I filled her in on your side of the scandal and asked her not to focus on that."

"What'd she say?"

"She wanted to know why you haven't told your side publicly. I explained about the children."

When we talk about this, his entire demeanor changes. I caress his face and compel him to look at me. "What you're doing here today is huge for the people you're seeing. That'll come through in the interviews she's doing with the patients. I have a good feeling about this."

Tension occupies every inch of him. "I'm glad you do."

I go to close the door and lock it before returning to him and placing my hands on his shoulders. "Breathe." I knead the tight muscles in his neck and shoulders. "Just breathe."

"So much at stake," he says softly.

My heart aches for him. "I know, and I have a feeling it's all going to work out."

"I wish I felt as certain as you do."

"Stick with me. I'll feel certain for both of us." I continue to massage the knots in his muscles until he begins to relax somewhat. "You've got this, Jason. Just be yourself. That's all you need to do to convince the board that you belong at Miami-Dade."

A warm smile lights up his gorgeous eyes. "You're making yourself completely essential to me."

"Is that right?"

Zeroing in on my lips, he nods.

If I start kissing him, I might never stop. With people waiting for him, we can't take the time right now. But later . . . I can't wait until later. "Let's do the interview so you can get back to the patients. It's hot out there."

"Lead the way."

I show him into the break room where Desiree's crew has set up lights and a camera.

"Desiree Rivera, meet Dr. Jason Northrup."

Desiree shakes his hand. "Great to meet you."

"Likewise. Thank you for this."

"No problem. Let's get you miked."

One of the technicians attaches a microphone to Jason's white coat and hands him the attached unit. "Clip that to your belt."

When he's ready, Desiree gestures for him to take the seat across from hers. "Let's roll."

The cameraman gives her a signal.

"This is NBC 6's Desiree Rivera with Dr. Jason Northrup, a pediatric neurosurgeon who recently relocated to Miami from New York. Today he's volunteering his services at the Our Lady of Charity free clinic in Little Havana. We caught up with him on a break. Welcome to Miami, Dr. Northrup."

"Thank you so much."

"Could you tell us a little about the circumstances that brought you here?"

The only sign of his feelings about that question is in the pulsing tension in his jaw. "I left my previous hospital in New York after a relationship with a woman I thought I loved ended in rather dramatic fashion. All I'll say about that is I would never, *ever* knowingly get involved with someone who's married. I hadn't been involved with anyone in years before this relationship."

"As I understand it, the Miami-Dade board has asked for some time to consider whether to extend privileges to you."

"That's correct."

"In the meantime, you've been getting to know the local area and volunteering your time here in Little Havana."

"Yes. I've really enjoyed seeing patients here today, and I'll be back again tomorrow for those who don't get in today. I'll keep coming until everyone who needs to be seen is taken care of."

I'm so proud watching and listening to him. He owns what happened in New York and is showing his dedication by volunteering his time for as long as it takes to see all the patients who've come to the clinic. I like him even more than I did this morning, and I wouldn't have thought that possible.

"I should get back to it. People are lined up outside, and it's broiling out there."

"Thanks for taking the time, Dr. Northrup. We wish you well in Miami."

"Thank you." He gets up, removes the mike and hands it to the cameraman. "Appreciate the opportunity," he says as he shakes Desiree's hand.

"Good luck with the board."

"Thanks."

"This'll run tonight at eleven and possibly again tomorrow."

"Sounds good." He squeezes my arm as he leaves the room to get back to work.

"Yum," Desiree says to me in a low, suggestive tone. "What a nice guy."

I bite back a stinging—and extremely unprofessional—retort. "Yes, he is. Thank you again for doing this."

"Definitely a pleasure. I hope the yummy doctor will be sticking around in Miami." She hands me her card. "Pass that along to him, if you would."

I take the card because there's no way not to without being rude. "Um, sure."

Desiree and her crew depart a few minutes later.

"How'd it go?" Maria asks as she pours water from a gallon jug into paper cups.

"Good, I think."

"I want to get some water to the people waiting outside. Some of them are wilting in the heat."

"Let me help."

We tuck more release forms under our arms and take trays of water cups outside into the damp, sweltering heat. At the end of the line, I encounter a young woman holding a boy of about four or five. He's draped over her and sound asleep. Sweat rolls down the woman's face as she struggles to maintain her hold on the child.

"Maria." I draw her attention to the woman.

Maria talks to her in Spanish and then leads her inside where window units help to cool the waiting room. The woman weeps with relief as she takes a seat and resettles her son. I overhear her telling Maria that he's had a severe headache for days and suddenly stopped talking. When he woke up this morning, he couldn't walk. She was afraid to call for rescue because she doesn't have insurance.

Maria hands her the necessary paperwork on a clipboard.

The woman shifts her child in her arms so she can complete the forms.

I sense Maria's alarm as she strides purposefully to the room where Jason is working, knocks on the door and asks him to see the boy next. I hear her use the word *urgent*.

Jason finishes with his patient and comes out to the waiting room, where I get to see him in action as he quickly evaluates the boy. Turning to Maria, he says, "Call for rescue."

While Maria hurries off, the young mother breaks down. "What's wrong with him?" she asks in halting English.

"I can't be sure until we get a full workup, and I don't want to speculate, but we need to get him to a hospital right away."

"I can't afford that!"

Jason puts his hand on the young woman's shoulder and looks her in the eyes. "I'll help you figure something out. The most important thing right now is getting your son somewhere that has the equipment to fully evaluate him. I can't do that here."

The child's mother, Sofia, weeps helplessly but nods in agreement.

I can tell that Jason is relieved that she's going to allow him to transport the child.

Paramedics arrive a few minutes later, and Jason directs them to take the boy to Miami-Dade. Before he follows them to the ambulance, he hands me the keys to Priscilla. Smiling, he says, "Don't get arrested."

"I'll try not to."

"I'll call you as soon as I can. Tell everyone I'll be back tomorrow." He runs outside and jumps into the back of the ambulance.

I have so many questions. He's instructed the paramedics to take the child to Miami-Dade, and he's going with him even though he doesn't have privileges there. What's his plan?

Maria tells the patients waiting for Jason that he had an emergency and they should come back tomorrow. She hands out numbers on yellow sticky notes to preserve their places in line. Despite having waited, in some cases, for hours in the heat, they're mostly good-natured about not getting to see him today.

"I handed out sixty-three numbers," she says when she comes back inside, wiping sweat from her face. "He's a godsend."

"He's enjoying it. He said he doesn't get to do a lot of basic patient care. When people come to him, they're usually having some sort of crisis, so he doesn't get much time with them."

"I really like him, and from what I can tell, you do, too."

"I do. A lot."

She offers a big silly grin. "Yeah?"

I nod.

"This is big news, prima."

"I know. I'm trying not to totally lose my mind, because who knows where he'll be in a month?"

"But the fact that you're even into him is huge."

"Yeah."

She takes me by the hand and tows me into the break room, which seems much bigger with the lights and cameras gone. After closing the door, she turns to me. "You have no idea how much we've all wanted this, for you to meet someone who makes you glow the way you do around him."

"I do not *glow*."

"Yes, you do, and it's awesome."

"I'm trying not to overthink it."

"Definitely don't do that. Enjoy it. You deserve it. Imagine how hot it'll be with him. I bet he knows what he's doing in bed."

"Maria! *Stop.*" The thought of being in bed with Jason makes the blood scorch my veins.

"Your face is bright red just thinking about it. Have you kissed him yet?"

"Maybe."

"I love this *so* much."

"Don't make it into a big thing, Mari, please?" I place my hand on my stomach, which suddenly feels unsettled. "I just don't know . . ."

She hugs me. "I understand why this is so difficult for you. I get that better than anyone. But I also know it's time for you to try again. It's been five years, C."

"Believe me, I know."

"You gotta let someone in there before it grows back."

I sputter with laughter. "Shut up."

"I'm serious! It can grow back."

"It cannot. A medical professional shouldn't lie about such things."

"It's a commonly known fact that the hymen regenerates just like the liver does."

I shake my head and roll my eyes as I try not to howl with laughter that would only encourage her outrageousness. "Lies."

"You also need to be concerned about dust and cobwebs. Nothing sexy about that."

"I'm leaving now."

"Hey."

I turn back to her.

"All kidding aside, I'm happy for you. Regardless of what might or might not happen with your sexy doctor, it's great to know that you can still feel that way for someone, you know?"

"Yeah, I do. It's been fun."

"It's okay to let it happen with him. Tony wouldn't want you to be alone forever. He loved you, and all he ever wanted was for you to be happy."

The reminder of my sweet husband's devotion brings tears to my eyes. "I know."

"I'm here if you need to talk about it."

"I know that, too."

"Especially if you want to share the dirty details."

"I'm out. See you tomorrow."

"I bet the details will be *extra* dirty with him," she calls after me.

CHAPTER 16

Carmen

Laughing at Maria's foolishness, I head out to the parking lot, the humidity like a slap to the face as I walk to Priscilla. "You'd better not get me arrested again," I say to the car as I start her up. I drive slowly back to Jason's hotel and breathe a sigh of relief when I park the car and turn it off. I debate whether to leave the keys at the front desk, but I don't trust them not to take it for a ride, so I decide to keep them with me.

My phone chimes with a text from Jason. *Heading into surgery. Will be 5-7 hrs. I'll hit you up after to see if you're still awake.*

I want to ask him if Miami-Dade extended privileges. They must have if he's operating there. What does this mean for his situation with the board? I'm dying to know, but he has more important things to focus on now. I reply with a thumbs-up.

I text Maria to confirm that the child's mother signed the release form. When Maria confirms that she did, I send a text to Desiree, letting her know what happened. I'm not sure if it'll impact the news story, but I figure it can't hurt to tell her about it.

I head home in my car, my mind racing with questions and excitement to see him again. Now I just have to report in to Mr. Augustino on what transpired today and get through the next five to seven hours.

⁓

He texts at nine forty-five. *Still up?*

Yes.

Can I come by?

Please do. I have your keys.

That's why I want to come by. For the keys. He adds the laughing emoji.

Do you need a ride?

Nah, I'm in an Uber. Be there soon. Can't wait.

I bolt out of bed and run for the bathroom to brush my hair and teeth. I'm wearing a robe over a long T-shirt, and I consider changing into something sexier.

Stop. Just stop. Breathe. Relax.

Easier said than done. When he gets here, I have no doubt we'll pick up where we left off in the car this morning—and we probably won't stop with kisses. I'm ready for more. I want more.

I just hope I can go through with it. I'm reassured by the certainty that Jason will follow my lead, that he won't push me for more than I can handle. I'm ready for this because it's him. Because I trust him. And because I want him. At the end of the day, it's really that simple.

By the time he knocks on my door, my heart rate is approaching the danger zone, and I'm lightheaded from failing to breathe. Good thing he's an accomplished doctor, because I might need one.

When I open the door, he fills the doorway. Once again, his arms are over his head on the doorjamb, dress shirt sleeves rolled up to reveal muscular arms. The look of blatant desire in his tired eyes makes my knees weak. For the longest time, we simply stare at each other.

"You going to invite me in, sweetheart?"

His question startles me out of the trance I slipped into at the sight of him. "Oh, um, yes. Of course. Come in."

The door clicks shut, and I turn to him. "How'd it go—"

He wraps his arm around my waist, pulls me tight against him and kisses me.

Hours of anticipation and desire come together in the most passionate kiss we've shared yet. We're ravenous for each other, his lips and tongue devouring me with a ferocity that has me clinging to him in order to remain standing. He presses my back to the wall in the foyer, tips his head and cups my cheek, his fingers sliding gently over my sensitive skin as his lips and tongue continue their sensual torture.

It's unbearable and necessary at the same time. Until he caressed me with such tenderness, I hadn't realized how much I've missed being touched like this.

"Tell me to stop, Carmen," he whispers gruffly in my ear, setting off a whole new calamity inside me.

With Tony, our physical relationship was a slow build as we went from children to adults and learned about love and desire together. This . . . This is an entirely different experience. I can't get close enough to Jason. I'm drunk on the way he makes me feel, alive in a way I haven't been in years, in a way I thought I might never be again.

I can't even find the wherewithal to feel guilty or conflicted about having these feelings for someone other than my late husband. The need for Jason is so consuming it drowns out everything else, even Tony. A week ago, I would've said that wasn't possible. Now I know otherwise.

He shifts his attention to my neck, and I strain to get closer to him, our bodies intimately aligned, the hard ridge of his cock pressed to my belly.

Though he has my brain completely scrambled, I still want to know how the surgery went. "Tell me about the boy," I manage to say as he kisses my neck. "Is he okay?"

"If you believe in things happening for a reason, I've got quite a story for you."

I grab his shirt to keep him close to me while he tells me his story. "The mother signed the release, right?"

"She did."

"Then I can tell you the boy had a tumor."

Gasping, I look up at him. "Oh my God."

He continues to kiss my neck and make me crazy. "He had a medulloblastoma, a tumor on the posterior fossa, the most common malignant brain tumor of childhood. It occurs exclusively in the cerebellum. It was a T2, which means it was greater than three centimeters in diameter, with no evidence of gross subarachnoid or hematogenous metastasis, which is the best news of all."

I shiver, as much from what he's doing to my neck as listening to him and realizing just how incredibly smart and talented he is. That's as attractive to me as his handsome face, warm smile and sexy body. "I have no idea what you just said, but it sounds serious."

"It's the exact tumor my team and I have been studying for the last three years."

I pull back again to look up at his face. "Seriously?"

He nods. "There is, literally, no one in this country better prepared to operate on that particular tumor than I am. What're the odds that I should encounter a child at your cousin's free clinic in Little Havana who needed exactly what I'm most uniquely qualified to provide?"

I'm flabbergasted by this turn of events. "That's incredible. Will he be all right?"

"I hope so, but he's got a long road ahead of him. We got almost all of it. With chemo and radiation, he has a very good chance of recovering, although he'll experience some impairments due to the location of the tumor as well as the treatment."

"What about the hospital and your privileges?"

"When I informed the chief of surgery of what was going on, he convinced Mr. Augustino to grant me temporary privileges to perform the surgery. He told him there was no one on the staff better qualified to handle this particular case. Because I was brought to Miami-Dade for a similar surgery in the past, Augustino gave the green light."

"I'm so glad he let you do it. What about the cost? Sofia was so upset about that."

"We're working on that. She's not going to have to pay for anything."

I brush the hair back from his forehead and let the silky strands run through my fingers. "When you think about it, maybe everything that happened in New York was so you could be there today to encounter a boy who needed you."

"Or," he says, nuzzling my neck and rolling my earlobe between his teeth, "it was meant to happen so I could find you."

"You're making my knees weak."

"We can't have that." He tightens his arm around my waist and lifts me off my feet.

I hold on to him as he transports us to my sofa where he gently deposits me before stretching out next to me. His arm encircles me, and I slide my leg between his. We come together effortlessly, as though this is a dance we've done together many times before. It feels right to be here with him, to touch him and kiss him, even if so much is still uncertain.

"What are you thinking?" I ask, noting his pensive expression.

"So many things, but first and foremost that I want you to be comfortable with whatever happens between us."

I press myself tighter against him. "I'm *very* comfortable."

He groans and buries his face in my hair, seeming to breathe me in. "You know what I mean, Carmen."

"I do, and because you care about the fact that this is the first time I've done anything like this since my husband died makes me far more comfortable than I'd be with anyone else."

"The thought of you with someone else makes me a little ragey, if I'm being honest."

I like hearing that he has a possessive side to him—more than I probably should. "Does it?"

"It does."

"Desiree Rivera gave me her card and asked me to pass it along to you."

"Did she?"

"Uh-huh. I ripped it up."

Laughing, he smooths his hand up and down my back as he gazes at me with eyes that see *me*, Carmen, not the sad young woman who lost her husband too soon. That's who everyone else in my world sees when they look at me.

I draw him into another kiss, using my lips, tongue and hands to tell him exactly what I want. I don't want him to have any doubts that I'm right where I want to be.

One kiss becomes two and then another. We tug at clothes as desire strikes an urgent need in both of us. My robe is untied and removed. The T-shirt clears my head as I pull at his shirt, trying to get to his chest without tearing the buttons off. The sensation of my bare breasts pressed against his chest takes my breath away.

I forgot how it feels to be consumed by desire. I forgot what it's like to be touched by a man who wants me the way Jason does. This part of me has been sealed off for years. Jason is bringing the sensual side of me back to life one kiss and caress at a time. He cups my breasts and runs his thumbs over the tight points of my nipples.

"You're so lovely, sweet Carmen. I thought so the first time I saw you looking so prim and proper in your suit as you waited for me to arrive the other day."

I arch into him, wanting more of what he's doing to my breasts. "I wasn't prim *or* proper."

"You were both those things and so much more. I was immediately intrigued by you. I wanted to know everything about you."

"I thought you were with Betty."

He shakes his head before lowering it to take my nipple into the heat of his mouth. "I was never with her."

I grasp a handful of his hair to keep him from getting away, not that he's trying to. The rush of emotion is so intense it forms an ache in my heart, which has taken such a beating in the past. Not that I want to think about that when every part of me is engaged in what he's doing to my nipples. He kisses a path down the front of me, dipping his tongue into my belly button, making me cry out from the craving need he inspires in me.

"So sexy," he whispers, his warm breath against my skin setting off goose bumps that make me shiver with delight.

Back when I was newly widowed, I used to try to picture being with someone else this way, and I never could get far enough past the agony to see it actually happening. I imagined it would be awkward, that I would cry, that I'd regret it afterward. But there's nothing awkward about being with Jason, and I already know I'm not going to regret it. Whether or not there'll be tears remains to be seen.

Jason's golden eyes go dark with desire when he sees the white cotton bikini panties I intentionally wore under the T-shirt. "So fucking sexy," he says in a low growl as he cups me over the panties, pressing his fingers against my clit and making me squirm as I chase an orgasm that feels so close. "I knew you'd be impossibly sexy in white cotton."

I release a ragged laugh as the orgasm lingers just out of reach.

"Easy, love. Don't worry. I won't leave you hanging."

As the panties slide down my legs, I close my eyes and try to prepare for whatever is about to happen. But nothing could prepare me for the slide of his lips up my inner leg or the press of his fingers against my incredibly sensitive flesh. He's barely touched me, and I'm about to combust.

His lips continue their journey up my leg while I hold my breath in anticipation. He arranges me so my legs are splayed open, making me thankful for the time I spent with my razor earlier. And when he opens me to his tongue, I'm completely lost to the dazzling array of sensations that overwhelm me to the point of madness. His fingers are deep inside me as his tongue swirls over my clit.

Dear God, I can barely breathe, and then he sucks hard on my clit. I scream from the powerful release that rocks me. I've barely recovered my senses when he starts the whole thing over again, taking me up so quickly I'm coming a second time before I know what's hit me. My body is a quivering, trembling collection of nerve endings, every one of them tuned to him. I hear the crinkle of the condom wrapper in the second before he covers me, kisses me with lips that taste of me and pushes into me a little at a time while staring down at my face with sexy golden eyes that ruin me.

"God, Carmen," he says on a long exhale. "Nothing has ever felt this good. *Ever.*" He holds me close to him, his lips pressed to the pressure point in my neck as he works his way inside me. "Talk to me. Tell me how you feel."

"I feel . . . full."

He laughs softly while leaving a line of kisses along my collarbone. "Does it hurt?"

"No." I raise my legs and wrap them around his hips, which sends him deeper into me. "Feels so good."

His low groan makes me shiver as he grips my ass to tilt me for an even better angle. I dig my fingers into the muscles of his back, needing to hold on to him, to keep him close, to ride the waves of this exquisite perfection for as long as I possibly can.

He tightens his arms around me and picks up the pace. "Carmen." The face that has become so dear to me in the time we've spent together is tight with tension. His eyes are heated as he gazes at me, and his lips are swollen from our frantic kisses.

I tighten my internal muscles around his cock, and he groans in the second before he pushes deep into me to find his release.

"Holy shit, woman," he says, gasping. "You finished me off before I had the chance to tend to you."

"You tended to me beforehand."

"Still . . . I don't want you feeling cheated."

"Trust me. That's the last thing I feel right now."

He kisses my cheek and the end of my nose before finding my lips in another soft, sweet, sexy kiss. "What're you feeling right now?"

"Wiped out. Exhilarated. Happy. Relieved."

His left brow lifts ever so slightly. "You're relieved?"

"I didn't cry."

"Did you think you might?"

"I wasn't sure what to expect."

He brushes a strand of hair back from my face and tucks it behind my ear. "Thank you for choosing me to take this big step with you. I'm honored to be the first."

My eyes fill, but these aren't sad tears. They're "life goes on" tears, and yes, that's a thing. "I'm glad I waited for you."

"I'm so glad you did, too."

Thinking about him possibly leaving if the board doesn't grant privileges leaves me feeling deflated.

He traces the outline of my mouth with his fingertip. "What caused the frown?"

"Did I frown?"

Nodding, he kisses me until I smile again. "What're you thinking?"

"About how we're starting something without knowing where you'll be in a month."

"And that worries you."

"Kind of. I don't go around having sex with random people."

He scowls playfully. "I would hope not."

"I guess what I'm trying to say is that this, what we did, spending time together . . . It means something to me."

"It does to me, too. Like I said, from the first minute I saw you waiting for me outside the hospital, I was interested. And then when I had to bail you out of jail—"

I slap his back lightly. "*Stop!* Oh my God! You can't make that part of our story."

"Too late. It's already one of the best parts of our story. I'll never forget how cute you were in that cell while you tried not to freak the fuck out."

"I was freaking the fuck out! From the second the cop stopped me."

Laughter lights up his face and makes my mouth water with lust. I already want him again. "Cutest jailbird I ever met."

I cover my ears. "Lalalala. I can't hear you, and if you ever tell my grandmothers or parents that I was in jail, I'll never speak to you again."

"I do so love a juicy bit of blackmail. I suppose you'll have to continue kissing me, frequently, to ensure my silence."

"You wouldn't dare!"

He points to his lips. "Better to not risk it."

Scowling, I push my lips hard against his.

Rocking with silent laughter, he wraps an arm around my neck to keep me anchored to him. "Yes," he says, his words muffled, "like that, only sweeter." He works on me until I yield to his persuasive lips and tongue, lost in a sea of desire that overtakes me once again.

I can't get enough of him or the way he makes me feel. I forgot the euphoric high that comes with connecting to someone this way. He withdraws only long enough to roll on a new condom before rejoining our bodies. As he makes love to me again, I surrender completely to the experience and the shuddering orgasm that rocks through both of us at the same time.

"You've bought my silence for another hour, sweet Carmen." His words, whispered against my neck, make me smile as I run my fingers through his hair.

I come back to reality slowly, my heart and mind resisting anything that would take me out of the most perfect moment I've experienced since I lost Tony. I glance at the clock. It's ten fifty-five.

"The news. We have to watch. They're going to air the interview."

He groans. "I don't want to watch it."

I give his shoulder a gentle push. "We have to watch it."

"Ugh." He withdraws from me and sits back against my sofa, blatantly unashamed of his nakedness while I'm hit with a fierce bout of shyness as I grasp my discarded T-shirt from the floor and put it back on. I turn on the TV to NBC 6 and scurry to the bathroom to clean up.

My hair is a wild nest of curls, mascara is smudged under my eyes and my lips are red and swollen from desperate kisses. I look as if I've been thoroughly ravished, and I decide it's a good look on me. I clean the makeup off my face, put my wild hair up in a bun and use the toilet before rejoining him in the living room.

I'm praying this interview doesn't make anything worse.

CHAPTER 17

Carmen

While I was gone, he put on his boxers. He stands to kiss me before taking a turn in the bathroom.

"Jason, hurry. They just said we're going to meet Miami's newest neurosurgeon after the break."

When he returns, I notice the tension is back in his shoulders and face. He sits next to me but keeps a bit of distance between us, as if steeling himself for whatever he's about to see and hear.

I place a hand on his back, wishing there was something more I could do to put him at ease.

He gifts me with a small smile while keeping his eyes on the TV.

"Our own Desiree Rivera spent some time today with Dr. Jason Northrup, Miami's newest pediatric neurosurgeon, and learned he's already making an impact in our community. Desiree?"

"Thank you, Jim, and indeed you're right about that. I met Dr. Northrup today at the Our Lady of Charity free clinic in Little Havana where he was spending the day volunteering his time and expertise to a wide range of patients. But his day at the clinic took an unexpected turn when Sofia Diaz and her son, Mateo, arrived, hoping to be seen by the doctor."

Desiree's live shot cuts to the footage she and her team recorded at the clinic, which shows Jason with patients and the line outside the door. It then shifts to Miami-Dade and an interview with Sofia Diaz, who's weeping as she details the surgery Jason performed on her son.

"He's been very sick." Sofia dabs at her eyes with a tissue as she speaks in halting English. "I hoped the doctor would tell me he had a virus, but Dr. Northrup took one look at my Mateo and called for rescue to bring him to Miami-Dade. They did an MRI and found he had a cancerous brain tumor. Dr. Northrup operated on him, and . . ." Her voice breaks. "He saved his life," she says in a soft whisper.

A shot of Mateo resting in his hospital bed is shown. He looks so tiny and defenseless in the big bed.

The footage cuts back to Desiree. "Ms. Diaz and her son found themselves in the right place at the right time today, and little Mateo is resting comfortably tonight after surgery to remove the tumor. Dr. Northrup told Ms. Diaz that with follow-up treatment, her son has a good chance of recovering from his ordeal. No doubt that chance was made better by Dr. Northrup, a nationally recognized expert in this particular pediatric brain tumor, which makes the citizens of Miami lucky to have him in our community. This is Desiree Rivera reporting from Miami-Dade General Hospital for NBC 6 News."

"What an incredible story, Desiree. Thank you for bringing that to us."

"Holy crap." I look at Jason, who seems as stunned as I feel. "She never even mentioned New York! This is best-case scenario, Jason." I whip out my phone. "I've got to get that story linked to the Instagram account." It takes a few minutes of clicking around on my phone to locate the video on the NBC 6 website and get it loaded on Jason's Insta account. I make liberal use of hashtags, including Miami, newdoc, pediatricneurosurgeon and lifesaver.

"How did Desiree know we'd transported him?"

I can't tell if he's happy she knew or pissed. "Um, I might've texted her to let her know you identified an emergency at the clinic and were taking him to Miami-Dade. I hope that's okay."

"Yeah, of course. The mother signed the release, so it's fine. And it was good thinking. That story was just . . ."

"It was *just* what we needed."

He puts his arm around me and brings me into his warm embrace. "I'll never be able to thank you for what you've done. You've brought about a miracle in a few days' time."

"You brought about your own miracle with what you did for that child today."

"It's all you. Without you, I'd be sitting in a hotel room spinning in my own misery while people I've never met debate whether my career should continue. But you . . . Look what you've done, Carmen."

I bask in the glow of his praise. That someone as accomplished as he is should think so much of me professionally is a heady moment. "We've done it together."

He squeezes my shoulder. "Yes, we have, and we're going to do it again together."

I give him my best sexy coy look. "Are we still talking about redeeming your reputation?"

He runs his hand up and down my arm in a gentle caress I feel everywhere. "Among other things."

I'm crazy about him. I've lost all perspective where he's concerned. What took years to happen with Tony has occurred in a matter of days with Jason. Granted, I'm fifteen years older than I was when I met Tony. I was still a child then. Our relationship came from a place of friendship first and grew into much more as we got older and became more aware of all the things it could be.

This, with Jason, is far more immediate and urgent. The more time I spend with him, the more time I want with him. I rest my head against his chest as the TV weatherman drones on about another South Florida scorcher on tap for tomorrow.

"I should go and let you get some rest," he says after a long period of quiet.

I don't want him to go, but I can't seem to get the words out at first. "You . . . You don't have to. Go, I mean. If you don't want to." I cringe at how silly I must sound to him.

"I don't want to be anywhere but with you, but only if that's what you want, too."

I raise my head off his chest to look him in the eyes. "It's what I want. Stay."

He smiles and leans in to kiss me. "Can I borrow your toothbrush?"

"I can do you one better. I've got a brand new one with your name on it."

"See? It's meant to be."

I'm beginning to think he might be right about that.

Jason

Being in bed with Carmen is surreal and exciting, so exciting that sleep is the last thing on my mind while she's warm and cozy in my arms. I breathe in the fresh, clean scent of her hair and nuzzle her satiny soft skin. Her skin is to die for. My hand slides under her T-shirt to cup a breast that fills my palm to overflowing. I've had her twice, and I want more. I'm addicted to her. Carmen has blotted out Ginger, like a total eclipse of the sun, or in this case, a total eclipse of the mess I left behind in New York.

When I pinch her nipple lightly between my fingers, she squirms in my arms and presses her ass against my hard cock. I should be exhausted after the day I put in. I usually crash and burn after a long, intense surgery like the one I performed earlier, but I'm wide awake, keyed up and incredibly turned on.

I couldn't believe that news story she orchestrated or how perfectly it worked out to put the emphasis on my skills rather than the scandal. I'll send the link to my mom tomorrow. She'll love it and will be relieved to see things moving in the right direction. It's all thanks to Carmen. I suppose I need to tell Mom about her, too.

"Jason!"

"Sí, bebé?"

She goes still in my arms.

"I've been practicing my Spanish."

"When have you been practicing your Spanish? You haven't had time to breathe."

"In between things. Mostly I'm looking for a special name for you. How do you feel about bebé?"

"What're my other options?"

I continue to toy with her nipple while I recall the list of words I committed to memory while I waited for Mateo to stabilize to the point where I felt comfortable leaving him in the capable hands of the surgical nurses. They know to call me if his condition changes.

"There's corazón." *Sweetheart.* "Bonita." *Beautiful.* "Hermosa." *Gorgeous.* "Cariño." *Honey.*

She inhales sharply. "Not that."

That must be what Tony called her. Cross that off the list. "Querida." *Darling.* "And my personal favorite, Rizo."

She cracks up laughing as I hoped she would. Rizo means *curly*.

I twirl a wild curl around my index finger. "I think that might be our winner." For now, anyway, because it's probably too soon for mi amor. *My love.* But I already suspect I could love this extraordinary, courageous, smart, inventive, resilient woman.

She's an intriguing mix of innocence and worldly experience. I've never met anyone quite like her. I've certainly never met anyone I admire as much as I do her. What she survived at such a young age would've ruined a lesser person. But not mi tesoro, *my treasure*. She picked herself up from the ashes of her husband's tragic, senseless death, finished college and graduate school and has made such a huge difference in my life since we met with her skill and passion for the task at hand.

I want to do something to show her how thankful I am. No matter what happens with Miami-Dade, the first chance we get, I'll whisk her away to the Bahamas for a long weekend or something else that will tell her how much her efforts mean to me.

One minute I'm caressing her breast and thinking about the Bahamas, and the next minute, or so it seems, the alarm on Carmen's phone is going off. I can't recall the last time I slept as soundly as I did with her in my arms, steeped in the bewitching scent of her hair. Her hand is entwined with mine, and the sweet intimacy of that touches me profoundly.

"Carmen." I kiss her shoulder and work my way up to her neck. "Wake up, Sleeping Beauty."

"Not yet."

"Is my Rizo grumpy in the morning?"

"Go away."

I laugh and kiss her some more until she groans. "Is this an everyday thing or just a workday thing?"

"Every."

"Good to know, but we need to get going. I have to go home and change before the clinic. And I assume you need some of Juanita's special brew to overcome your morning grumpiness."

She grunts out a reply and snuggles deeper under the covers.

"Oh no you don't. Get that sweet, sexy ass out of this bed." I give her a pat on the bum to encourage her to move.

Giving me a stormy look, she says, "Are you always so freaking cheerful in the morning?"

"If I say yes, is that a deal breaker?"

"Potentially."

"Then no, I'm not cheerful in the morning. I'm a nasty bastard. Better?"

"Much."

"Get your ass out of bed so I'm not late for work."

Groaning, she does as directed and drags herself into the bathroom, taking her phone with her to silence the alarm.

When the door slams behind her, I crack up laughing. I love discovering this new side to her, one that no one else has gotten to experience since she lost her husband. I can't wait to discover every side of her—the good, the bad and the grumpy.

Carmen

I'm barely awake when my phone chimes with a text from Mama D, who's Tony's mother, Josie. *How's the new job? Hope you're loving it. Let me know when you can—and let's do lunch. I'll come to you!*

Seeing her name on my screen fills me with an overwhelming feeling of guilt after what happened with Jason last night. Of course, I know that Tony's family will support me in anything I do, but are they ready to see me with someone new? Am I ready for them to see that?

Yes, dammit. I'm ready, and I want this with Jason, even if he's relentlessly cheerful in the morning. I shower and dry my hair, once again leaving it curly in deference to his affection for my curls.

I love that he's calling me Rizo, that he took the time to learn terms of endearment in Spanish. I loved having sex with him last night, and I can't wait to do it again. In my closet, I find a dress that'll allow me to appear professional but won't cause me to overheat at the clinic.

I'm about to leave the bathroom when I remember the text from my mother-in-law. I lean against the vanity for a minute as I stare down at the screen and think about what I want to say to her. *The job is great. I'm on a special assignment helping one of the new docs this week. Will call you later!*

Jason is dressed and ready to go when I emerge from the bathroom. The sight of his handsome, smiling face makes my stomach flutter with excitement for another day with him. After he takes a turn in the bathroom, he studies my face as he steps up to me, putting his hands on my hips. "Is it safe to kiss the sleeping dragon?"

"Yes, she's fully awake now." I pucker up to make my point.

Still smiling, he comes in slowly, letting the anticipation build before he touches his lips lightly to mine and then takes them away before I have a chance to fully enjoy the kiss.

"More."

"Not now."

"Yes, now."

"Grumpy and demanding in the morning. I'm learning a lot about you, and it's only eight o'clock." He kisses my forehead, the tip of my nose and my lips again quickly—far too quickly for my liking. "If I start kissing you again, I won't want to stop, and we've got somewhere to be." He releases his hold on me and steps back.

I'm gratified to see the sizable bulge in his pants.

"Stop looking at it."

"Don't want to stop."

"Gotta stop. You know the number for Miami-Dade, by any chance? I need to check on Mateo."

"I do." I rattle off the number for him.

He asks for surgical ICU and is connected to the nurse's desk. "This is Dr. Northrup checking on Mateo Diaz."

I try not to listen too closely as he talks to the nurses, but hearing and seeing him in doctor mode only adds to my interest in him. As he asks complex questions and listens to answers, he's competent and concerned for his patient. After five minutes on the phone, he thanks the nurse and ends the call.

"How is he?"

"Doing great. He had a good night. I'll swing by later to see him in person."

I grab my purse and head for the door, aware of him following me. I can't be anywhere near him and not be aware of him, even when we're doing nothing more exciting than walking to the stairs. When we're on the way down, I hand him my phone to hold while I dig through my purse, looking for his keys.

"You got a text from Mama D."

"Oh. Okay." I find the keys, take the phone from him and read the text. *Can't wait to catch up.* I have to tell her about Jason. Abuela invited him to Sunday brunch, and Tony's parents always come. I have to tell them about him before Sunday. I can't believe what's happened since this past Sunday.

"Everything okay?" Jason asks when we're in the parking lot.

"Uh-huh." I feel queasy at the thought of managing Tony's family in the context of my new relationship. And is this a relationship or a fling? I'm not entirely sure, which has me wondering if I should even be mentioning it to them. Ugh.

He holds the driver's door of my car and waits for me to get settled before closing it. After he gets into the passenger seat, he turns to me. "Tell me what's wrong."

"Mama D is Tony's mother."

"Oh." He takes a minute to process that. "Are you feeling, you know, guilty . . ."

"No!" I sigh. "Maybe a little. I don't know how I'm supposed to feel."

He reaches for my hand and cradles it between both of his. "I assume you're still close to them?"

"Very."

"And is it safe to assume that they love you and want the best for you?"

"Yes," I say softly. "They've been incredibly supportive of me."

"So would it also be safe to assume that they'd be glad to see you happy, even if it's still a raw wound for all of you and probably always will be?"

I appreciate that he gets that Tony's death is still a raw wound for us, that it probably always will be. I nod in response to his question. "It's hard."

"I know, sweetheart. Well, I don't know. Not really. I can't possibly know what it was like for all of you to lose him the way you did. I only know that I really like you. I may even more than like you, and I want to be with you. But I also want to be respectful of how difficult it is for you to take this step with me and for those who love you to see you with someone new."

My heart trips over the words "more than like you." My gaze connects with his. "It means a lot to me that you get it."

"I'm trying to get it. Tell me if I screw up?"

"I'd be happy to."

We share a warm smile that leads to another kiss.

"Are you going to tell her about me?"

"I want to."

"But?"

"I guess I'm not sure if it's too soon to be saying anything to anyone. We don't even know where you'll be next week, and I just don't want to get too far ahead of myself."

"I suppose that's fair enough, but you should know . . . Regardless of what happens with Miami-Dade, I want to be wherever you are."

I'm dumbfounded by his candor. "Oh. Um, you do?"

"Yeah, I do." He presses his lips to mine once again, this time sliding his hand around my neck to kiss me for real. By the time he pulls back, I'm dizzy and drunk on whatever it is that comes over me when he kisses me that way. "I wish we had nowhere to be today so we could go back upstairs to your bed and I could show you some of the many ways I want to be wherever you are." More kisses, more dizziness. "This weekend . . . Can we please spend it together?"

I'm nodding before he finishes asking the question.

"Every minute?"

"Yes, every minute."

"Now I have something to look forward to."

He resettles himself in the passenger seat, and I somehow manage to start the car. After a quick trip to his hotel so he could shower and change, we arrive at Juanita's ventanita in Priscilla. He made a case for driving me since I wasn't caffeinated yet, and it might be safer for both of us. He thinks he's funny after finding out I'm grumpy in the morning.

When Juanita sees me with Jason for the second morning in a row, she raises a brow. In Spanish, she asks if there's anything I want to tell her.

"No," I reply, "nothing to report."

She laughs and calls me a liar. "I know something when I see it, amiga, and I see *something*. And before you can deny it, just know I'm happy for you. No one deserves it more."

Jason stands by my side while I shamelessly talk about him in a language he doesn't understand. He pays for two cortaditos and two dozen pastelitos for us and the clinic staff.

"Saw you on the news last night, Doc," she says to Jason. "Thank God you were able to help that sweet child."

"I'm glad I was in the right place at the right time."

"We're all glad for that."

Twenty minutes later, we arrive at the clinic to find an even longer line than yesterday.

"Holy shit," he whispers.

"You're in hot demand, Doc."

"I see that."

"If it's too much, you can still say so. No one says you have to be here indefinitely."

"I'll be here until every one of these people is seen."

CHAPTER 18

Carmen

It takes three days for Jason to see all the patients who come to the clinic. He treats everything from gout to hemorrhoids to asthma to diabetes complications to scabies. According to Jason, he's heard from almost everyone he's ever known since the news segment went live, which he attributes to my posts about it on Instagram as well as his mother posting the link to Facebook.

We fall into a routine that includes long days at the clinic followed by daily stops at Miami-Dade for him to check on Mateo and for me to brief Mr. Augustino on our progress in person.

"The coverage on NBC 6 was huge," Mr. Augustino says on Friday evening. "I've heard from several members of the board about it. Keep up the good work, Carmen. It seems to be having the desired effect."

Jason is thrilled when I tell him that, but he's not himself after having been to see Mateo. He's met me in my office, where I've been killing time looking at emails detailing other projects that'll require my attention when this one is finished and reading documents the former director of public relations left for me. As I read, it occurs to me that I still haven't called Tony's mother, and I'm running out of time before Sunday brunch.

"What's wrong?" I ask him.

"Mateo has an infection. We're working on it, but it's worrisome."

"Do you need to stick around?"

"No, they know to call me if anything changes. It's a waiting game right now. Hopefully the antibiotics will do the trick."

"Is this a common thing?"

"It happens." He waits for me to gather my belongings and gestures for me to lead the way to the elevator. In the parking lot, he takes hold of my hand the way he does every chance he gets. "Can we run by my hotel on the way to your place? I want to pick up some clothes and running shoes. I need to get in a run at some point."

"I didn't know you were a runner."

"Any chance I get, which isn't as often as it used to be. Exercise helps me manage stress."

"Tony was a gym rat. He was always trying to get me to go with him, but I sucked at it. He would try not to laugh at me, but *he* sucked at not laughing."

Jason laughs as he holds the car door for me. I've told him he doesn't have to do that every time, but he says he does have to. "Now I want to take you to the gym to see this comedy routine for myself."

"That's not happening."

When he gets in the car, I turn so I can see him. "Is it okay that I mention Tony and our relationship to you?"

"Of course it is. He's part of you, and I want to know every part of you."

"I went to this grief group for widows after it happened. I was the youngest one there by decades, but those ladies helped me a lot. They taught me that grief is love with nowhere to go. They helped me accept that I'll never stop loving him. I might love someone else someday, but I'll always love Tony, too, and it's okay to let that happen."

"I'm glad you were able to get that kind of support when you needed it."

"They also said that when my Chapter 2 came along, which is what they call the first significant relationship after the loss of a spouse, that I'd know he was the right one for me because he would understand that I'll always love Tony, and the new guy wouldn't be threatened by that."

"Does this, with me, count as your Chapter 2?"

"I think it might." After several nights in bed with him, I'm completely addicted to him and the way he makes me feel.

"I promise I'll never be threatened or annoyed by the love you have for Tony, Carmen. I think he must've been a really special guy to have a woman as fantastic as you are care so much for him."

"He was," I whisper as I blink back tears that are equal parts sadness and joy. I never dared to dream that I'd meet someone like Jason. I thought I'd had my one chance at great love, that it was too much to hope for more.

"I always want you to feel like you can talk about him with me."

Smiling, I decide to lighten the mood. "You can talk about Ginger with me, too."

He scowls. "No, thanks. I'm good."

I laugh as a lighthearted feeling of pure joy comes over me. That feeling has been close at hand during the week we've spent together. I want to hold on to it with everything I've got, even with so much still uncertain. I'm sure about one thing: I'm falling hard for my sweet, sexy doctor, and falling has never felt so good.

~

While Jason goes for a run, I decide I have to call Josie. One of the things she and I have in common is our heritage. She, too, is half Cuban and half Italian. Her parents left Cuba around the same time as my grandmother did, and the two families knew each other in Havana. I also have texts from my parents and grandmothers, who're wondering where I've been all week.

I can't exactly tell them I've been in bed with Jason every chance I've gotten . . .

Josie picks up on the first ring. "Hi, sweetie. How was your first week?"

"It was good."

"They already gave you a special project with one of the doctors? What's that about?"

I tell her about Jason and what happened in New York.

"I saw him on the news! Was that your doing?"

"Along with my cousin Maria, who set him up to work at the clinic and suggested we contact Desiree Rivera. Maria gets most of the credit for that."

"It was a wonderful story. I'd heard about the fancy doctor helping at the free clinic. Agnes said people were lining the streets."

Agnes is her next-door neighbor and source of all information. "He got a good turnout. He treated more than two hundred patients."

"That's incredible. I'm sure it meant so much to people."

"It did. He wants to continue to volunteer there at least one day a week if he's able to stay in the area."

"The Miami-Dade board would be crazy to pass on him."

"I agree, but it's up to them." I'm suddenly overwhelmed by anxiety as I try to find the words to tell her about my personal relationship with Jason. "There's something else I need to tell you."

"Is everything all right?"

The poor woman is conditioned to expect disaster. "Everything is fine. It's just that . . ."

"What, honey? What is it?"

"Dr. Northrup . . . Jason . . . He and I have been, well . . . I'm sort of seeing him." My face burns with mortification over the stumbling words as I'm gripped with sadness so profound it touches the very deepest part of me.

"Sweetheart, that's wonderful news. I've so hoped you would meet someone special."

"Oh. You have?" I've never once spoken to her about the possibility of me dating again or anything close to that topic. While everyone else in my life has been eager to set me up on dates, as her son's widow, I've avoided discussing that aspect of my life with Josie.

"Of course I have. You've got so much life left to live and so much love to give. Tony would want you to find someone who makes you happy. He loved you so much."

A sob catches me off guard.

"Carmen, honey . . . It's okay. Really."

"I'm sorry. I don't mean to be so emotional. It's just . . ."

"It's hard to talk about moving on from Tony."

"Yes." I'm a sniveling, snotty mess as I reach for a tissue to mop up the damage. "I hope you know that no matter where I go or who I'm with, Tony is always going to be part of me."

"I do know that. Without a doubt. You have a right to be happy after everything you've been through. You've been so incredibly devoted to his legacy and his memory."

"That won't change. Ever."

"I know that, too. Will we get to meet your Jason at brunch on Sunday?"

"Yes, he'll be there."

"We'll look forward to meeting him."

"I just want to thank you for always being so supportive of me."

"You're one of my kids, Carmen. I'll always be supportive of you and whatever you choose to do. Your future children will be my grandchildren."

Her sweet kindness sends new tears sliding down my cheeks. "Thank you. I love you."

"I love you, too. So very much. I'll see you Sunday?"

"See you then."

Long after I end the call, tears continue to stream down my cheeks. Telling Josie about Jason has opened the door to so many emotions I locked away long ago in an effort to survive the crushing loss. When it first happened, the part I had the hardest time with was knowing how long I'd have to live without him. It seemed unfathomable then that I would most likely continue to exist for decades while he was gone forever.

When Jason comes in from his run, I try to frantically clean up the last of the tears. I glance at the clock and am surprised that it's already after nine. He goes right for water in the kitchen before coming to find me, stopping short at the sight of my tear-swollen face.

"What happened?"

He's sweaty and gorgeous and makes me feel better just by walking in the room. "I talked to Tony's mother."

"You told her about me?"

"Yes."

"Did she upset you?"

"Not the way you think. She was amazing. Super supportive of me, as always." I wipe new tears that won't quit as much as I wish they would. "I'm sorry. I don't know why I can't stop crying."

He kneels in front of me and takes hold of my hands, kissing the backs of both of them. "It was a hard conversation. I'm not surprised you're feeling emotional."

"Are you always this amazing, or just with damsels in distress?"

"You're the only damsel I'm concerned with, and if I didn't stink so bad, I'd hold you until all the distress is gone."

I cup his face and kiss him. "Go take a shower so you can hold me all night."

He groans and leans into the kiss. "I'm going." Another kiss. "In a minute." Five full minutes of tongue-twisting kisses later, he pushes to his feet. "I'll be right back. Don't go anywhere."

"Nowhere else I'd rather be than right here with you." I force myself to shake off the malaise and to focus on the present rather than wallowing in the past. My present is looking rather promising at the moment, and it's that thought that has me standing and pulling off my clothes as I head for the bathroom to join Jason in the shower.

He startles with surprise when I step in behind him and wrap my arms around him. "Well, hello there."

"Hi."

"What's up?"

"Nothing much. You?"

He laughs. "Nothing was up until you pressed your sexy self against me. And now . . ." He guides my hand to his hard cock.

"All that for me?"

"For you and only you."

I rest my cheek against his back as the warm water rains down upon us. He moves my hand up and down the long length of his shaft. He's rougher than I would've been without his guidance, but I let him take what he wants and needs while I run my free hand over the dips and cuts of his muscular abdomen. I'm obsessed with his six-pack and the ropy V of muscles over his hips. He's muscular in a leaner way than Tony was, not that I'm comparing. That's a rabbit hole I refuse to fall into, because if I were to go there, I'd also have to acknowledge the difference of being in bed with a man who has much more experience than my husband did.

So not going there. Uh-uh. No way.

Jason's muscles tighten, and his breathing quickens. "Carmen."

"Hmm?"

"Let's do this together."

"Next time. Take one just for you."

His deep groan makes me smile and has me deciding to sweeten the pot. I release my hold on his cock and turn him to face me, glancing up at him as I drop to my knees to take him into my mouth.

I love the shock that registers in his eyes, his sharp intake of breath, the rough grip on my hair and the way his entire body goes tense as I take him as deep as I can. The head of his cock nudges against my throat, and I swallow convulsively, drawing a shout of pleasure from him.

"Carmen," he says, sounding desperate. "Babe . . . *Fuck*."

Despite the warning I hear in his voice, I lick and suck gently, focused entirely on him and his pleasure.

In the second before he comes, his cock gets harder and bigger, which fascinates me. After years of not giving sex a thought, it's all I seem to think about since he came into my life.

"Shit," he whispers as he sags against the wall.

I lick my lips and stand on shaky legs.

He wraps his arms around me as his chest rises and falls rapidly.

"Was that okay?"

He laughs as he seems to fight for breath. "Ah yeah, you could say that. You wrecked me."

As we stand there under the warm water, clinging to each other, I'm content in a way I haven't been in years. It's a feeling I want to hold on to with everything I've got, as I know now how fleeting such things can be. And when I feel his reawakened cock pressing against my belly, I laugh. "That didn't take long."

"He's under your spell." Jason shuts off the water, steps out of the shower and has a towel waiting for me when I follow him. He wraps it around me and nuzzles my neck, giving a gentle bite that electrifies me.

"Don't leave any marks." I can just imagine what my grandmothers would say if I showed up with love bites on my neck.

"I won't. Don't worry." With his hands on my hips, he directs me toward the bedroom. On the way, the towel falls to the floor, and I find myself facedown on the bed. "Like this." His hand slides from my back to my ass, which he's mentioned a few times is the finest ass he's ever seen. Any inhibitions I might've had about being naked in front of him quickly disappeared in the face of his desire for me.

I've always been conscious of what Tony once referred to as my extravagant curves. I'm not fat so much as "lush," as Maria describes us both. I could stand to lose some weight, but I try to eat healthy, exercise when I feel like it and maintain a healthy body image. Although, this week, the only exercise I've gotten is in bed with Jason.

Next week, I tell myself as I wait to see what he has planned, I'll get back on the treadmill, which is the one machine at the gym I can handle.

His lips land on the center of my back and work their way down. It takes him only seconds to have me quivering with desire and anticipation. He raises me to my knees and uses his tongue to intensify the quivering and the desire. I'm a trembling orgasmic mess of nerve endings on fire for him by the time he pushes into me from behind. Grasping my hips, he thrusts in deep before retreating almost completely and then repeating the whole thing again and again until I'm desperate to let go of the intense pressure that's building like a steam engine about to burst from internal combustion.

When he grazes a fingertip over my clit, I explode, screaming from the release that rocks through me.

He's right there with me, coming with a grunt and a moan that vibrates through the lips he's pressed against my back.

We tumble onto the mattress, still joined as we ride the waves that follow epic release.

He mumbles all the Spanish words he practiced on me the other day, calling me every term of endearment he can think of as he caresses my breasts and belly.

I break out into goose bumps that make me shiver as much from the words as his tender touch.

Jason withdraws from me, disposes of the condom in a tissue and grabs the throw blanket from the end of my bed to cover us, keeping his body curved tightly around mine. "How you doing over there?"

“Very, very good. You?”

“Same. Very, very, *very* good.”

I reach for his hand, which is flat against my abdomen, and hold on tight to him, overwhelmed by everything that’s already happened while wondering where we’ll go from here.

CHAPTER 19

Carmen

The news from the nurses on Saturday is good—Mateo is responding well to the antibiotics and doing much better.

Jason is visibly relieved after he gets that update.

We spend much of the day working on the PowerPoint presentation for the Miami-Dade board of directors, which includes testimonials from former patients as well as Jason's colleagues in New York. His assistant came through with plenty of both, so we've got a lot to work with in addition to what we've done together here.

The NBC 6 story is included, along with the photos I took of him with patients at the clinic, playing dominoes in the park, eating at the bar at Giordino's and sitting on Miami Beach.

"It's really great, Carmen," he says when we review it from the beginning.

"We had lots of good stuff to work with." I glance at him, leaning over my shoulder to view the laptop screen. "I hope this helps you see that the scandal is only a tiny part of your story."

"It does. I just hope the board sees that, too."

"They will. How could they not?" I get up and stretch, my muscles protesting from spending hours at the computer, not to mention the hours in bed with him. "How do you feel about cigars?"

"Medical school ruined my enjoyment of many things, including cigars. We learned all about how unhealthy most of the best things really are."

"That's a drag."

He smiles at my pun. "A huge drag. I'll never look at cigars, booze, fried food or red meat the same way again. Why do you ask about cigars?"

"I want to take you to the Little Havana Cigar Factory. I thought you might find it fun to check out how they're made."

"That does sound fun. Can we have dinner at the restaurant after?"

"We're going there for brunch tomorrow."

"Is there a limit on the number of times we're allowed to go there? I want to see your family again. I like them."

"They like you, too. In fact, I've been getting texts from them asking when you're coming back."

He puts his arms around me and kisses me. "Are you ashamed of me, Rizo?"

"Of course not. Don't be silly."

"Then what're you thinking?"

"I'm getting attached to you." The words are out before I can take even a second to decide whether I should say them.

"I'm getting attached to you, too."

"Are we setting ourselves up for disaster here?"

"Maybe, but disaster has never felt so good." He kisses me again, and like always, the second his lips connect with mine, I lose myself in the magic we create together.

By the time we finally come up for air, I've forgotten what we were talking about. Oh. Right. Attachment . . .

Jason's phone rings, and he reluctantly releases me to check it. "It's Terri, the nurse administrator from New York."

She's the one who sent us the testimonials from former patients and colleagues.

He takes the call. "Hey, Terri." As he listens to what she has to say, he walks toward the window in my living room. "When did this happen?"

My stomach tightens with nerves as I wonder what new disaster might have occurred. As I watch him, I realize it's far too late to be worried about anything as simple as attachment. I'm falling in love with him. If I haven't already completely fallen. His fate is now tied to mine, and whatever news he's getting from Terri, I only hope it doesn't make anything worse for him.

After a tense ten-minute conversation in which he does more listening than talking, he thanks Terri for calling and asks her to keep him posted. Long after he stashes the phone in the pocket of his basketball shorts, he continues to stare out the window.

"What's going on?" I ask when I can't wait another second to know.

"Apparently, Howard resigned as chairman of the board in New York to, and I quote, 'spend more time with his family.' After hearing from my lawyer earlier in the week, apparently Ginger wrote a letter to the remaining board members, telling them I had no idea who she really was or that she was married with children. The new board chair, a woman named Dr. Linda Adams, wants to talk to me on Monday. Terri thinks she's going to ask me to come back."

The news hits me like a punch to the gut. "Oh. Wow. That's a lot."

"I know." Apparently sensing my immediate dismay at this turn of events, he comes to me and puts his hands on my shoulders. "Take a breath. Nothing is decided."

Six days ago, I didn't know he existed, and now . . . Now I wonder if I can ever again be truly happy if this man isn't in my life. That's a lot for six days, especially considering the five years that preceded them. "Maybe we should, you know . . ."

His brows furrow with concern that's adorable on him, but then again, everything about him is adorable. "What?"

I lick my dry lips and force myself to look at him while trying to remain unemotional. "Take a step back until we know what's going to happen?"

He shakes his head. "I don't want to take a step back from you."

"I don't want that, either, but I also don't want to be left crushed or heartbroken when you resume your life in New York."

"Do you honestly think I'd just walk away like you never happened?"

"I don't know what to think."

"Let me put your mind at ease. Nothing will be decided without your input."

"You have to do what's best for your career, Jason. Your entire life is in New York—"

"Not anymore it isn't."

"You've known me for *six days*! You can't make huge career decisions based on six days."

"Yes, I can."

"No, you can't."

He nods in the second before he kisses me and once again wipes my brain clear of any thoughts that don't involve more of him and the way I feel when he kisses me so passionately. With his arms tight around me, he walks me backward to my bedroom, where he comes down on top of me on the bed without missing a beat in the kiss.

I know I should stop kissing him and go back to discussing the fact that he can't make career decisions based on a woman he's known for six days. But since that woman is me and I'm crazy about him, I decide to keep kissing him while I can, even if I already feel heartbroken at the thought of him going back to New York.

He shifts from my lips to my neck, leaving a trail of hot kisses that have me shivering and dying for more. "How can you think you won't factor into whatever happens next? Of course you will."

"It's been *six days*, Jason."

"I knew in six minutes that you were special, that I wanted to know you and be with you. Every minute I've spent with you since then has only made me want more of you. So, yes, six days later, it does matter what you think about whatever happens next."

I'm ridiculously moved, as much by the words as the kisses that set my body on fire.

He pulls back from me only to grab a condom, and then he's back to remove my T-shirt and panties. "This," he says as he enters me slowly and carefully, "is everything."

"Not everything."

"*Every* fucking *thing*." He's fierce and sexy and everything to me, too. Even as I tell myself to hold something back so there'll be something left just in case this goes bad, I can't do it. I give him everything I have as he makes love to me. And that's what this is.

I know what love feels like, and it's this all-consuming, must-be-with-him-or-I'll-die feeling that overtakes common sense and every other kind of sense as it invades with the power of a tsunami, overtaking your life and reshaping it to fit his presence.

He feels it, too. I know he does. I can tell by the way he looks at me, by the way he kisses and touches me with so much reverence. I can tell by the way he values my opinions and listens to me when I talk to him. I can tell by the way he respects and welcomes Tony's presence in my life. I can tell by the way he can't be near me without touching me in some way.

Yes, it happened fast, but the end result is very similar to what took years to happen in the past.

Love is love, and this . . . This is love.

Jason

We end up spending the rest of Saturday in her bed. We talk about getting up to go do something or to have dinner at the restaurant, but in the end we order takeout, eat in bed, watch movies and make love. It's the most perfect day and night I've ever had with anyone.

Carmen has been quieter than usual since the call from Terri opened the possibility of me returning, eventually, to New York. That news would've thrilled me a week ago, but now the thought of leaving Carmen has become unimaginable. The very real possibility exists that New York will ask me to come back and Miami-Dade will deny privileges in deference to its sister facility.

If that happens, I'll have little choice but to return to New York to pick up my career and research already in progress. After meeting Carmen's family, seeing how close she is to them and how tied she is to her community, I can't picture her anywhere but here, not that I'd presume to make that choice for her. I just wonder if she could be truly happy living so far from her family and home.

These are the thoughts that run through my mind Sunday at noon as I drive us to her family's restaurant. As always, the scent of Carmen's hair and skin makes me crazy for more of her even after the decadence of the last twenty-four hours.

I downshift, slowing the car to a stop at a red light. As soon as the light changes and we're moving again, I reach for her hand.

She looks over at me, a small smile curving her sexy lips. It's not the usual smile that lights up her entire face. I haven't seen that one since Terri called yesterday and gave Carmen reason to worry about where this relationship of ours may be headed.

I want to reassure her, to tell her she has nothing to worry about, but I won't do that until I know for sure it's true. If I end up going back to New York, I'll ask her to come with me, even if I know that's a long shot. She just landed her dream job at Miami-Dade.

Ugh, I wish it didn't all seem so hopelessly complicated. All I want to do is celebrate the fact that I've found her, that I've fallen for her. I want to say *fuck it* to everything that isn't her, even if I know I can't do that with all the time and energy I've invested in my career. It was a huge deal for Carmen to get involved with me in the first place, and the last freaking thing I want to do is make her sorry she took a chance on me.

That's my greatest fear—that I'll make her sorry, and this interlude with me will turn out to be a setback for her.

I can't let that happen, no matter what else might transpire.

We park in the lot outside the restaurant, which is currently closed to the public. Carmen told me that Sunday brunch is for family and friends, the only time Vincent and Vivian reserve for themselves in the hectic running of the restaurant. Carmen also prepared me for a curious crowd who'll ask inappropriate questions about our relationship as well as their own medical issues.

I'm ready for whatever they're dishing up. They're important to her, so they're important to me. I'll also be meeting Len and Josie, who are Tony's parents, which makes this brunch an even bigger deal for all of us. It's a good thing I don't have issues with my stomach, because if I did, I'm sure it would be acting up as I follow Carmen in through the back door.

She's wearing another of those wrap dresses, this one red with flowers on it, that accentuate her curves to delicious perfection. Her long hair is down and curly, and sky-high sexy-as-fuck black heels click on the terra-cotta tile floor. She's dazzling, and I can't keep my eyes off her. I'm wearing a pin-striped dress shirt and navy pants, even though she said I could wear jeans if I wanted to. Somehow jeans didn't feel appropriate for this occasion. I feel like a boring accessory next to the magnificence that is Carmen.

Abuela is the first one we see. She's coming out of the kitchen carrying a platter bigger than she is laden with food that has my mouth watering.

I step up to help her. "Let me take that for you."

She hands it over to me and kisses Carmen and then me on the cheek I lower so she can reach me. "Thank you, honey. Take it into the dining room if you would."

"Follow me." Carmen leads the way into the cavernous dining room on the Cuban side of the house, which I didn't really get a good look at the last time I was here. It's much bigger than I expected.

"How do you decide which side brunch is on?"

"We rotate each week. Abuela and Nona decide on the menu and supervise everything."

"I love that." Their traditions are charming and endearing and make me wish I was part of a family like theirs.

At Carmen's direction, I put the massive platter on a table in the middle of the big room. The second the food is out, people migrate toward us. I receive kisses from Vivian and Nona. I meet Vivian's sisters, Vincent's brother, Navarro cousins and Giordino cousins. I meet so many people I can't possibly remember all their names.

Vincent presses a Bloody Mary into my hand as the women buzz around Carmen and me like flies on fresh game. I suppose that's what I am—the fresh game, a thought that makes me smile.

Carmen looks at me, raises a brow in question.

"This must be what fresh game feels like."

She laughs at that, her hand on my back letting me know she's right there, by my side, as we're swarmed by her family members.

I can tell something significant is happening when the buzzing dies down and the sea of women parts to admit newcomers.

Carmen's hand leaves my back as she goes to greet the couple with hugs and kisses. The woman says something to Carmen that has her nodding and reaching for the older woman's hand. She leads them to me.

"Jason, these are my in-laws. Josie, Len, meet my friend Jason Northrup."

I shake hands with both of them. Carmen told me they're younger than her parents, but they don't look younger. They look at least ten years older. Both are mostly gray, and their eyes—brown for her and hazel for him—carry the weight of their tragic loss. "It's so nice to meet you both."

Josie cradles my hand between both of hers. "Likewise."

Unlike his wife, Len doesn't seem all that pleased to meet me, but he's polite for the sake of his wife and Carmen. I try to put myself in his place, meeting the man his son's widow is now seeing, and decide he can think whatever he wants to about me. My heart goes out to him. No one should have to go through what he and his family have endured. "I'm very sorry for the loss of your son."

"That's very kind of you," Josie says softly. "Thank you. We enjoyed the story on the news about you. It was nice of you to give your time to the clinic."

"It was a pleasure. I enjoyed it very much." Which is absolutely true. I forgot what it's like to deal with basic, easily solved medical concerns. I've become accustomed to the harder cases, the ones that are never easily solved and often have less-than-ideal outcomes.

After Len and Josie wander off to talk to other people, Maria approaches me, Bloody Mary in hand. She nods toward Tony's parents. "How'd that go?"

"Okay, I guess."

"They're good people. If Carmen is happy, they're happy. Don't worry."

"That's good to know."

"All these people . . . These are her people. We love her."

"I know."

"You aren't going to hurt her, are you?"

"I'm going to try like hell not to."

She nods, seeming pleased with my response. "It's a very big deal that she brought you to brunch. I hope you realize that."

"I do."

Carmen joins us, and I put my arm around her, aware of everyone in the room watching us, getting a sense of how we are together. I want them to know I care about her.

"Everything all right?" she asks, her gaze encompassing me and Maria.

I give her a reassuring smile. "It is with me."

"Me too," Maria says. "The board of the clinic wanted me to pass along their thanks for what you did for us this week. They said you're welcome to come back anytime you'd like."

"I've got most of another week to kill before my meeting with the Miami-Dade board on Friday. I'm all yours if you'll have me."

"Yes, we'll have you," she says, laughing. "I'll let them know, and I'll see you in the morning." She starts to walk away but turns back. "For what it's worth, I think it's amazing that you're continuing to volunteer at the clinic when you got what you needed from us on the first day."

"I genuinely enjoy it."

"I know you do, and that makes you truly awesome." To Carmen, she adds, "He's a keeper, prima."

Carmen curls her hands around my arm. "I agree."

A powerful feeling of yearning comes over me, to be kept by her, to attend brunch at Giordino's every Sunday, to be part of this amazing, loud, boisterous family. I can picture myself with Carmen years from now, still going strong with a couple of adorable, rambunctious curly-haired kids who look like their mother along for the ride as we join her family for Sunday brunch. Seven days after meeting her, I can see all that and so much more.

However, I need to figure out my own life before I can think about disrupting hers any more than I already have. So I tamp back the yearning and focus on today and the coming week, during which much will be decided.

I try not to think about that as I enjoy the Cuban-themed feast, featuring many of the dishes I had the first time I was here and a few new things. Carmen explains everything to me, and I try it all. I've yet to have anything here that isn't delicious. We're seated at a big horseshoe-shaped table next to Carmen's parents and Nona. Abuela clearly relishes her role as the hostess.

Between courses, Carmen reaches for my hand under the table. The sense of connection I feel with her is powerful, so powerful in fact that only a few weeks after another woman upended my life in the worst possible way, I'm fully prepared to allow that to happen again.

Carmen is more than welcome to upend my life in any way she sees fit.

Everything would be different this time. I know that with a certainty I've never felt with anyone else.

"Are you okay?" Carmen asks.

"I'm great. You?"

"It's nice to have you here."

"Thanks for inviting me."

"I know we can be a lot . . ."

"I was thinking how lucky you are to have such a great family. They must've been an enormous comfort to you." I don't have to say when. She knows what I mean.

"They were. They surrounded me and held me up in every possible way. Mami slept in bed with me for the first month. Maria took the second month. My cousin Delores, who we call Dee, took the third month. She's one of the cousins that lives in New York now. I was never alone, unless I wanted to be. I've always been thankful for them, but never more so than I was then."

"I can't imagine what it would be like to have people like that, who swoop in and try to make it all better."

"You didn't have that in New York?"

I shake my head. "I have friends, most of them colleagues who think I've gotten a raw deal, but no one who swooped in the way your family would have."

"You haven't seen true support until you've seen it from this clan."

"I'm sure it's formidable."

"They saved my life. Without them around to remind me of my many blessings, I'm not sure I would've survived losing Tony."

"I'm very glad your life was saved so I would get to meet you and spend this time with you."

"Me too." She smiles, but it's tinged with wariness that I wish I could do something about. However, until I know where I'm going to end up and whether we're going to be able to make something of this, she'll remain wary and guarded, and I can't blame her for that.

After brunch, we go grocery shopping. As I watch her carefully choose produce, I discover yet another layer to this woman who has me completely fascinated.

"Why're you staring at me?"

"I'm not staring so much as ogling you as you ogle the avocados."

"Choosing avocados is very serious business."

"So I'm learning."

"They can't be too firm, and you don't want them too soft. There's a sweet spot right in the middle." She hands one to me. "Feel that? It's perfect."

While trying not to let my mind wander in lascivious directions, I take it from her and give it a gentle squeeze. "I'll never look at avocados the same way again."

"Have you ever actually bought one before?"

"I can't say that I have."

"Savage."

I crack up laughing. "What are you going to make with those avocados anyway?"

"I put them on salads mostly. Avocado is an excellent source of good fat."

"Is it now?"

"It is. And good fat helps to get rid of the bad fat." She pulls a face. "I like to think of it like a Pac-Man in there, gobbling up all the fat I don't need." She puts four avocados in her basket.

"You don't think you're fat, do you?" I'm not at all sure if I should ask that, but curiosity wins out.

"I think I'm curvier than I should be."

"I completely and *adamantly* disagree."

She rolls her eyes at me. "Stop."

"I will not stop. I think your curves are luscious, delicious, sexy perfection, and you'll never convince me otherwise."

"You're very good for a girl's ego."

"Your ego should be very, very healthy."

I love the way she smiles at me and continues on her way, list in hand like the well-organized woman she is.

We return to her place, and when I tell her I want to check out the gym in her complex, she frowns. "Enjoy that."

"Come with me."

"No way. I've already told you I suck at the gym. I don't need you seeing that for yourself."

"Then let's go for a walk or something."

"It's too hot." She looks up at me. "You go. I have some things I need to do around here, such as laundry. I can toss yours in, too, if you want."

"I don't expect you to do my laundry."

"I know you don't. I offered. Put it in the bathroom if you want me to do it, and go have your run."

"I'd rather hang with you than go run."

"You can do both. I'll still be here when you get back."

"You promise?"

She kisses me. "I promise."

I gather my laundry and put it in the bathroom, as directed, before changing into running shorts and a tank top. This is going to be quick because I don't want to waste whatever time I have with her doing something as mundane as running.

I want to be with her every minute that I can for as long as I can. Who knows where I'll be a week from now? All I know is the thought of being anywhere but with her is suddenly unfathomable to me.

CHAPTER 20

Carmen

In the morning, Jason and I take two cars to get cortaditos from Juanita before parting company to spend the day apart for the first time in a week. He's heading to the clinic, and I'm going to my office at the hospital to fine-tune his presentation to the board that's set for Friday at four.

I show it to Mr. Augustino that afternoon, and he agrees it's excellent.

"Can you think of anything else that ought to be included?" I ask him.

"Perhaps more about the details of his research and how that could bring national and international prestige to our hospital."

"Good point." I make a note to ask Jason for more information about the specifics of his research.

"This is very well done, Carmen. Great work."

"Thank you. Dr. Northrup made it easy by giving me so much to work with."

"Is it true that he's back at the free clinic in Little Havana this week?"

"He is."

"Well, that's good of him to do."

"He really enjoys working there. If he's granted privileges here, I think he'll continue to volunteer there as often as he can."

"I received an interesting email today."

I experience a twinge of anxiety from the way he says that.

"It was from the woman Dr. Northrup was involved with in New York. She explained the circumstances of their relationship and confirmed that he had no idea who she was or that she was married with children. She took the blame for the entire mess."

"Oh. Well, that's good news."

"Apparently, she also sent the letter to the board of the hospital in New York."

Even though I already know this, hearing it from Mr. Augustino makes it more official. Of course he'll go back to New York. I've been such a fool to think he'd do anything but that if offered the opportunity.

"Are you all right, Carmen? I hope you know this is all about courtesy to our sister facility and is no reflection at all on the terrific work you've done."

I look up at Mr. Augustino, my boss, the hospital president, the man who must never know that I've fallen hard for the doctor he assigned me to work with. I clear the emotion from my throat and keep my face expressionless when I look at him. "Yes, of course. I'm fine, and I'm glad you're happy with my work."

But one thing is abundantly clear to me in light of this development. I have to take a step back from Jason, and I have to do it now while I still can.

I'm on my way home from the hospital when he calls. I think about letting it go to voice mail, but after spending almost every minute of the last week with him, I at least owe him an explanation.

"Hi."

"Hey. How was your day?"

"Good. You?"

"Busy. We saw fifty-two patients."

"Wow. That is busy."

"I'm starving. What do you feel like for dinner?"

"I, ah, did you talk to the new board chair in New York?"

"I did. I was going to tell you about it when I see you. Is everything okay?"

I pull into a parking lot in front of a coffee shop and a thrift store because I don't trust myself to have this conversation while I'm driving.

"Carmen? Are you still there?"

"I'm here."

"What's wrong, Rizo?"

Hearing that nickname brings tears to my eyes that I try—unsuccessfully—to contain. "What did the new board chair say? Did you get your job back?"

"She offered me the opportunity to come back if I want to."

That news strikes like a knife to my heart. I want to ask him if he still plans to meet with the Miami-Dade board, but why would he? He got back the job he really wanted in the first place. "That's wonderful news, Jason. You must be thrilled."

"A week ago, I would've been thrilled, but now . . ."

"You have a chance to get your career back on track. That's what you said you want."

"It was what I wanted. Before."

"Before what?"

"Before you."

My heart does a little happy dance at hearing that, but then reality smacks it down. "You cannot make major life decisions based on someone you've known for a week."

"Why not?"

"Because! People don't do that!"

"Some people do."

"I don't. I *can't*. You can't."

"May I please see you so we can talk about this face-to-face?"

"I can't do that, either."

"Why?"

"Because if I see your face, I'll forget about protecting myself in this situation, and that has to be my top priority. It just *has* to be, Jason."

"So that's it? We're over, just like that?"

"I . . . I don't know."

"Do you think I'd just go back to New York and not at least ask if you'd like to come with me or figure out some way to make this work between us?"

"As much as I love being with you, and I really do, I'm not moving to New York. I just got my dream job. My whole life is here. I couldn't do that to my parents or Tony's parents or my grandmothers. I can't move. I *won't* move."

Tears run down my face, and the pain in my chest reminds me far too much of how I felt after losing Tony. Not that this is anything like that. Jason is still alive and well, but his life is going to happen far away from mine. And that hurts. It hurts bad. As bad as anything has hurt in a very long time. "I have to go."

"Please don't go. Let's talk about it."

"There's nothing left to talk about. My life is here. Yours is somewhere else. I had so much fun with you, but I have to stop this now before it leaves me in ruins." I'll probably be in ruins anyway, but he doesn't need to know that.

"I never intended for that to happen."

"I know."

"Carmen—"

"I have to go now. I'll hope for all good things for you, Jason. You deserve the best of everything." I end the call before he hears me break down into heartbroken sobs. My body shakes with the force of my despair. I'm absolutely sure it's the right thing to stop this now, because it's not going to be any easier in a week.

But good God, it hurts now, too. It hurts so bad.

My phone rings, and my heart lurches with hope that it might be him calling me back. I tell my lurching heart to knock it off, wipe my face and take the call from my mother, who'll keep calling until I answer. Such is life for the adult only child of a woman who suffered nine miscarriages. "Hey."

"Hey, yourself. What's wrong?" She probably got a readout on her ESP-o-meter that tells her whenever I'm in distress.

"Nothing is wrong. I said one word."

"That's all it takes for me to know something is wrong."

I should've let the call go to voice mail and texted her. "I'm fine. What's up with you?"

"Where are you?"

I look around, trying to figure out where exactly I am. "On the way home."

"Come by for dinner. We'll talk."

The last thing I feel like doing is talking about it, or explaining to my family why I'm heartbroken once again. "Mami, I—"

"I'll see you when you get here."

The line goes dead.

I could text her and tell her I'm simply not up for dinner at the restaurant, but she would leave work and come to my place to check on me, and I don't want her doing that, either. "Ugh." I start the car, back out of the parking space and head toward the restaurant, feeling dead inside. The elation of the last week has been overshadowed by devastation.

I wouldn't have missed spending the time I did with Jason for anything. He made me feel alive again and showed me that I can still have strong feelings for a man. That's all good news. But the thought of never seeing him again . . .

My eyes flood with more tears that make it hard for me to see where I'm going. I fumble around in the console and find a pack of tissues. At a red light, I mop up the tears and give myself a stern talking-to about getting it together so I won't have to explain red, puffy eyes to my family.

I take a deep, shuddering breath, hold it and then release it slowly, repeating the process several times until I feel calmer. The light changes, and I accelerate through the intersection, intent on keeping my focus on the traffic while trying to ignore the ache in my chest.

The last place I feel like being is at the restaurant where I'll be the center of attention, but if I don't go to them, they'll come to me. They're too busy at this hour to leave work, so I go to them. This reminds me of being summoned to appear every night at dinnertime as a teenager so we could pretend to be a normal family that ate dinner together.

I used to hate that I had to go there every night at six o'clock or run the risk of being tracked down by one or both of my parents. Rather than face their wrath, I did what I was told and showed up on time, especially after they got me a car and told me I was to use it to get to dinner on time or lose the privilege of having my own car.

Now that I'm older, I realize the value of what they did by making sure I wasn't home alone every night while they were at work. I did most of my high school homework while sitting at the bar at Giordino's, which was as much my home as our house was. The habit of stopping in for dinner continued after Tony and I were married. We both enjoyed spending time with my family—and not having to cook on our rare nights off.

I did a lot of my college and grad school homework there, too, more out of habit than anything. I discovered I wasn't as efficient at home alone, so I found myself right back there long after the choice was mine to make. Not to mention my parents kept me in food and drink while I worked, so there was that. That's why they joke that they got me through college and grad school, which isn't far from the truth.

They've gotten me through everything, and as I pull into the parking lot behind the restaurant, I'm comforted to know they'll get me through this new heartache, too.

I pull down the visor to view the damage in the mirror. My eyes are a little red and watery, but overall, it's not as bad as I expected. Although, my appearance doesn't matter much, because the people closest to me will take one look and know that something has happened.

Resigned to my fate, I grab my purse and head inside through the back door, which takes me past the bustling kitchen. The smells coming from there make my mouth water, reminding me that even in the worst of times, my appetite is always robust. That became a joke of sorts after Tony died, and I ate as if nothing had happened. Food has always been my friend that way.

My stomach rumbles in anticipation of dinner as I make my way to the bar. My dad is holding court, as usual, and leans across the bar to kiss my cheek. "What's wrong?"

"Nothing."

"Don't lie to your old man."

"There's nothing old about you."

He raises an eyebrow, letting me know he's not letting me off the hook.

I take a seat at the bar. "Bump in the road with Jason. Nothing to worry about. What're the specials tonight?"

He puts a glass of chardonnay in front of me and hands me the printout of specials.

I appreciate that he doesn't immediately start peppering me with questions the way my mother and grandmothers would. "Where're the ladies?"

"Tending to a private party upstairs, which buys you a little time."

I share a smile with him, appreciating that he gets that I need that bit of time before the inquisition begins.

"It's not terminal, I hope." He speaks quietly so he won't be overheard by the other patrons at the bar. "I like him."

"I do, too, and I'm not sure if it's terminal. He might be going back to New York." I shrug as if that's not the worst possible outcome—for me. "It's the best thing for him. That's where his life is."

"Nothing says your life couldn't be there, too."

I glance at him and catch the hint of sadness in warm eyes the same shade of brown as mine. "You trying to get rid of me, Pops?"

He leans his elbows on the bar. "Not even kinda, but it's been nice to see you sparkle again."

"It's been nice to feel that way, but nothing says he's the only one who can make me happy." The words are no sooner out of my mouth when I call myself a liar. I don't want anyone else but him.

"True."

I can tell my dad wants to say more but is hesitant to say too much. I nudge his hand. "What?"

"It's just that it took five years for you to meet someone who made you want to take a chance again."

"And look at what happened when I took that chance."

"If you don't mind me saying, you seem to be giving up rather easily, sweetheart."

That has me sitting straighter. "I'm not giving up so much as taking a step back out of self-preservation. I don't want to live in New York, especially after I just got this job and finally started my career."

"Jobs are replaceable. People aren't. You know that better than anyone."

"Jeez, Dad, go for the jugular, why don't you?"

He shrugs. "Just speaking the truth. If you care about this guy, and I think you really do, don't let him go without a fight. Tell him what you want. You might be surprised to discover he wants the same thing you do."

"As I said to him, we can't make huge life and career decisions based on someone we've known a week. That's insane."

"I knew two days after I met your mother that I'd never be happy without her in my life. Did I know for sure that I'd marry her and have this amazing life with her? Nope, not yet, but I knew I could not and would not be happy without her."

Of course, I know my parents were instantly attracted to and smitten with each other, but their story takes on new meaning for me in light of current events.

Dad wipes down glasses coming out of the steaming dishwasher. "I'm just saying, if he's the one for you, you'll figure it out. Don't give up on him, sweetheart. He's a good guy."

"I know he is, and that makes everything so much harder. I'd love the chance to get to know him better and to spend more time with him, but I'm not willing to move to New York for a guy I just met."

"So do the long-distance thing for a while and see what happens."

"And how will that go when he works eighty hours a week?"

"I have a feeling he'd make time for you. The man never takes his eyes off you."

"That is not true!"

"It's absolutely true." He tosses the dish towel over his shoulder. "What do you want for dinner? Dante's marsala is outstanding tonight. Had some earlier myself."

"That sounds good."

"House salad, too?"

"You know me." I love our house salad with its crispy romaine, tasty roma tomatoes, cucumbers, carrots, black olives, house-made croutons and shredded parmesan cheese. I get it without the red onion.

"I know you as well as I know myself, and seeing you with him . . . I liked the look of that. Be right back with your salad, love."

His sweet words bring new tears to my eyes. While he's gone, I take the time to check my phone and find a text from Jason that I devour.

I'm so sorry this has gotten complicated, but one thing isn't complicated. I like you. A LOT. A LOT. A LOT. I think about you all the time. In one week, you've made yourself essential to me in so many ways, most having nothing at all to do with our "project." I've got a lot to figure out, and I completely understand your need to protect yourself in the midst of my madness. I get it, even if I already miss you like crazy.

"I miss you, too," I whisper, rereading his message at least ten times before my dad returns, bringing my salad with the house Italian dressing on the side, just the way I like it.

Dad lifts his chin to ask what's up.

I hand over my phone to show him the text.

He reads it quickly and hands the phone back to me. "Have I mentioned I like this guy?"

"You might've said something about that."

"Sometimes it's hard to be patient and wait to see what'll happen. I have a good feeling that having some patience in this situation might serve you well."

"Maybe."

He goes off to tend to other customers while I eat my salad and think about Jason's text and what my dad said. I was doing okay before I met Jason, and I have to believe I'll be fine if he goes back to New York. But nothing will be as bright or as interesting as it was with him around. It'll be difficult to go on knowing he's out there somewhere, too far away to be part of my daily life.

For once, my formidable appetite is letting me down as I pick at the salad and try to work up interest in anything.

My mother slides onto the stool next to me. "What's going on?"

Since there's no point in trying to dodge her, I give her the summary. "Jason may be getting his old job back in New York."

"Oh crap. Well, good for him, but not so good for you, huh?"

"Something like that."

Abuela and Nona are right behind her, and my mother fills them in, which saves me the trouble of having to explain it yet again.

"Ay, mija, that boy is *loco* for you," Abuela says. "He's not going anywhere."

"It's not that simple, Abuela. His whole life, his research, everything is in New York. He only came here because he didn't have any choice. Or he thought he didn't."

"That's nonsense," Nona says. "His work isn't his whole life, and he's smart enough to know that."

I should've known they'd make me feel better. They usually do. And Dad was right about Dante's marsala. It's delicious. I box up half of it to take for lunch tomorrow.

"My boss wants to bring his wife in for their anniversary. He asked if I could pull some strings for him."

"Eh," Nona says with a wink. "We'll see what we can do."

I smile at her, and when she holds out her arms to me, I lean into her embrace. "After brunch, I said our little girl is falling in love with that handsome doctor."

I start to protest, but she hushes me.

"I said she's falling in love, and so is he. I only hope they can figure it out so no one gets hurt." She runs her hand over my hair the way she used to when I was little. "I also said if he hurts you, I might have him killed, but I didn't mean that. Well, not *really* . . ."

I'm laughing even as tears roll down my cheeks.

"If it's meant to be with him, my sweet girl, it will be. But no matter what happens with your Jason, you're a strong, capable woman, a survivor of much more difficult things than this'll ever be. You, my love, will be *fine*, no matter what."

"What she said." Abuela uses her thumb to point to Nona in a rare moment of total agreement.

I want to luxuriate in the warm embrace of my grandmothers and parents, but I need to go home and get ready for work and prepare to move on with my life. Nona is right—if it's meant to be, it will be. "Thank you, Nona. I needed to hear that tonight, and you're right. It'll work out the way it's meant to."

"And you will be *fine*," Abuela says emphatically, "because we say so."

I hug her and my mother—and my dad when he comes around the bar to get his share. "Love you guys. Don't know what I'd do without you, which is why I can't even think about living somewhere else."

"We love you, too, but you're *not* to make decisions based on us." Dad gives Mami a quelling look that has her thinking better of what she was going to say. "You would be fine without us, and we would be fine without you—if we have to be. We want you to be *happy*, Carmen. That is *all* we want for you."

I appreciate that he's given me the freedom to do what's best for me, even if it wouldn't be what's best for them. I've got a lot to think about. That's for sure.

CHAPTER 21

Jason

I stop for dinner at an Italian place that has nothing on Giordino's. I may be ruined forever for Cuban and Italian food after eating there. I may be ruined for everything if I've lost Carmen, which is a profoundly depressing thought that sucks the life out of me as I drive back to the hotel where I haven't slept in days.

A lot of my stuff is at Carmen's, which means I'll have to see her at some point. But out of respect for her wishes, I buy a toothbrush, toothpaste, razor and comb in the hotel gift shop, along with a bottle of water. I pay for the items, take the bag from the clerk and turn to head toward the elevator when I see her.

Ginger.

Sitting in my hotel lobby waiting for me, looking as always as if she just stepped off a runway in Milan. She once told me that her color palette was autumn, which is why she wears tans, oranges and browns exclusively. I should've taken one thing from that information—that she's shallow and concerned with all the wrong things. Hindsight is indeed twenty-twenty. Today she's wearing orange, but all I see is red.

For a second, I'm so surprised to see her that I'm speechless. She looks at me with those big green eyes that used to move me, and it's all I can do not to lose my shit. "What do you want?"

"Can we talk? Please?"

"Absolutely not." I wonder how she found me, but that's secondary to getting rid of her. "Go home. There's nothing for you here."

"Jason, I want to apologize."

"Good, thanks. All set. Go away." I head for the elevators, hoping she got the message.

She didn't. She grabs my arm to stop me, and since I'm not up for a nasty public scene, I glare at her until she releases me.

"I have less than nothing to say to you."

"I have things I need to tell you. Give me five minutes, please?"

"I'm not giving you thirty seconds. Go back under the rock you crawled out from under and leave me alone. Your scheme has been a roaring success. I hear Howard quit the board. Congratulations on ruining the lives of two people. You should be very pleased with yourself."

To my great horror, she begins to cry. "I'm so, so sorry. I never intended—"

"*What didn't you intend?* For the whole sordid mess to get plastered all over the New York media, or for me to lose my job, or for your kids to find out what a shameless bitch their mother is?"

"Any of it. I didn't intend for it to go as far as it did."

I stare at her, incredulous. "What did you think would happen when your husband, who runs the hospital where I work, walked in on us when my dick was down your throat?"

A guy from the hotel approaches us, his expression stormy. "That's enough, folks. Take it upstairs or outside unless you want me to call the cops."

"I apologize." I notice there're kids in the bar area, too far away to have heard what I said but close enough that I shouldn't have said it. Why am I even talking to her? "I'm going upstairs. Alone."

"Jason . . ."

"I really ought to thank you, Ginger." I've turned down the volume considerably, but I hope the glare I direct her way is as frosty as I intend it to be. "If you hadn't blown up my life, I never would've come here and met the most extraordinary woman I've ever known. So thanks for that, for leading me to her. She makes this entire nightmare worth every bit of hell and heartache you put me through." The elevator dings when it arrives. "Have a nice life."

Her tear-stained face is the last thing I see before the doors close and the elevator gets me the hell away from her. As the car ascends, I realize my hands are shaking, and every muscle in my body is tight with fury. How dare she come here to find me, hoping to do what? Reconcile? As if that's ever going to happen.

My heart is beating so fast I fear it's reaching the danger zone. Naturally, the fucking keycard picks that moment not to work, but there's no way I'm going back to the lobby while she might still be lurking about. I slide down to the floor and bust out a beer from the six-pack of Sam Adams I bought on the way back to the hotel, realizing it's not a twist-off and I don't have a bottle opener.

"Motherfucker."

Remember a month ago when your life wasn't a complete disaster? The thought has me pulling out my phone to check what I was doing a month ago today. I scroll through the calendar app and find the date on which I had three back-to-back surgeries, a two-hour meeting with my research team and a late dinner with Ginger at my place. I remember that particular night. I tried to get her to tell me more about herself, but she dodged the questions the way she always did.

I was too tired to care. All I wanted was to eat, have sex and sleep. Looking back, picking apart every minute I spent with her, I can see the signs were there. I just chose to ignore them. For the first time in years, I was in an actual relationship, having regular sex with someone who seemed to like being with me as much as I liked being with her.

Why would I blow that up by making an issue over her not wanting to talk about herself? Wasn't that a refreshing change of pace? I'd found a hot, sexy woman who preferred to talk about me rather than herself. She was a true unicorn. What more could I possibly want?

So much more, as it turns out. She might've played me for a fool, but I was rather easily played. I've never been one to be led around by my dick, but that's exactly what she did, and I let it happen. With ninety percent of my mental energy expended at work on any given day, the ten percent I had left wasn't enough to delve deeper into the inner workings of my relationship with her or to come up with questions I should've been asking.

That's my bad. Not that I'll ever think I deserved what she did, but for someone who's always been told he's freakishly smart, I was anything but when it came to her. I was a typical dude who didn't care about the details as long as he was getting laid on a regular basis.

In my heart of hearts, I knew something about us wasn't quite right, and I didn't care enough to figure out what.

My phone chimes with a text. I pull it out of my pocket and experience a moment of pure elation when I see it's from Carmen. *Mr. Augustino reviewed the PP presentation today and said we need more about your research. Not sure if you still plan to meet with the M-D board, but if you do, send me more on that.*

I read the message three times, looking for something extra that isn't there. She's all business, and I can hardly blame her for that. Since she can tell I read the message, I respond with, *Will do.*

Do I still plan to meet with the Miami-Dade board of directors? I turn it over and over in my mind. It would be so much easier to go back to New York, to pick up where I left off as if none of this ever happened. Before I met Carmen, that's exactly what I would've done. I would've been on a plane within hours of hearing from the new board chair.

But here I am, still in Miami, and why is that exactly?

I think about the first time I saw Carmen, standing in the blazing sun waiting for me outside the hospital. I think about going to get her out of jail and how adorably undone she was by spending time in that cell. I smile, recalling how her hair had gone from ruthlessly straight to wildly curly in the two hours since I'd last seen her thanks to my convertible and the humidity. I thought she was stunning the first time I saw her, but even more so the second time, when her prim, perfect veneer had been upset by her time in jail.

I remember her telling me she'd never even been to detention before she met me and landed in jail less than an hour later. God, she was adorable that day, so frazzled and worried about her parents finding out she'd been detained. What a refreshing change of pace she was from the start, unlike anyone I've ever met.

I recall finding out she is a widow and wanting to know everything about what she went through and discovering, one detail at a time, how she survived it with her particular brand of strength, courage and determination. In many ways, she reminds me of my mother. She would love Carmen. Almost as much as I do.

That thought stops me short.

Hell, *I love her*. Is it too soon? Absolutely. Does that matter? Absolutely not. I love her, and I think, maybe, she may love me, too. Why else would she feel it's so vital to take a step back, to protect herself from whatever damage I may inflict on her with my ongoing turmoil? If she didn't care, she wouldn't do that. She would've stuck around, enjoyed the time we have left, and walked away unscathed when I leave.

After the amazing time we've spent together, neither of us will walk away from this unscathed. The thought of never seeing her again is unimaginable to me, and the possibility of that fills me with panic. I pick myself up off the floor and, hoping Ginger has taken off by now, go downstairs to get a new key.

I've got a lot to do and not much time left to do it.

How Much I Feel

Carmen

I hardly sleep, tossing and turning and thinking of Jason and Tony and dreading having to put my life back together once again. I hate being back in this place of grief and loss. No, it's not the same as when I lost Tony, but the ache is all too familiar and unwelcome. I try to shake it off as I go through my morning routine, which includes a stop at Juanita's.

She immediately senses something is up. "Oh no. What happened? Where's your sexy doctor?"

"I . . . Um . . ."

Juanita surprises me when she shuts her window, flips the Open sign to Closed, comes outside to take my hand and marches me inside. In all the years I've been buying coffee from her, I've never been inside.

"What're you doing? This is the busiest time of day for you."

"They'll wait. What's wrong?"

"He's probably going back to New York."

"Que lástima." She hugs me tightly. "Lo siento, mi vida."

I'm determined not to break down, to soldier through this and get to the other side of it as quickly as possible. Two weeks ago today, I didn't even know he existed. I refuse to allow him to ruin the life I worked so hard to put together for myself after the last time my heart was shattered. "I'll be okay. I promise."

Angry customers are knocking on the window, but Juanita doesn't seem to care in the least as she hugs me long and hard. "So many people admire you, amiga. The way you've carried on after losing your sweet husband. Everyone wants to see you happy and smiling the way you've been with that hot doctor. It was a sight for sore eyes."

I frantically blink back tears, determined to press on without them. "Thank you, Juanita. I truly appreciate the support."

"If it doesn't work out with him, you're going to find someone else. I know it. A heart like yours is too big to hold all that love you have inside you. You gotta give it away, amiga."

I didn't know she felt that way about me. "Thank you. That means so much to me." I hug her again. "Now get back to work before you have a riot on your hands."

"Eh." She waves a hand at the window as she hands me my cortadito. "They'll wait. They're addicted."

I laugh because that's the God's honest truth. Like me, they can't get through the day without a shot of Juanita's magic. When I try to pay her, she scowls fiercely at me. I send her a grateful smile and emerge from the shop, feeling the glares from everyone in the long line directed at me as I make my way to my car.

"Don't you be looking at her that way," Juanita says. "I brought her in here, and if you want your fix, you'd better be nice to mi amiga. Now, who's next?"

I smile at her sauciness as I get into the car, perching my coffee carefully in the cupholder because God forbid I should spill it. Juanita's cortadito is liquid-gold deliciousness.

I'm getting ready to pull out of my parking space when Priscilla roars into the lot and comes to a stop next to my car. I'm frozen in place, unable to move or think or breathe or do anything other than drink in the sight of Jason's gorgeous face. I'd have to be blind to miss the yearning in the lovely eyes that always look at me with affection and desire. Now is no different. He conveys so much with just a look.

He gets out of his car, comes over to mine, and knocks on the passenger window. I eye the unlock button warily. It took every ounce of fortitude I could summon last night to take a step back from him. If I let him into my car, I'll be right back to square one.

I glance at the passenger window. He's bent at the waist, staring at me imploringly through the glass. Every part of me wants every part of him. Even as I curse my own lack of willpower, I unlock the door.

He gets in, closes the door and turns to face me.

I crank the AC so we won't roast to death.

A quick glance tells me he's tired—as tired as I am. He didn't shave, and his hair looks like he "brushed" it with an impatient sweep of his fingers.

"Are you okay?" he asks.

"Sure. Never better." I take a sip of my coffee so I'll have something to do with my hands besides reach for him and beg him to stay with me forever.

"You willing to share your fix?" Offering a small smile, he tips his chin toward the cup.

I hand it over to him and try not to react to the moan that's become far too familiar to me for reasons that have nothing to do with cortadito.

He gives the cup back to me. "Ginger was at my hotel last night."

I gasp, nearly spill the coffee all over myself and realize my efforts to remain detached from him are for naught. I can no more remain detached from him than I can suddenly decide to quit breathing. "What did she want?"

"Who knows? I told her to get lost."

"How'd she find you?"

"That's a very good question, but I didn't care enough to ask. I just wanted her gone."

"Wow, she came down here to find you. That's pretty crazy." Suddenly, I'm chilled to the bone and not just because of the AC, which I turn down to low.

"She's nothing to me, Carmen. Surely you have to believe me when I tell you that."

I tell myself it doesn't matter. He's leaving. I'm not. I know he doesn't feel anything for her, so I want to not care that she came here looking for him. Except I do care. I care more than I've cared about anything in years, despite my futile effort to step back from him and this crazy situation. With him sitting next to me, his familiar scent filling my senses and reminding me of so many intimate moments with him, remaining removed is all but impossible. "I do. I believe you."

"I miss you."

"You saw me yesterday."

"I missed sleeping with you last night. I slept like shit."

"I did, too."

"I know it's a lot to ask of you, but will you please give me a couple of days to figure out my life before you write me off forever?"

"I haven't written you off forever. I'm just trying to avoid, you know . . ."

"Heartbreak?"

"Yeah," I reply, sighing. "I've had enough of that for one lifetime."

"The very last thing I want to do is cause you more. I hope you believe that as well."

"I do."

"The offer from New York was unexpected. It's thrown a wrench into things, and I'm trying to figure out how to proceed. You're very much a factor in my decision-making process."

"Which I absolutely should not be. Nine days, Jason. You've known me for *nine days*."

As if he can't resist the need to touch me for another second, he takes my hand and brings it to his lips, kissing my palm and the inside of my wrist, where he has to feel the thundering beat of my heart in the throbbing pulse point. "The best nine days of my whole life, Carmen. Hands down."

"Really?" My voice sounds high and squeaky.

"Really. I need you to have some faith in me, and in us. We're going to figure something out, okay?"

Hope swells within me, a wave of happiness so big I couldn't hold it back even if I wanted to, which I don't. I nod, because what else can I do but put my faith in him?

He leans across the center console but can go only so far.

I have to meet him halfway, so the choice is mine to make. As if there's any choice at all. I lean in.

His hand curls around my neck as his lips meet mine in a kiss that starts off sweet but quickly becomes about frenzied need and intense desire.

We resurface many minutes later, hands buried in each other's hair, lips tingling and other parts on fire for more.

"Whoa."

His single word sums it up rather well.

"I have to go to work." I glance at the clock. I have fifteen minutes to get there on time and will need every one of them at this hour.

"Me too." He kisses the back of my hand and lets it go, seeming reluctant. "Can I call you later?"

I think about that before shaking my head. "Call me when you figure out what you're doing. We'll go from there."

He groans dramatically and drops his head back against the seat. "You drive a hard bargain, Ms. Giordino, but okay. We'll do this your way." He rolls his head my way and looks at me with those beautiful eyes. "Don't fall for someone else before you hear from me, okay?"

My lips quiver from the effort not to laugh. I sense he wouldn't appreciate that right now. "I'll try not to."

"You do that." He reaches for the door handle but looks at me one more time, seeming to take visual inventory, before he gets out of the car and closes the door behind him.

I watch him walk over to join Juanita's line, noting the subtle hunch of his shoulders as he goes. While I hate to see him hurting, it helps to know we're both unsettled. I'm thankful for that as I leave the parking lot and head for work, running frightfully late.

CHAPTER 22

CARMEN

Traffic is more of a monster than usual, and I end up jogging on heels from the parking lot, juggling my cortadito, my work bag and my purse. The effort is worth it when I roll into the executive suite five minutes after nine.

Fortunately only Mona sees me come in late, and I doubt she'll tell anyone.

"Good morning," she says, apparently chipper in the morning, which is super annoying to a non-morning person.

"Morning."

"Did Dr. Northrup's sister find him last night?"

That stops me dead in my tracks. "His *sister*?"

"She's very pretty. I could see the resemblance, actually."

"That's interesting, because Dr. Northrup doesn't have a sister."

Mona stares at me, her eyes wide. "He *doesn't*?"

"He only has a brother, so it seems you gave his location to someone who isn't actually a family member, Mona. That could've been very dangerous if she'd been looking to harm him."

I feel like shit when her eyes fill with tears, but it's true. She can't just give out a colleague's personal information without their permission.

"Is he . . . He's all right?"

"He's fine, but he was extremely unhappy to be confronted by the woman who caused the scandal in New York."

"*That's* who she was?"

"That's who she was."

"Oh my goodness. I'm so sorry. I feel terrible." She looks up at me with eyes gone shiny with tears. "You won't tell Mr. Augustino, will you?"

I offer a smile and a wink. "You kept my secret, and I'll keep yours."

"Oh, thank you, Carmen. You're the best. I'm so glad you've joined our team."

"Me too." I go into my office and get settled for the day. I send Jason a quick text to tell him that Mona was the one who gave his "sister" the address of his hotel.

Well, that's one mystery solved. Leave it to Ginger to lie about everything.

I told Mona she shouldn't be giving out that info without permission. She's very sorry.

Tell her no worries.

I put down my phone and get started with my email where I find a message from Terri, the nurse administrator friend of Jason's from New York.

Hi Carmen,

Here are some more testimonials that came in from former patients and colleagues of Dr. Northrup's. I heard the board here has offered him his job back. Tell him we're all elated to hear that and can't wait to have him back where he belongs. I texted him, but haven't heard from him. Hope he's holding up all right in the midst of all this nonsense. Anyway, I'm not sure if you still need the testimonials, but figured I'd send them along. Thanks for all you've done to help Dr. Northrup.

All best,

Terri

I feel absolutely dead inside reading that message, hearing how excited his former colleagues are that he's returning to them. I read through the testimonials from thankful patients, family members of patients who died despite Jason's heroic efforts and colleagues who sing his praises as a physician and human being.

I add each one of them to the PowerPoint presentation, which includes a cascading array of testimonials. I realize there're probably too many of them, but in light of what we're trying to accomplish, I include them all.

I add the bullet points Jason emails me about his research, save the file on our internal server and share a link to the latest version with Mr. Augustino.

An hour later, he comes to my office, knocking on my open door before he steps inside. "Good morning."

"Morning."

"I saw the latest version of the presentation. It's outstanding. Kudos, Ms. Giordino."

"Thank you. I'm glad you're happy with it."

He sits in my visitor chair, seeming morose. "It may all be for nothing. Did you hear that New York invited him to return?"

"I did hear that."

"I spoke with the chair of our board earlier, and she feels it would be inappropriate for us to proceed with him in light of this development."

My heart sinks. "So that's it? It's over, then?"

"I believe it is."

"Oh, well." I can't break down in front of my boss. I won't cry at work. But I want to. I really, really want to.

"You did great work on this project, and I'm pleased to offer you the director's position if you're still interested. You'd be charged with hiring your own assistant to replace yourself."

Crushing lows, soaring highs. I can't keep up with this roller-coaster ride I'm on. "I . . . Yes, that would be wonderful. Thank you for the confidence you've placed in me."

"The board is interested in doing more of the kind of community outreach you coordinated for Dr. Northrup. I'd like you to oversee that as part of your new duties."

"I can do that."

"Excellent." He leans across my desk to shake my hand. "Congratulations, Ms. Giordino."

"Please, call me Carmen."

"I'd be happy to. I'm Roy."

I should be thrilled. I've been promoted in my second week, I get to hire my own assistant and I'm on a first-name basis with the hospital president. But I'm not thrilled. I'm heartbroken for myself while happy for Jason. The wide array of emotions is almost too much to process.

A wrong has been righted. That's what matters here, or so I tell myself.

I force myself to keep my emotions locked away until I can fully wallow in them later. "I talked to my parents, and they said to let them know when you and Mrs. Augustino would like to come in for dinner. They'd be delighted to have you."

"That's wonderful. My wife will be so excited. She loves the Cuban food at Giordino's. I'm partial to the Italian myself. Our anniversary is on July twelfth."

"I'll get you a reservation for seven?"

"That's perfect. Thanks again."

"Anytime."

Mr. Augustino—Roy—leaves my office, and I try to refocus on the notes the former director left me about ongoing projects, upcoming events and other things that'll require my attention as the new director.

I can't concentrate on anything, so I decide to take a walk to clear my mind. I wander through the hospital, getting to know the place as I go. In the elevator, I randomly choose the fourth floor, which is labor and delivery. I pass the closed doors to the neonatal intensive care unit where premature babies fight for life. I watch as an elated couple is escorted to the elevator from the other side of the long hallway. The woman is in a wheelchair with a baby in her arms as the man follows behind her, carrying the baby's car seat.

I wonder what it would be like to be that woman, on my way home to start the next phase of my life with my child and the man who loves me. If Tony had lived, that would've been us, at least twice by now, if not three times. We debated how many children we wanted. Two for sure, with more open for negotiation we never got to have.

On the sixth floor, where the oncology department is housed, I encounter a young male patient attached to a rolling IV stand, walking with a nurse, who encourages him to take a few more steps as he grimaces in pain. I say a silent prayer for his full recovery.

On the seventh floor, I land in the pediatric ICU where I ask for Mateo Diaz at the nurses' station. They direct me to room 718. I knock on the door, and Sofia jumps up to greet me with a hug. She speaks to me in Spanish, thanking me for coming by and singing the praises of Dr. Northrup, who saved her little boy's life.

Mateo, dwarfed by the big hospital bed, is awake and alert.

"How's he doing?" I ask her in Spanish.

"So much better. Thank God."

"That's wonderful news. And how are you?"

She hesitates before answering. "All that matters is that my baby is alive."

"What do you need, Sofia? What can we do to help?"

With tears in her eyes, she leads me to the doorway so we won't be overheard by her son. "I lost my job because I was absent, my rent is due and I have no idea what to do."

I pull out my phone. "Give me your number. I'll talk to some people and see what can be done to help."

"You've already done so much. I heard you're the one who arranged for Dr. Northrup to come to the clinic. Without him . . ." She glances at Mateo. "I don't know what we would've done. He donated his services and paid for the hospital costs out of his own pocket. Did you know that?"

"I didn't, but I'm not surprised." If I hadn't already been most of the way in love with Jason Northrup, I would be now.

"It's enough, Carmen. I'll figure out the rest."

"Give me your number anyway. People will want to help."

Reluctantly, she gives me her number, which I type into my contacts. "I'll see what I can do."

"God bless you."

I hug her, and when I pull back, Jason is standing there. For a second, I'm confused because I thought he was going to the clinic this morning.

"How's my friend Mateo doing?" he asks Sofia.

"He's so much better."

"I heard that. I'm so glad. I'll be in to see him in just a minute. Carmen, may I have a word, please?"

"Sure." I squeeze Sofia's arm as I follow Jason into the hallway.

I want to hug him and kiss him and thank him for what he's done for Mateo. I want to ask him if he's heard that the Miami-Dade board has deferred to New York's wishes to have their star pediatric neurosurgeon back. But I don't do any of those things. Rather, I wait to hear what he has to say.

"I've got to go to New York."

My heart drops like a lead sinker in a murky pond. "Okay."

"They've got a three-year-old girl with the same tumor Mateo had. I'm flying up to operate on her, but I'll be back as soon as I can."

I bite my lip and nod, intent on getting through this without becoming emotional. "I hope it goes well."

"I do, too. Her situation is a bit more complex than Mateo's was."

His golden eyes gleam with the anticipation of a complicated new case. He's clearly in his element.

"Mr. Augustino offered me the PR director's job this morning."

"Seriously? Carmen, that's amazing. Congratulations." I can tell he wants to kiss me but restrains himself out of deference to where we are. "One week on the job and you're already getting promoted."

"I think it's more because the director decided not to come back after her maternity leave."

"That's not why. It's because Augustino knows what an asset you are to his team. He never would've offered it to you if he wasn't pleased with your work."

"I suppose that's true."

"It's entirely true. I'm really happy for you and super proud."

"Thanks." I bask in the glow of his approval for a few final seconds while wondering if I'll ever see him again. When he gets back to New York where his old job is waiting for him, what reason will he have to come back here? I can ship him the stuff he left at my place, I guess. "Good luck with the surgery."

"Thanks. I'm going to leave Priscilla in the parking lot here and take an Uber to the airport. Just in case you see her out there."

"Okay."

"I'll text you when I can."

I nod and start to walk away, determined to hold my head up and soldier on even if my heart is breaking.

"Hey, Carmen?"

I turn back to him, raising a brow while drinking in the sight of him and trying to commit him to memory. As if I could ever forget.

"I *will* be back."

I nod and continue on my way, clinging to my composure as I go. I can do this. I've been through worse. I'll get through this, too. When I return to my office, I text Abuela and Nona, telling them about Sofia's situation and asking what we can do to help.

Abuela responds first. *We're on it, querida.*

Thanks for letting us know, Nona adds.

Next question, Abuela says, *is how are YOU?*

I'm ok. Jason is going back to NY to do a surgery, but he said he'll be back. I guess we'll see.

Ay, mija, Abuela says, *I know this is so hard, but that boy is falling for you. We all saw that. He'll be back.*

I hope you're right.

When have you ever known me not to be?

You had to toss her a softball, Nona says in her usual dry way.

I laugh out loud, delighted as always by them. *Love you guys. Thanks for always being there for me—and everyone else, too. I want to be you two when I grow up.*

You're already the best part of us, Nona says. *We love you, too. We'll get something going for Sofia.*

I reply with the kiss-face emoji. Sofia won't know what hit her when the two of them mobilize on her behalf.

I force myself to focus on work, to push everything else to the side and give my all to the job I'm being paid to do. I want to make Mr. Augustino glad he asked me to be the director. I work with HR to start the recruiting process for an assistant. I write a press release about one of our cardiologists winning a prestigious award and another for a nurse supervisor who's retiring after forty years at the hospital. I interview them both and pour my heart and soul into telling their stories.

Both releases are picked up by various local media outlets, which is a win for me—and the hospital. I also contact Desiree Rivera to thank her for the wonderful story about Jason and his work at the clinic and suggest a follow-up on how well Mateo is doing. She agrees to pitch the idea to her producers.

Days pass in which I do little more than go through the motions—get up, get ready for work, stop at Juanita's, go to the office, chat with Mona, devote all my attention to my work, sit through meetings, rinse and repeat. Several days after Jason left, I have dinner at the restaurant. I'm treated to the full rundown of fundraisers and efforts my grandmothers have put together to help Sofia, who is overwhelmed by their generosity. All the while, I try not to think about Jason, which is easier said than done.

I got one brief text from him the day he left—letting me know he arrived safely in New York and was heading into surgery. Since then? Nothing.

I tell myself he's busy saving lives, doing what he was put on this earth to do. It's the way things should be, even if I miss him more than I ever thought possible. I feel a little guilty about how badly I want him back in Miami, because I know his work and research would probably be better served if he stayed in New York. Guilt aside, though, I miss him so badly I ache with it.

On Friday, the board meets for the day as scheduled. According to Mona, who helped to prepare for the meeting, the matter of Dr. Jason Northrup is not on their agenda. I process that information with the sinking feeling inside that's become all too familiar to me during this seemingly endless week.

The one bright spot is that I get my first real paycheck and stare at the details with a sense of disbelief. I always did well at the restaurant, but this is even better, especially after how hard I worked to get through school. I pay my rent, pay down a chunk of my credit card balance and wallow in the sense of accomplishment that comes with ridding myself of debt.

I spend the weekend alone, holed up in my apartment, licking my wounds and wondering if Jason meant it when he said he'd be back. I relive every minute we spent together, wallowing in details I never want to forget. I watch Desiree's interview with him a hundred times and scroll through the photos I took of him playing dominoes with the old men, eating at Giordino's, drinking at the Fontainebleau bar and sitting on Miami Beach.

When I realize I don't have a single photo of the two of us together, I'm gutted by a feeling of loss so intense it takes me back to the darkest days of my life. I hate returning to that place, even if I continue to tell myself this is nothing like that. I'm learning that heartbreak is heartbreak, regardless of what causes it. With all the photos I took of him for Instagram, how could I not have thought to take a selfie of us together? I call in "sick" to Sunday brunch because I just don't have it in me to answer questions from each of my overly concerned family members.

It doesn't surprise me when my parents and grandmothers arrive at my door Sunday afternoon bearing brunch leftovers, enough food to get me through the week without having to hit the grocery store. That's a welcome relief, as I don't feel like doing anything.

I appreciate that they stay for only half an hour, during which we talk about everything other than the elephant sitting on my chest, before they depart to open for dinner at the restaurant. Once again they give me reason to thank my lucky stars to have been born into a family that cares the way they do, even if there are times I wish they cared a tiny bit less.

By the following Wednesday, I'm convinced my relationship with Jason was nothing more than a figment of my overactive imagination. If it hadn't been for the clothing and personal items he left at my apartment, I'd think I dreamed the entire thing. I've taken to sleeping in one of his dress shirts that still bears the faint scent of his cologne. Don't judge me. I'm trying to be strong, but I miss him, even if my rational self is convinced it's absolutely crazy to feel this way about someone I spent one week with.

It was a really, *really* good week.

I'm at my desk on Thursday when Mona comes into my office and closes the door. I can tell with one look at her that she's bringing me a scoop.

"What's up?"

"The board is meeting in executive session."

"About what?"

"Mr. Augustino said it's a personnel matter and that he couldn't say anything else."

"Okay . . ."

"Debby in the cafeteria said she heard it's about Dr. Northrup."

My heart stops. "Really?"

Mona nods. "She heard he requested the meeting."

I can't. I just can't. If I allow myself to go there . . . "Thanks for letting me know."

"Have you heard anything?"

"I haven't." Mona is dying to know what went down between me and Jason, but I'm not telling her or anyone about that. It's our business, and it's in the past now, anyway.

Her cherubic face falls with disappointment. "Oh. Okay." She clears her throat. "I'll, ah, let you get back to work."

"Thanks, Mona. Close the door when you leave?"

"Of course."

When the door clicks shut, I release a long exhale. My skin feels hot and tight, my heart is beating fast and my mouth is dry. I want to text him and ask if the rumors are true, but if he wanted me to know, he would've told me. I haven't heard anything from him since that one text more than a week ago.

I stand and stretch, walking over to the window that looks down upon the circular driveway where we first met. I think about Priscilla and Betty and my trip to jail, about Jason bailing me out and asking for my help in restoring his damaged reputation. I dream about kissing him and touching him and making love with him, of sleeping in his arms and waking to his handsome face on the pillow next to mine.

I blink back tears and give myself yet another pep talk, the hundredth one in the last week. I was fine before him. I'm determined to be fine after him. It was fun, and I'm glad I met him. I'm relieved to know I can have feelings for a man other than my late husband. These are all good things, and maybe if I keep reminding myself about them, I might just survive this.

CHAPTER 23

Jason

This has been a week straight from hell. The surgery was a cluster that included two follow-up surgeries, and we still didn't get it all, which complicates the child's prospects for recovery. Sometimes it comes down to a choice between getting all the tumor but leaving the patient with no quality of life. I did the very best I could for her, but sometimes my best isn't good enough. At those times, this job can be tough to take.

I met with the new chair of the New York hospital's board of directors, who issued a formal apology for the way I was treated and offered my job back along with a promise that I'll be appointed head of neurosurgery when the current chief retires late next year.

It's a good offer, and I promised to give it careful consideration. I think she expected me to jump at the opportunity to come back. She has no idea that my heart now lives in the Miami sunshine. I miss Carmen so much. More than I've ever missed anyone. I think about her all day every day. I dream about her at night, and I marvel at the way she came stampeding into my life and wiped just about every other thought out of my head that doesn't involve her.

If I'm not working, I'm thinking about her. I wanted to reach out to her, to text her, to call her, to let her know I'm thinking of her and missing her and basically dying for her, but I can't do that until I've made some decisions about where I'm going to work and live. More than anything, I want to be fair to her.

When I learned that the Miami-Dade board took my petition for privileges off their agenda last Friday after hearing New York wanted me back, I panicked that Miami was no longer an option. What did Carmen think when she heard that? Does she even know? Of course she does. Mona knows, so she would've told Carmen if Mr. Augustino didn't.

And then it occurred to me that I needed to take control of this situation and stop letting others make decisions about my career for me. I reached out to Mr. Augustino, told him what I wanted and asked if he could help to make it happen. He said he'd do his best, which is why I'm back in Miami in an Uber on my way to the hospital to meet with the board.

My driver, a young man named Carlo, has the radio cranked to a light rock station and is singing rather loudly in broken English. What he lacks in talent he more than makes up for in enthusiasm.

The traffic is bad as usual. Thanks to Carmen, I know what *usual* looks like around here, and as we make the slow crawl toward the hospital exit, all I can think about is seeing her again, holding her and hoping she still wants me as much as I want her. And more than anything, I hope the presentation she put together on my behalf will sway the Miami-Dade board and convince them to allow me to join their team so I can live and work in her town—the only place in the world where she can truly be happy.

That's what I want for her—happiness. She deserves it more than anyone I've ever met, and I want to be the one to give that to her for the rest of our lives. Of course, I can't tell her that. Not yet anyway. But that's what I want, and if things go well today, I may be able to offer her the first steps toward forever.

I just hope she still wants me after the turmoil I've brought to her life since we met.

A new song comes on the radio, something familiar, but I can't quite place where I've heard it before. Probably in my mom's minivan back when she was driving my brother and me to school and practices and everywhere else. We used to make such fun of the "dorky light rock" she made us listen to in the car. "My car, my music," she used to say, telling us we could pick the songs when we had our own cars.

The song tells the story about a guy whose girl left him because she thought he'd been untrue to her, how he's haunted by her, would give anything to be with her. I'm riveted as I listen to Carlo sing the chorus, "That's how much I feel." But it's the last verse that really gets to me, the part where we find out the guy is married now, has been for years, but sometimes when he makes love to his wife, he still sees the face of the one who got away.

I'm struck by complete and utter panic, knowing that'll be me if I lose Carmen. I'll be haunted by her forever.

No matter what happens today with the board, I have to find a way to work it out with her. After spending this last week without her, I have no doubt that what I feel for her is a forever kind of love.

"Sir?"

I snap out of my thoughts to realize Carlo has been trying to get my attention.

"We're here. Miami-Dade General Hospital."

"Thanks, Carlo."

"My pleasure."

I grab my backpack and get out of the air-conditioned car into the stifling heat that I'll forever associate with Carmen and my first week in Miami. I'm wearing a light-blue dress shirt with a navy tie and khakis. Inside, I find the first men's room and pull the white coat I brought from New York out of my backpack. It has JASON NORTHRUP, MD embroidered on it. I put it on and check my reflection in the mirror. If I'm going to meet with the board and ask for a job on their neurosurgery team, I'm going to do it looking like the highly qualified physician I am.

I want to go straight to Carmen's office to tell her what's going on, but I recall my vow to stay away until I have something definite to report. I take the elevator to the executive offices on the fifth floor and take a right toward the boardroom when everything in me wants to go left to her.

First things first.

With my hand on the boardroom door handle, I take a deep breath and release it before entering the room where Mr. Augustino asked me to meet him ahead of the board members joining us.

He shakes my hand. "Good to see you again, Dr. Northrup."

"You as well. Thank you for seeing me and arranging the meeting."

"I'll confess to being surprised to hear that you still wanted to meet with our board. I was under the impression that you'd be resuming your duties in New York."

"They've offered me my old job back and promised a promotion to department head when the current chief retires at the end of next year."

"That's a pretty sweet offer. Our department head is around your age, so I'm afraid she's probably here to stay for a while."

"I understand."

"You have the chance to be the department head next year in New York."

"Yes."

"And you still want to meet with our board?"

"Yes, sir. Very much so." I suppose he'll find out soon enough why I want so badly to work here.

He gives me a curious look before nodding. "All right then. Have a seat. The board will be joining us in thirty minutes."

"And the presentation Ms. Giordino put together?"

He points to the spot above us where a camera is trained on the screen at the other end of the long table. "It's set to go."

"Thank you again."

"My pleasure. Make yourself comfortable. I'll be back shortly."

While I wait, I pace the length of the long room, thinking about what I want to say to the board and wondering if I'll have something to report to Carmen as soon as today. I sure as hell hope so. I can't wait another day to see her.

I stand at the window, looking out at the driveway where I first laid eyes on her, and think about the conversation I had with my mom last night. I told her about Carmen, caught her up on the goings-on in New York and told her of my plan to ask the Miami-Dade board to consider hiring me after all.

"You're making an awfully big decision based on a woman you've known a very short time. After what happened with Ginger, I just hope you know what you're doing."

I smile, recalling her concern and how I set her mind at ease. "Carmen is nothing like Ginger," I told her. "You're going to love her. This feels right to me, Mom. Nothing has ever felt as right as being with her does. That's all I can tell you." I can't wait to introduce the two most important women in my life to each other.

The minutes go by slowly, as if the clock is moving in the opposite direction. Twenty-five minutes after Mr. Augustino left the room, the door opens and Mona comes in carrying a tray of cookies and other snacks for the meeting. She lets out a gasp when she sees me there.

"Debby in the cafeteria was right! The meeting *is* about you!"

I'm not sure how I feel about being the source of cafeteria gossip, but after withstanding the New York tabloids, that's nothing. "It's good to see you, Mona. Do me a favor?"

"Anything."

"Don't tell Carmen I'm here. I want to surprise her."

"Of course. My lips are sealed." She leans in to whisper. "Good luck, Doc. I hope you get whatever it is you want."

"Thank you."

A short time later, Mr. Augustino returns, and the board members begin filing into the room, a mix of races, genders and ages. I've done my research and know that half of them are physicians, the other half prominent members of the community.

The board chair, a black woman named Dr. Felicia Rider, calls the meeting to order after everyone is seated. "Dr. Northrup, welcome."

"Thank you, Dr. Rider. I appreciate the opportunity to meet with you all."

"You asked for this meeting, so the floor is yours."

Well, here goes nothing. Or everything . . . "Just over two weeks ago, I arrived at Miami-Dade after leaving behind a bit of a mess in New York. You know the details of what happened there. Since that time, the other party involved has reached out to the boards here and in New York and provided updated information about what transpired, so I won't belabor the point. Upon my arrival at Miami-Dade, I was told the board wanted some time to consider my application for privileges. Mr. Augustino assigned the supremely competent new director of public relations, Carmen Giordino, to assist in helping me to acclimate to the local community and to make a case for my employment at your hospital. What follows is the presentation Ms. Giordino prepared for that meeting."

Mr. Augustino signals the person in the AV room. The lights go dark and the screen comes to life with the presentation, which now includes music to accompany the photographs, testimonials, NBC 6 footage and details about my research project.

Then, in a part I haven't seen before, Carmen's voice is recorded to accompany the next few slides. "The American Board of Neurological Surgery defines neurological surgery as constituting 'a medical discipline and surgical specialty that provides care for adult and pediatric patients in the treatment of pain or pathological processes that may modify the function or activity of the central nervous system.'

"Certification requirements by the ABNS include eighty-four months of neurosurgical residency, two years as chief resident, as well as training in a wide variety of disciplines, such as neuropathology, neuroradiology, endovascular or pediatric neurosurgery, to name a few. Neurosurgeons undergo months of training in general patient care areas including trauma surgery, orthopedic surgery, otolaryngology and plastic surgery. To achieve board certification, a neurosurgeon undergoes written and oral exams. In preparation for the oral exam, a neurosurgeon has to log one hundred and twenty-five cases and, after successfully completing the exam, must embark on a quest for lifelong learning and continuous certification.

"Dr. Jason Northrup became board-certified two years after completing his residency and is considered one of the nation's foremost experts in the area of pediatric medulloblastoma, overseeing cutting-edge research into the cause and treatment to combat these common pediatric tumors."

The presentation ends with a photo of me smiling at the group of men at the dominoes table in Little Havana, the picture taking me right back to that wonderful day with Carmen. As the lights come back on, I hold my breath, waiting to hear what their reaction will be.

"Thank you for that outstanding presentation, Mr. Augustino, and pass along our compliments to Ms. Giordino," Dr. Rider says. "Dr. Northrup, I have one remaining question for you, one that I'm sure must be on the minds of my fellow board members. With an offer on the table to return to your previous position, why is it that you're still interested in working here?"

I anticipated this question and thought about how I might reply on the two-hour-and-twenty-minute flight from LaGuardia to Miami. I go with the answer that occurred to me then. "My reasons for wanting to live and work in Miami are personal."

"Fair enough. We appreciate the information as well as your interest in joining the team at Miami-Dade. We'll discuss your application in executive session. Mr. Augustino will notify you of our decision. Thank you, Dr. Northrup."

"Thank you all for your time today."

With Carmen's incredible help, I've done what I can. It's out of my hands now.

CHAPTER 24

Carmen

Concentration is nonexistent when your whole life and any chance at true happiness are on the line. I'm dying to know what's happening in that boardroom, and I'm getting less than nothing done while I wait. Surrendering to the reality that I'm completely useless today, I've again turned my desk chair toward the window that overlooks the parking lot and the activity at the main entrance.

I stare out that window for what has to be an hour as I try to remain calm while I wait to hear something.

"Do you even know what otolaryngology is?"

The sound of his voice electrifies me, and my mood swings from the lowest of lows to the highest of highs in a whiplashing second. Smiling, I say, "It's a medical specialty focused on the ears, nose and throat or, as it applies to you, head and neck surgery." I turn my chair to find him leaning against the doorframe looking handsome, relaxed and dare I say happy.

His smile lights up my world. "Hi."

"Hi there."

"How's it going?" he asks.

"Oh, you know, just another day in paradise. You?"

"Eh," he says with a shrug. "Nothing special except for right now."

"Are you going to tell me how it went with the board, or are you going to make me suffer?"

He raises a brow. "How do you know about the board? I told Mona not to say anything."

"She didn't. Turns out Debby in the cafeteria is an excellent source of information around here."

"So I've heard." He pushes off the doorframe, closes my office door and comes over to sit on my desk, facing me. "It went well with the board, thanks to you and that incredible presentation you put together."

"You gave me a lot to work with." I bite my lip as I stare at him greedily and contemplate the question I most want to ask.

"What?" he asks, giving me an inquisitive look.

"I was just wondering . . ." I clear my throat and force myself to look directly at him, which for me is akin to looking directly into the sun. He makes everything brighter in my world, just by walking into the room.

"What are you wondering, Rizo?"

As always, the nickname makes me swoon. "If you were offered your job back in New York, why did you meet with the board here?"

"You really have to ask that question?"

"Well, yes, I guess I do."

He pushes himself off the desk and surprises the living crap out of me when he drops to his knees in front of me and wraps his arms around me, resting his forehead against my chest.

For a second, I'm too stunned to move, but then my fingers find their way to his hair, and my heart starts beating so fast I fear I might need medical attention. Good thing I'm in a hospital.

After a long moment in which we simply coexist in the relief of being back together, he pulls back to look up at me. "I met with the Miami-Dade board because I want to work *here*. I want to live *here*."

I know the answer to my own question, but I ask it anyway. I want to hear him say it. "Why?"

"Because you're here."

My heart skips a happy beat, and the surge of joy that floods through me leaves me breathless. "You can't make major career decisions based on someone you've known less than a month."

"Too late. I already have."

"Jason . . ."

"Carmen . . ."

I can't believe this is happening, that he's in my office telling me he's rearranged his career and life for me. "This is insanity."

He shakes his head. "No, it's not. It's love. I love you. I want to be with you. I want to be part of your big, fabulous Cuban-Italian family. I want to burn my ass with you on Priscilla's leather seats in the hot South Florida sunshine. I want to be wherever you are."

Overwhelmed by everything he said, I cup his face and stare into the golden-brown eyes that've dazzled me from the start.

"You know what would make this moment absolutely perfect?" he asks with a teasing grin.

"What?"

"If you were to tell me you love me, too, so I'll know I didn't just make a complete fool of myself in front of the Miami-Dade board."

I kiss him with all the love I feel for him, with days' worth of pent-up desire and the elation that comes with seeing a once-hopeless situation become the promise of a future I never dared to dream possible. "I love you, too. I think I have from almost the first second I ever saw you."

"I fell for you when I saw you in that jail cell."

I play-punch his shoulder. "I'm going to murder you if you tell people that."

His laughter is everything. It's my favorite sound. "No, you won't. You love me too much to murder me."

"If you tell my parents I was in jail, I *will* murder you."

"Your secret is safe with me, mi amor. *You* are safe with me. Siempre." *Always.*

I hug him as tightly as I can from my desk chair.

Apparently, that's not good enough for him. With his arms wrapped around me, he stands and brings me with him, leaning back against my desk and holding me close to him as he seems to breathe me in. "I told myself I wouldn't come to you until I knew for sure I was going to be able to work and live here, but I lacked the willpower to stay away after missing you so much."

"I'm glad you didn't stay away. I missed you, too. So, so much."

"I don't know what's going to happen with the board. They might say no out of deference to New York. I honestly have no idea how it's going to play out. All I know is I want to be with you, and if I can't work here, I'll find something else."

"But your research . . ."

"I'll start over if I have to."

"I can't believe you'd do all this for me."

"Really? You can't? Do you not have any idea how awesome you are? How smart and funny and sexy and courageous? If you could see yourself through my eyes, you'd have no doubt whatsoever as to why I'm willing to chuck it all so I can be with you."

"That makes me feel very lucky."

"We both got lucky the day Mr. Augustino sent you out to babysit me."

"God, I was so mad that he made me do that. The last thing I wanted to be told to do on the first day of my first real job after years of school was to babysit the new neurosurgeon. And then when you showed up in Priscilla, with Betty riding shotgun, and slipped me a fifty to deal with her . . . You're lucky I didn't stab you right then and there."

He rocks with silent laughter. "I had no idea my life was in danger that morning."

"Be glad I didn't have a knife with me."

"My little hellcat. Just when I think I've seen all sides to you, here comes another one."

"Don't mess with me."

"Duly noted. Besides, I'd much rather kiss you."

I know I should stop this, since I'm at work after all, but I don't stop it. Rather, I fully participate, wrapping my arms around his neck, opening my mouth to his tongue and rubbing shamelessly against his erection. It's the best kiss with him yet, because it's laced with the promise of forever.

"We need to stop before this gets out of hand," he whispers against my lips.

"It got out of hand about ten minutes ago."

His low chuckle rumbles against my kiss-swollen lips. "How do you feel about taking sick at work?"

"In general or today?"

"Today in particular."

"I'm feeling rather lightheaded, short of breath and feverish. My heart is acting up a bit, too."

He affects a solemn expression as he places one hand on my forehead and the other against the throbbing pulse point in my throat. "I prescribe an afternoon in bed to deal with these worrisome symptoms. Doctor's orders."

"If we do this, Mona will never let us forget it."

"I have a feeling Mona loves a good happy ending as much as the next gal."

"You want to find out?"

"More than I've ever wanted anything."

"Let's do it."

"Oh, we're going to do it, all right."

"Jason! Stop. Let me get out of here with a shred of dignity, will you?"

"You might have to go ahead of me. You've got me all worked up."

"I've got *you* worked up? I was in here minding my own business before you showed up."

"You, ah, might want to fix your hair, and your blouse is all . . ." He rolls his hand as he points to my top, which is indeed askew.

I do the best I can to put myself back together, tucking my black-and-white polka-dot blouse back into black dress pants and running my fingers through my hair to restore order. "Better?"

"Well, no. I like you better when you're all messed up. But it'll do to get you out of here with your dignity intact."

I grab my purse, keys and phone. "Let's go."

He follows me out of my office. We catch a lucky break that Mona is away from her desk when we reach the outer lobby.

"How much you wanna bet she's in the cafeteria telling Debby that you're in my office?" I ask him.

"You'd win that bet."

We're in the elevator before I release the breath I held while we made our escape. On the walk to the parking lot, I send an email to Mona, letting her know I've left for the day because I'm not feeling well.

"It's the only time I'll ever ask you to lie for me," Jason says, tuning in to my discomfort.

"This is what happens when I get in bed with the devil. I do time in jail, lie and play hooky."

"You know what rhymes with hooky?"

I lose it laughing and elbow him in the gut. "Shut up."

"Admit it. Life is more interesting with me around."

"I'll admit no such thing so as not to encourage you to lead me even further astray."

"Oh, baby, the places I want to lead you." He takes my hand and walks toward Priscilla. Before I can ask about my car, he says, "I'll bring you back in the morning."

With an entire afternoon and evening to spend with him, work is the last thing I care about. When we're in the car, I text my mother to tell her that Jason is back in Miami and angling for a job at Miami-Dade because *he wants to be wherever I am*. I send that text and smile at the thought of the news ripping through my family.

They'll be as thrilled as I am, which makes me even happier than I already am.

"What're you doing over there?" he asks when we're stopped at a light.

"Telling my family you're back so they'll leave me alone."

"Good thinking, because we're not going to want to be disturbed for a couple of days."

"A couple of *days*? I have to work tomorrow!"

"You're very sick. You need rest and fluids. Lots of fluids."

I snort with laughter. "That is so *disgusting*!"

"Nothing disgusting about it, baby."

He gets us back to my place as fast as he possibly can and parks in my space. Then he looks over at me. "You haven't had anyone else parking in my visitor spot while I was gone, have you?"

I roll my eyes. "Please. It took me five years to find you. It would've taken me longer than a week to replace you."

"You're never replacing me."

As we get out of the car and go upstairs, we manage to keep our hands to ourselves. But once that door clicks shut behind us, all bets are off. We pull at clothes and yank on buttons and zippers and swear like sailors with frustration when the clothes fight back against our clumsy attack.

I laugh when my head and right arm get stuck inside my blouse.

"It's not funny!" he says. "Do something!"

"You're the surgeon. Figure it out."

He gets me free of the fabric and makes love to me the first time right there in the foyer, with me pressed against the wall still wearing my bra and with his pants around his ankles.

"Oh God, Carmen." He releases a deep breath. "I've been a fucking mess thinking I blew it with you."

"I'm still here, and I love you. I love you, Jason."

Now that I can tell him that, I want to say it so many times he won't ever forget it.

The second time we make it to my bed. We're napping after the third time when Jason hears his cell phone is ringing in the other room. He disentangles from me and runs naked from the bedroom as I laugh at him from the bed.

He brings the phone back to bed. "Three-oh-five area code."

My heart stops.

He puts the call on speaker. "Dr. Northrup."

"I'm so glad I caught you. This is Roy Augustino."

Jason sits on the bed and takes hold of my hand. "Hi, Mr. Augustino."

I grip his hand, close my eyes and hope for the best.

"The board has asked me to extend an offer of employment. I've emailed a formal offer that I hope will meet with your approval. I consulted with the board in New York. We agree that we need to keep you in our family, and you should be able to decide where it is you want to work."

I open my eyes to look into his, which are glowing with happiness.

"Thank you. I'll take a look and let you know."

"Outstanding. Assuming the offer is sufficient, we set your official start date as a week from Monday, to give you time to work out housing."

"Perfect. Thank you very much."

"My pleasure. I hope I'll soon be saying welcome aboard, Dr. Northrup."

"I'll be in touch and hopefully will see you next Monday."

"Sounds good."

He puts the phone on the bedside table and slides into my outstretched arms.

"Congratulations."

"There's no way this would've happened without you and everything you did."

"I don't believe that."

"It's one hundred percent true. You make the difference in every possible way."

We kiss like two people who just got the keys to forever.

"I love you, Carmen."

"I love you, too, Jason."

"That's the best news I've had all day."

EPILOGUE

Jason

Two days before the one-year anniversary of meeting Carmen, I wake up in bed with her like I do every day now that she's unofficially officially moved in with me. Since her grandmothers would, in her words, "have a brain hemorrhage that you'd have to operate on" if they knew we're living together, we haven't actually told them we're cohabitating.

Carmen thinks we're fooling them, which is what she needs to believe in order to actually live with me. I'm under no such illusions where her grandmothers are concerned. From what I've observed, they know everything before it happens, but far be it from me to say or do anything that would make Carmen uncomfortable in our new home.

After I bought the condo we both loved in Brickell, I asked her to move in with me almost right away. She turned me down repeatedly, even as we spent every night together, either at her place or mine. We kept clothes, toothbrushes and personal items at both places, and as I told her, we were wasting money by paying for two homes when we need only one.

On the six-month anniversary of the day we met, I took her to the Bahamas for a long weekend, during which I presented her with her own set of keys to my condo over a romantic dinner on the beach. "Move in with me. *Please.*"

I could tell from the way she looked at me that she was wavering, so I went all in.

"I love you more than Priscilla. I want us to have every minute we can together."

"You really love me more than Priscilla?"

"I've told you that before."

"No, you haven't."

"Well, I do. You should know that."

"We don't already spend every minute we can together?"

"It could be more." I stuck my lip out. "Don't you *want* to live with me?"

"Of course I do, but . . ."

I groaned dramatically. "Ugh, the worst word *ever* invented. *But.*"

She laughed at my agony. She does that a lot, but that's okay. She can do whatever she wants as far as I'm concerned. I reached across the table for her hand. "Talk to me, Rizo. Tell me what's on your mind."

"It's really important to me that I pay my own way. If I move in with you, you'll want to pay for everything, and I don't want that."

"Fine. Negotiate." At this point, I would have signed the deed to the place over to her if it would mean we'd share an address.

"You paid for the condo. I pay for everything else."

"No."

"Just no?"

"I'm not letting you pay when we go out for dinner or when I take you away to the Bahamas or anywhere else for that matter."

"I pay for utilities, cable, Wi-Fi, groceries. Nonnegotiable."

"Do I get to pay for my own dry cleaning?"

She raised the eyebrow that cuts me down to size every time. "You aren't making fun of me by any chance, are you?"

"Never."

"Sure you aren't . . . You can pay for all the dry cleaning since your guy got that veneer stain off my navy suit. Clearly you're better at picking dry cleaners than I am."

"All right, but I'm allowed to pay for surprise extras anytime I want. Nonnegotiable." Have I ever had more fun in my life than I do with her? Nope. Never.

"Fine."

"Fine." And then the sand beneath me seemed to shift. "Wait . . . Did you just agree to move in with me?"

"I think I did."

I let out a whoop that had other beachfront diners looking at us.

"Sit down, Jason."

I didn't realize I'd jumped out of my seat. "Yes, dear."

"One more thing."

"What's that?"

"You cannot, under any circumstances, tell my grandmothers."

"They won't hear it from me."

"And you can be the one to tell my father."

"Wait, *what*?"

She lost it laughing, and sure enough, she made me tell Vincent we were moving in together.

"What took you so long to convince her?" Vincent asked, shocking me. I was prepared for disapproval, but I suppose when you've watched your only child go through the pits of despair, seeing her happy again mellows a guy.

"She drives a very hard bargain."

"That's my girl," Vincent said, glowing with paternal pride.

I love him and Viv, as well as Nona and Abuela, as if they're my own family. Vincent has been giving me bartending lessons so I can "make myself useful" around the place. It's nice to have a father again after so many years mostly estranged from my own.

I hear from Terri, my former colleague in New York, that Howard and Ginger are "working on their marriage." I give the guy credit. He's far more forgiving than I would've been in his position, but I'm not one to judge. Besides, I've got far bigger things to think about today than people who no longer matter to me. I've got so many new people in my life I can hardly keep them all straight. But I do make the effort, which Carmen appreciates.

I've asked the entire family to come to brunch today, even the cousins who live in New York. I think they know why I asked, but the one person who hasn't got the faintest clue is my beloved. Carmen thinks they're all here on a routine visit. She even organized an outing with her cousins last night to the iconic Ball & Chain nightclub on Calle Ocho and actually made it to midnight before telling me I had twenty minutes to get her to bed before she fell over.

My girl can't hang late at night, which is fine with me. There's nowhere I'd rather be than in bed with her.

Today I'm wearing one of the four-pocket guayabera shirts she bought me for Christmas, but she's had no luck convincing me to try Cuban cigars. You can take the doctor out of New York, but he's still a doctor *and* a nonsmoker. My Spanish has gotten much better and my comprehension improves with every month I spend living in Miami. The more I hear, the more I understand, and Carmen enjoys teaching me.

My mom and brother are in town, too, but I wisely keep them hidden until it's showtime. Carmen met them when we went home to Wisconsin for an after-Christmas visit last winter, and just as I predicted, my mom adores her—and vice versa. Having them here would be a dead giveaway that something's up, and I want Carmen to be completely surprised.

I'm quite sure she's actually forgotten that Tuesday is our one-year meet-iversary, but I'm used to her forgetting. I'm the one who's reminded her the other eleven months. My plan is actually contingent on her not remembering.

I also invited Mateo and his mother, Sofia, who now works as a waitress at Giordino's, to join us for brunch. Carmen's family has fully embraced the single mother and her son, who's doing so much better. In consultation with his oncological team, I keep a close eye on him with regular exams and scans. So far, so good.

It's Nona's turn to host, and she's gone all out with the eggplant parm I'm addicted to, along with Carmen's favorite, chicken marsala, as well as a massive antipasto that everyone attacks before we're seated for the main courses.

Somehow, I manage to actually eat, but only so Carmen won't be suspicious. I've become well known around here for my ravenous appetite. I think that's the thing her grandmothers love best about me, that I'm always hungry for whatever they're dishing up. I've become a complete snob when it comes to Cuban and Italian food. Nothing ever measures up to Giordino's.

I spend more time than ever at the gym to offset the uptick in delicious food I'm consuming these days at the restaurant and at home. Carmen is an amazing cook, and long before she officially moved in, she said my kitchen inspired her, which is fine with me.

She loves to cook. I love to eat. Win-win.

I look over at her, talking in her animated way with her cousin Dee. I first met Dee when we went up to New York for a long weekend in the spring so I could officially move out of my apartment there. We also had dinner with many of my former colleagues, who wanted to meet the woman who'd lured me to Miami.

She told them I was easily led, which is true. I had a choice between being happy with her or miserable without her. In the end, it was a no-brainer.

I'm so glad Miami-Dade came through with privileges, because commuting to Fort Lauderdale or Palm Beach would've been a bitch.

I would've done it if I'd had to. We're both thankful I don't have to and that we can grab lunch together a couple of times a week in the hospital cafeteria, where we're careful not to give Debby anything new to talk about.

She's a good egg, who's become a friend to both of us, as have Mona and many other people we work with.

Apparently, Mr. Augustino suspected that Carmen was the reason I wanted to relocate, but we had no idea until Carmen finally worked up the nerve to tell him we're involved, and he said he'd known that for months. He congratulated her on finding new love after everything she went through in the past.

It's going to have to be one hell of a wedding to accommodate Carmen's massive family and all the friends we've made together and separately.

Yesterday afternoon, I took care of one last thing that had to be done before today. I went to see Tony's parents. I've gotten to know them fairly well over the last year, as they're very much in Carmen's life. I wouldn't have it any other way, and I want them to know they'll always be important to both of us.

I thought about calling first but decided to just drop by the way Carmen does anytime we're in the neighborhood.

When she came to the door, Josie seemed surprised to see me there alone. "Come in." She kissed my cheek and took me by the hand to lead me into the cool comfort of her home. "This is a nice surprise."

"Is Len home?"

"He is. Let me get him."

She told me to have a seat in the family room, where I was hit by a flurry of nerves as I took in the handsome, smiling face of Carmen's first husband. They have Tony's official police photo and a shadowbox containing his awards on display on the mantel over the fireplace. I studied the man whose likeness has become so familiar to me and hoped he'd approve of me being in his parents' home to talk about my plans to propose to his beloved wife.

"Hey, Doc," Len said when he came in from the pool area.

I stood to shake his hand. A lot of the people in Carmen's life call me Doc, which is fine with me. I like that they've given me a nickname. That means they like me. After some initial hesitation on his part, Len has come around to being happy for Carmen—and for me. At least I think he is. "Good to see you."

"You too. How about a cold one?"

"I won't say no to that."

He got beers for the two of us and an ice water for his wife. "Is everything all right with Carmen?"

"She's great. Maria and Dee have her out shopping this afternoon, so I figured I'd come by."

"We're so glad you did," Josie said.

Here goes, I thought. "I want you both to know how much I appreciate how welcome you've made me feel since Carmen and I have been together. That means so much to me, and I know it does to her, too."

"She means everything to us, and you make her happy," Len said. "That's obvious to everyone who knows her."

"She's the best thing to ever happen to me." I paused before I added, "I'm painfully aware that the only reason I get to be happy with her is because of the worst thing to ever happen to you."

"Life goes on," Josie said softly. "Somehow the sun keeps rising and setting, and the years go by, and you keep breathing. Our Tony loved Carmen with his whole heart. The only thing he'd care about is her safety and happiness. We both think he'd like you."

"I'm glad you think so." I rubbed my damp palms on my shorts. "I wanted you to know that I'm going to propose to her during brunch tomorrow."

Josie gasped, and at first I wasn't sure if it was a happy gasp. "That's so wonderful, Jason. I told Len after brunch last week that it was only a matter of time before you two tied the knot."

"Congratulations," Len said. "That's great news."

"Thank you for coming here to see us first," Josie said. "It means so much to us."

"Carmen loves you. You'll always be part of us. I give you my word on that. Our future children will be very lucky to have you as grandparents."

Josie wiped away tears and came over to me.

I stood to hug her.

"Take good care of our beautiful daughter."

"I will. Always."

Now the big moment is upon me, and I'm hit with a crisis of confidence. Is proposing to her in front of everyone really the right thing to do? I debated this for months and decided she'd want the people we love to be part of this moment. I just hope I'm right about that.

Nona crooks her finger at me, in on the surprise since I spoke to her, Abuela, Viv and Vin two weeks ago to ask for their permission to propose. They were so excited that I'm not sure how the four of them managed to keep the secret for so long.

"I need to help Nona with something," I tell Carmen.

"Okay."

She's so happy to have Dee in town that I've hardly gotten a word in with her since we sat down to eat. Dee looks like her sister, Maria, and Carmen, but I see Nona in Dee, as well.

"You ready?" Nona asks me.

"I think so."

"Why do you look like you might be having a stroke?"

"Um, because I've never done this before, and I'm rethinking whether I should do it here."

"Pshaw. She'll love it."

"You're sure about that?"

"Hundred percent."

"Well, it doesn't get any more reassuring than that."

"What really matters is that *you're* sure about her."

"One million bazillion percent."

She kisses my cheek. "Then go get your girl."

Fortified by Nona's encouragement, I step into the open part of the horseshoe of tables that's become a familiar part of my weekly routine. I'm at home in this place with these people, and more than anything, I'm at home with the extraordinary woman I met a year ago.

"If I could have your attention, please."

Getting this group to shut up is not a simple task, but since I've never asked for their attention before, they go silent far quicker than expected.

"Carmen, could you come here for a second, please?"

She glances at Maria and at Dee, both of whom shrug. They have no idea what I'm up to. It was a big enough risk to tell her parents and grandmothers. I didn't dare tell her closest cousins.

Carmen gets up and comes around the long table to join me in the middle.

I offer her my hand, and after giving me a confused look, she takes it.

Over my shoulder, I look toward the kitchen where my mom and brother are hiding. "Hey, Mom, Benny, you can come out now."

"What's going on?" Carmen asks, seeming shocked as my mother and brother join the party.

"Everyone, this is my mom, Donna, and my brother, Ben. Mom, Ben, meet Carmen's family—and this isn't even all of them."

Carmen looks up at me, a baffled expression on her gorgeous face. "Jason, why didn't you tell me your mother and brother are in town?"

"Because I wanted to surprise you."

"Well, you have."

"Good, because they're not the only surprise I have for you today." Here we go. As I look at her, at that one-in-a-million face I saw for the first time one year ago this week, all the nerves fade away. The only thing that matters is telling her what she means to me and asking her to be mine forever. "Betty, you're on."

From the kitchen comes the sweet woman I met the night before fate brought Carmen into my life. My beloved is speechless at the sight of Betty, who's wearing the same red dress she had on the day we met Carmen and teeters on her signature spike heels. After Betty sent me a sweet thank-you note and fifty dollars to reimburse me for the money I gave her, Carmen and I have kept in touch with her ever since.

Carmen can't believe what she's seeing. "What the . . . *Betty* . . ."

Betty hugs my shocked beloved and then hands me the velvet box containing the ring. "Love you guys," Betty whispers.

While Carmen is still processing the fact that Betty is here, I drop to one knee.

Carmen lets out an inelegant squeak and then covers her mouth as tears fill her eyes.

"We met one year ago this week."

She shakes her head. "No, it's next week."

I shake my head. "One year ago this coming Tuesday, a momentous day in many ways."

She gives me a stern look, putting me on notice that I'll blow the most important moment of my life if I mention the word *jail*.

"Since that first day when you made me a *prisoner* to your love . . ."

Of course she gets my joke and gasps at how close I came to spilling secrets she's locked into the vault.

"You've changed my life in every possible way in the last year. You turned my nightmare into a fairy tale so beautiful I still can't believe this is my life, that *you* are my life. I love you more than Priscilla, and you know that's a very high honor that only you will ever achieve."

Carmen is laughing even as tears spill down her cheeks.

"I promise to always accommodate your morning crankiness and to fetch the cortadito on the weekends."

As planned, Juanita comes out of the kitchen bearing a take-out cup of her wonder brew that she hands to Carmen as she leans in to kiss Carmen's cheek. "You go, amiga!"

"I can't believe you're here!" Carmen says, clearly astounded.

"I wouldn't have missed this for anything."

I give Carmen's left hand a squeeze to remind her of what we're in the middle of here. "Will you marry me and allow me to spend the rest of my life with you, which is the only place in this world I want to be?"

She's crying and nodding before I'm even done asking. "Yes. *Yes.*"

I slide the two-carat stunner I've had for months onto her finger and stand to hug and kiss her as the family goes crazy clapping, cheering and whistling.

Nona wipes away tears and gives the waitstaff a signal. They come out carrying trays full of champagne flutes that are distributed to the family.

Vincent and Vivian stand next to us and raise their glasses.

"To our beautiful daughter and future son-in-law, Carmen and Jason. Congratulations." Vincent's eyes are bright with unshed tears. "We love you both so very much. May you share a long and happy life together."

"Hear, hear," Len says, raising his glass to us in a toast that means everything to Carmen and to me.

The celebration goes on so long we have to scramble to clean up and get the restaurant ready to open to the public at four. Everyone pitches in, and we make it just in time to admit the first customers.

Carmen and I have barely had a second alone since the big moment, but she's been right by my side as we accepted congratulations and wallowed in the excitement of our loved ones. My mom and Ben left at three to catch a flight home but promised to be back for a longer visit soon.

"Second-best day of my life," I tell her when we're finally on our way home in Priscilla, laden with leftovers that make it so we don't have to grocery shop. We have much better things to do today than squeeze avocados, which has become part of our Sunday ritual.

Her left hand is flat on my leg, the ring sparkling in the late afternoon sun. In another few weeks, it'll be too hot for the convertible. "What's the number one best day?"

"A year ago this coming Tuesday."

"That was better than today?"

"Hell yes. Will we ever forget your two trips to jail in the same day?"

"I would love to forget it. I just need to do something about you."

"Mmm, I have a few ideas of what you can do about me."

"Believe me, I know all about your ideas."

"You've only seen the start of them. Wait until we're married." I glance over at her. "Today was good?"

She gives my leg a squeeze. "Today was beyond amazing. Thank you for all you did to make it happen."

"I was hoping it'd be okay to do it there."

"It was perfect."

"I wanted it to be perfect for you."

"You did good." I feel her gaze on me as I drive. "When Tony died, one of the things that made me the saddest was losing the person who knew me better than anyone else. Today, when you asked me to marry you in front of all the people I love the most, you showed me I'm known that way again, and that means so much to me."

I bring the car to a stop at a red light and lean across the console to kiss her. "I'm glad to know you in *every* way." I waggle my brows playfully, because today is not the day for sadness of any kind. "The ring is okay?"

"The ring is exceptional. I love it."

"Good," I say, releasing a deep breath. "I'm glad you love it."

"I can't believe you were worried about any of it. You knew I was a sure thing."

"No way! You've made me work for it every step of the way. I was afraid you'd turn me down in front of everyone."

"You were not!"

"Nah," I say, laughing, "not really. But I'm glad the deed is done, that ring is on your finger and you've agreed to spend forever with me."

"I can't wait to spend forever with you." She looks over at me with love in her gaze. "I heard you went to see Len and Josie yesterday."

"Of course I did. They deserved to know what I had planned, and I wanted their support. I knew it would matter to you."

"You got it just right, Jason. Thank you for doing that."

Her approval means everything to me. "I want to get married soon."

"How soon?"

"This fall?"

"That's in, like, *three* months!"

"Sounds about right."

"You want to get married in three months."

"I'd do it tomorrow, but something tells me you won't go for that."

"You're correct about that."

"So three months?"

"You really can't wait any longer?"

"I really can't."

"Then I guess it's a good thing my parents own a restaurant."

AUTHOR'S NOTE

Thank you for reading Carmen and Jason's story! I hope you enjoyed it as much as I LOVED writing it. I wrote the opening chapters (everything up to the first time they go out for dinner) more than ten years ago and have wanted to do something with the story I started then ever since. South Florida has played an important role in my life, and I've always wanted to set a book there. My dad attended Embry-Riddle Aeronautical Institute in the 1950s, when it was located in Miami (it's now a university and has since moved to Daytona Beach). He fell in love with South Florida and would've stayed there permanently, except he was the only child of a widowed mother at home in Rhode Island. So luckily for me (and my brother), he moved back home to RI, where he met my mother and went to work as an aviation mechanic, eventually owning his own FAA-certified aviation repair station.

But every chance he got, he returned to South Florida. As a child, I swam in the pool at the Fontainebleau that Carmen recalls from her childhood and spent time in Key Biscayne and Fort Lauderdale, where my parents wintered after they retired. My dad loved it there so much, and so did we. During the writing of this book, I made two trips to Miami and loved every minute of bringing Carmen and Jason's story to life in a place that has meant so much to me.

I'm thrilled that Alison Dasho and the Montlake team were as excited about this story as I was. After you finish reading, join the How Much I Feel Reader Group at facebook.com/groups/HowMuchIFeelReaderGroup to discuss the book with spoilers allowed. Also make sure you join my newsletter mailing list at marieforce.com and follow me on Facebook (facebook.com/marieforceauthor) and Instagram (@marieforceauthor) to keep in touch.

A huge thank-you to Laura Ortiz, who grew up in Little Havana and helped me with a million details and even sent me a Cuban care package while I was writing the book. Thank you to my longtime reader friend and Miami resident Mona Abramesco, who introduced me to Laura. Mona and Laura also did advance reads for me, which were enormously helpful, and Mona plied me with delicious Cuban food in Miami. Special thanks to Tracey Suppo and Joyce Lamb for early reads and cleanup!

While I was in Miami, I held a luncheon for area readers. This was after I had finished writing the book and was in town to add some additional local details. Attending the luncheon was Carmen Morejon, who came to Miami from Cuba when she was ten years old, accompanied only by her five-year-old brother. I had so many questions about her experience, and Carmen generously shared her story with me and agreed to do an advance read of the book. Meeting such incredible people and hearing their stories is the best part of this amazing job, and it was truly a pleasure to get to know Carmen and other Miami-area readers who contributed to this story. I appreciate your generosity and your willingness to help me with large and small details.

Sincere thanks and appreciation to my sensitivity readers: Gwendolyn Neff, Lizbeth Silva Costa, Carmen Morejon, Dinorah Shoben, Tia Kelly, Miriam Ayala, Emma Melero Juarez, Stephanie Behill, Angelica Maya and Isabel Acevedo. As always, a special thanks to my primary beta readers, Anne Woodall and Kara Conrad. And a shout-out to Angel, my wonderful tour guide in Little Havana. I enjoyed our afternoon together so much!

To the many readers who responded to my queries for insight into hospital politics, I appreciate your input. And to Sarah Hewitt, family nurse practitioner, for helping me to flesh out Jason's career and research. I'm so thankful for Sarah's many contributions.

A huge thanks to the fantastic, dynamic team that supports me every day—Julie Cupp, Lisa Cafferty, Holly Sullivan, Nikki Haley, Tia Kelly and Ashley Lopez—and lots of love to the home team—Dan, Emily, Jake, Brandy, Louie and Sam Sullivan.

Finally, to the readers who support my books no matter where my muse leads me, you make me feel lucky and blessed every day of my life.

Much love,

Marie

ABOUT THE AUTHOR

Photo © 2014 Pamela Sardinha

Marie Force is the *New York Times* bestselling author of contemporary romance, romantic suspense, and erotic romance. Her series include Gansett Island; Fatal; Treading Water; Butler, Vermont; and Quantum.

Her books have sold more than 10 million copies worldwide, have been translated into more than a dozen languages, and have appeared on the *New York Times* bestseller list thirty times. She is also a *USA Today* and *Wall Street Journal* bestseller as well as a *Spiegel* bestseller in Germany.

Her goals in life are simple—to finish raising two happy, healthy, productive young adults; to keep writing books for as long as she possibly can; and to never be on a flight that makes the news.

Join Force's mailing list on her website at www.marieforce.com for news about new books and upcoming appearances in your area. Follow her on Facebook at MarieForceAuthor and on Instagram @marieforceauthor. Email Marie at marie@marieforce.com.